CREATURE
FEATURES

CREATURE FEATURES

Strange and Monstrous Beasts in Classic Science Fiction

EDITED BY
CHAD ARMENT

COACHWHIP PUBLICATIONS

Greenville, Ohio

*Creature Features: Strange and Monstrous Beasts in Classic
    Science Fiction*
© 2018 Coachwhip Publications

No claims made on public domain material.
Cover image: spider © Michal Sochor
CoachwhipBooks.com

ISBN 1-61646-437-2
ISBN-13 978-1-61646-437-0

CONTENTS

THE IGUANODON
ROBERT DUNCAN MILNE

PART I. THE IGUANODON'S EGG
A Primeval Monster Now at Large in the Jungles of New Guinea

"THE SCHOONER *AILEEN*, just returned from the Bay of Papua with a cargo of nutmegs and massay bark, reports having sighted an extraordinary monster in the swamps which line the eastern shore of the bay. It was plainly visible at a distance of four miles from the spot where the schooner was lying off, breaking and tearing its way through the camphor-trees and sago palms with, as Captain Biggs describes it, the same ease, as 'a pig through a potato patch.' The captain says that, judging from its appearance at that distance, it can not have been less than from eighty to a hundred feet in length. He says that sometimes it would rise on its hind legs, and that then its head would stand far clear of the tops of the palm-trees. He examined it through his glass, and says that he never saw any animal like it, but compares it most nearly to a bear in general characteristics. Captain Biggs is a sober, reliable man, not much given to 'yarning,' and, as the circumstance is attested by his crew of six, we offer no comment. Here is a chance for our local Nimrods."—*Brisbane Courier, January 6, 1882.*

The above paragraph, taken from a Queensland (Australia) paper of a recent date, sent me by a friend, attracted my attention when I read it to the extent of my exclaiming, "Bah! have these sea-serpents and boojum-snarks begun to attack the hard-headed Australians with their leaven? Well!" And the next

7

minute it passed from my memory. I should probably never again have thought of it, had not a singular circumstance brought it to the surface, and given it sufficient importance in my eyes to make it the text, as it were, of the following narrative.

The other morning I happened to stroll casually into the Mercantile Library, on Bush Street, and noting several ladies coming up from the basement, curiosity prompted me to find out what was going on there. On entering the hall I found that it had been converted into a species of museum; full of specimens of the animal and mineral kingdoms, many of them so deftly imitated and so preternaturally natural as to deceive, if it were possible, even one of the elect, biologically speaking. Bones of long-vanished animals were grouped on the floor; tusks of as-tounding development, purporting to be fac-similes of originals in European galleries, lay beside them. In the centre of a railed enclosure towered a monstrous and gigantic elephant, which a placard announced to be an exact reproduction of the mammoth which was found imbedded in the ice of the river Lena, where its crystal coffin had preserved it intact for—who shall say how many thousand years? A creature twenty-six feet long by sixteen high is worthy of more than a passing glance, and I stood ex-amining the pillar-like legs, the shaggy hide, and the enormous tusks, and calculating whether or not the original of the massive hulk would have tipped the beam at a hundred tons, when I was aroused from my reverie by a voice at my side:

"A purty big beast, sir; but I seen bigger."

Mechanically I turned and inspected the speaker. A bronzed, bearded, and weather-beaten man of, I should say, about fifty, dressed in sailor fashion, leaned carelessly against the railing, and looked up at the mammoth.

"You've seen bigger? Ah!" I repeated in a preoccupied way, catching vaguely, at first, the purport of the remark.

"Yes," said the man, with rather more emphasis, "I seen big-ger. An' what's more, ten times bigger. Why, that there mammot ain't a patch on the beast I once seen. It was purty near's big's that when it was a babby."

I now turned and faced the man square.

"Look here, my friend," I said, "I don't know what you take me for, but I can assure you that there is very little use in spinning yarns of that sort to me. I flatter myself that I have too much knowledge of natural history, and the laws regulating the development of animal life upon the surface of our planet, to give them credence." And after delivering myself of this announcement, I paused to witness its effect. There was no effect. The man merely looked me in the face and said:

"I can see you're a man of eddication, sir, an' a better scholar, an' has more book larnin', no doubt, than me; but I tell you, jest as sure as you're a-stannin' there, that I'm speakin' the pure truth when I say I seen a beast ten times as big's that there mammot, an' I was at the hatchin' of it, too."

I looked at the man closely and critically to detect, if possible, what object he could have in playing upon my credulity, but I could gather nothing from his frank countenance and apparent sincerity of expression. I determined, therefore, to seem to acquiesce, and draw him out.

"And, pray, in what part of the world did this strange creature live?" I asked.

"In Papua, or, as some calls it, New Guinea—a big island lyin' to nor'ward of Australey; maybe ye've heerd of it. An' for all I know the beast's there yet," replied the man.

Suddenly there flashed across my mind the remembrance of the paragraph in the Australian paper, just quoted, and I could not help connecting it with this man's assertion. Was it possible, thought I, that there might be some germ of truth in these strange and fanciful stories of uncouth and gigantic creatures in out-of-the-way wilds where men's footsteps rarely tread? Was it possible that under certain peculiar conditions and rare auspices some stray specimen of long extinct races might yet survive? Utterly improbable as the idea might seem, I was yet bound to confess that it was neither logically nor naturally impossible, and I determined to hear what this man might have to say, and derive, if nothing else, perhaps amusement from his story. Inquiry elicited the fact that Captain Sebright (he is now engaged as a pilot on the bay) resided on Jessie Street, and I accepted an invitation to call upon him the same evening, and hear his story, besides examining some documents in his possession which bore upon the subject.

During the course of the day I met my friend W—, one of the shining lights of the Academy of Sciences, and persuaded him to accompany me on my evening visit, though at the expense of a smile of pity and superiority. We accordingly called on the captain, and, after the usual preliminaries, our host entered upon his narrative as follows:

"I don't know if ye was ever in the South Seas, gen'lmen, but atween you an' me, there's more room for queer things there than any part o' the airth ever *I* was on. Talk o' yer vegetation, yer trees, yer funny birds, yer rummy beasts, I can bet that ye won't find the like nowhere elst, nohow. But the queerest thing ever I see in the beast line, I seen on the island of Papua. If ye got the time I'll tell ye how it was, an' then, I reckon, ye'll think the same's I do. It's jest sixteen years ago, mebbe a little more or less, that I shipped afore the mast on the barkentine *Mary Chester* from Wellington, New Zealand, with a cargo of coal for Singapore. It was in the month of October, an' the cap'n he took the north passage by way of Torres Straits. Well, we gets along all right as far's Cape Rodney, when a typhoon struck us, an' afore we could shift our canvas, we was on our beam-ends an' a-swimmin' for our lives. One o' the boats got loose in the upset, an' me an' Ben Baxter, the bo'sun, clumb into her, an' arter we was in we helped Mister Ince, that was the second mate, to get in, an' we never seen one o' the crew more, nowheres. There was oars in the boat, an' we made for land, but the wind blew us far up into the gulf of Papua. She kep' a-drivin' us for, I guess, a day an' a half, till we was stranded on a mud bank, an' had to wade ashore. The natives come down to look at us, afeard like, but gradooally they got less skeered, an' then we went up with them to a sort of village they had, some two or three hunderd yards from shore. Now, mind you, in them times nobody knew nothin' about them blacks that lived in Papua. There was no trade in them days with Australey, nor none with other countries, for folks could get their spices an' birds far easier in the islands to

the west, an' had no need to come to Papua. There was some
trade with the north coast o' the island, but this part as we was
stranded on was way down in the southeast corner, an' the breed
as lived there was as different from the folks as lived a thousand
miles off, at the other end o' the island, as a Negro from a Malay.
The report was that they was cannibals, an' we was a little afeard
at first that they might be out o' fresh meat; but they treated us
fust-rate an' no mistake. From the first day that we got there we
kep' a bright look-out for a ship, an' we axed 'em by signs if any
ships ever comed that way, an' Mister Ince he drew the picter of
a ship on a leaf of his note-book, but they shook their heads an'
larfed, an' it was clear no ship ever comed that way yet. The boat,
I must tell ye, had got washed off the mud-bank the first night,
an' spiked on a coral reef, an' was so stove in that we couldn't
do nothin' with her, an' the natives had no tools that amount-
ed to anything for carpenterin'. So there was nothin' for it but
either to stay where we was, or else make for some other part
o' the island. To nor'ward an' eastward ye could see nothin' but
snowy mountains, an' south'ard there was nothin' but swamps,
and mud-banks, an' forests o' camphor-trees an' sech like, while
goin' west meant getting away from the sea, so we jest concluded
to stay where we was, for a while, anyhow. The blacks guv us
a hut to live in, made o' double lateen sails o' matting—that's
the stuff them Malays make their huts on—and for grub we got
what they got. There was no lack of oranges, banannys, an' co-
coanuts; and for meat, kangaroos an' sech small game as they
could trap or shoot with arrows. An' don't ye forget that them
blacks lived purty comf'table for savages. It was the rainy season
there, an' the sun was d'rect over our heads, for Mister Ince, the
second mate, cut out a quadrant from a piece o' plank with Ben
Baxter's jack-knife, an' told us that we was about 70° 30' south,
by about 145° 30' east, an' consekently right in the bight of the
gulf of Papua. It was the twenty-third of October when we got
wrecked, an' Mister Ince said it was jest square midsummer for
that latitude, 'case the sun would travel south for the next two
months, an' the next midsummer would come 'bout the middle o' Febrooary, when the sun got on the zenith again, comin'

nor'ward. Well, gen'lmen, them savages was the ugliest people ye ever comed acrost. Thick lips? I guess not. Noses like a three-legged pot, beat flat, and two big holes knocked in the bottom of it? Oh, no! Paint? My stars! If they wasn' the most hijousest chromos I ever seen, you may swamp me dead. Why, they jest laid it on as if paint wasn't worth nothin', and no more it was; an' the women was wuss nor the men. But they was as kind-hearted a folk as ever ye see; an' if anybody goes for to tell ye that the Papooans is cannibals, leastways them as we was among, jest tell 'em for me that they're a longways out in their reck'nin', though they do say that the up-country fellers 'll gobble ye up quickerin 'scat. Them hut's o' theirs, made o' cocoanut mattin', keeps rain out a durn sight better nor canvas, as ye may jedge when they makes their pots an' buckets out o' the same stuff, too. Well, gen'lmen, arter about a month or so we began to pickup a smatterin' o' their lingo. Mister Ince, though he was a eddicated man, an' ye would ha' thought could ha' talked it to wunst, was the backwardest of all. I managed to git most o' the grub words purty quick, an' 'How de do?' an' 'Good-bye,' an' them sort o' tricks; but Ben Baxter, that was the ignorantest A. B. as ever shipped afore the mast, an' never knowed nuthin', an' couldn't write his own name, though he *was* bo'sun, he larned the whole of it to wunst. Ben got along with the lingo fust rate, an' bein' a big man, 'bout six foot four, I guess, an' broad in proportion, they was afeered of him, an' used to kneel down an' kiss his feet, but they didn't see nothin' in Mister Ince, that was a little man and sickly. Well, we'd been there 'bout six weeks, I reckon, when Ben says to us one night in the hut:

"'Boys,' says he, 'I'm goin' to get married.'

"'Yes,' says I, 'I thought so. I seen ye makin' up to that broad-beamed squaw with the yaller furbelows. Ye're goin' to do it, are ye? Well, I wish ye luck. Mebbe, ye want me for best man.'

"'Well, Ben,' says Mister Ince, 'I suppose we must make the best of it. Not a sign of a ship in sight, and no chance of one as far as I can see. I mean to try and find a passage to the south along the foot-hills when the rainy season's over, and I thought you would come along with us, but if you get married here we shall have to go without you,' an' Mister Ince coughed, an' I could tell by his cough that he wouldn't never make no passage along no foot-hills to the south in this world, for he was far gone in consumption, though he didn't know it.

"'Well,' says Ben, 'I don't know 'bout that, sir. 'Taint a regular marriage by a priest, ye know, an' I dunno if sech marriages is werry bindin'.'

"'You shouldn't look at it in that light, Ben,' says Mister Ince—he was allus sorter religious—'if the cerimony is p'formed accordin' to the customs of the people ye're livin' with, it is your dooty to abide by the contrack.'

"'Well,' says Ben, scratchin' his head puzzled like, 'I guess if that's the case I'm the wust Mormon in the South Seas; but a pusson mout as well be killed for a sheep as a lamb, an' one more or less can't make much diff'rence noways.'

"So next mornin', sure enough, Ben was married, an' I'll tell ye how the thing was done. There warn't no cerimony to speak on, but Ben an' the squaw stood facin' each other, and one o' the old men—I found out arterwards he was a kind o' high priest—took an' fried a bananny, an' guv one end to Ben an' the other to the squaw, and then broke it in two in the middle, an' each o' them ate their piece, an' arter that they was reckoned married as tight as airy parson in the world could do it. An' now you gen'lmen mustn't go for to think that them savages wasn't as vartuous as white folks, 'case I tell ye they was. Every man had on'y one wife, an' wunst she was his wife there was no divorcin' of her, nuther. Each pair ockepied a hut, an' the little picaninnies wollered in the sand outside. As I said before, it was the twenty-third of October when we got wrecked, an' it was the third of December when Ben Baxter got married."

"But, captain," I interpolated, getting somewhat tired of the rambling story, and observing W— smothering a yawn, "what has Ben Baxter's marriage got to do with the monster you asked us here to tell us about?"

"Jest everything in the world," responded the captain, with animation. "If it hedn't bin for Ben Baxter's marriage there wouldn't ha' bin no big beast a-cruisin around them Papooan swamps now."

This observation put a stopper on my objections as to the relevancy of the story, and with some dim idea that the captain was actually leading up to some conclusion by steps which were necessary to the intelligibility of his narrative, I determined to wait patiently.

"Ye see," proceeded the captain, "the squaw as Ben married was the chief's darter, an' out o' that there marriage Ben got bigger an' more popylar nor ever. Ye see, he could throw them savages a-wrastlin', give 'em the foot, an' beat 'em at the club game, an' they made a sort o' god out o' him. Now, I must tell ye that them savages hadn't no idee o' a soopreme bein', an' didn't keer nothin' for no kind o' wuship of anythin' they cuddn't see, but they wushiped Ben Baxter, 'case they respected his p'ints, an' he was suthin' afore their eyes. Well, it comed on t'ward the middle o' December when the people o' the village begins to make big prep'rations for some sort of a feast, as I could see by their carryin' on an' fixin' up o' all sorts o' grub, an' paintin' themselfs up fresh, an' a hull gang o' savages come in from the country, mebbe eight hunderd or a thousand all told. There was hurryin' around, an' beatin' o' drums, an' clashin' o' metal plates, till we all of us wondered what next. Ben had gone to another hut to live with his wife, an' me an' Mister Ince was left alone by ourselfs. Mister Ince's cough got wuss an' wuss, an' on the fifteenth of December (for we kep' the days notched on a stick) he died, an' me an' Ben Baxter dug a grave, an' we rolled him up in cocoa-nut mats an' put him in, the savages all stannin' 'round an' lookin' on; an' when we shoveled the sand over him Ben Baxter he cried, an' then all them savages began to blubber like babbies, an' ye never hear sech a hullabaloo in all yer life. An' afore Mister Ince died he guv Ben Baxter his pin an' his ring, an' he guv me his watch an' his pocket-book, for he said he had no livin' relatives in the world as he knowed on. An' here's a bit o' writin' which you gen'lmen 'll understand better nor I do, relative to the country we was wrecked in. It's a bit torn, but mebbe ye may get some facks out of it," and the captain handed us a sheet of note-paper written with pencil in a very small hand, partly indecipherable from age and wear.

W— took the manuscript, put on his glasses, and after examining it intently for a minute or two, read as follows:

> "October 23, 1865—B'ktine *Mary Chester*, Captain William Ayres; Wellington to Singapore, coal; foundered off Cape Rodney; all hands lost except self, Baxter, boatswain, and Sebright, seaman. October 24—Made land; natives kind and inoffensive; made quadrant; took latitude from known data and approximately known longitude—7° 30′ S., 145° 30′ E., giving N. coast of bight of Bay of Papua. * * * (here MS. becomes indecipherable) * * * geological formations peculiar; surface outcroppings of Jurassic Period; chalk rocks, lias, and inferior oolite; bluish and grayish laminated clays; cliffs characteristically striped and banded; arenaceous marls and argillaceous limestones; here and there a ferruginous bed; * * * conifera, araucaria; cycads abundant, pterophyllum and crossozamia; endogenous plants as well; *zamia spiralis* (Australian pine-apple) * * * both vegetable-eating and carnivorous univalves, limpets, and whelks; starfish, sea-lilies, sponges, corals, * * * inland beds of Jurassic fossils; whole mounds of bones of gigantic dinosaurian reptiles; particularly ichthyosaurus and iguanodon; thigh bones of latter eleven feet by * * * living vegetation as well as geological formation same as in Jurassic Period; most remarkable region; well worthy scientific investigation. * * * December 3d—Baxter married native woman today; shall try to make Cape Rodney when rainy season over; bad cough and very weak." * * * *

"I can make nothing more out of this manuscript," said W—; "the rest is either torn or blurred. What I *have* read, however, convinces me that the writer had carefully noted the natural characteristics of the country he was cast into, and that these

partook strongly of such as we know to have existed in the Juras-
sic Period. Strange," he mused, "that such a region should exist
unknown to the scientific world. Why, it would well repay inspection by government commission. Strange, too, that it should
lie in almost the sole spot of earth which still remains more of a
terra incognita than even the interior of Africa or the Antarctic
continent. And the fact that we *know* Australia to possess nu-
merous living representatives of the Secondary Period, both in
the vegetable and animal kingdoms, such as the araucaria, the
screw-pine, and certain classes of shell-fish, leads us to infer that
the island of Papua, lying in the same quarter of the earth, but
more tropical, may possess similar or even more marked zoolog-
ical characteristics. I must confess that the somewhat scattered
notes I have just read have given me a fresh interest in Captain
Sebright's narrative. I shall, with his permission, take much plea-
sure in submitting them to the notice of the Academy of Sciences
at our next meeting. Pray, go on, Captain Sebright. I am all ex-
pectation as to the *denouement* of your story."

I was secretly pleased at the turn affairs had taken, and that,
after all, my reputation for credulity, as deducible from this visit,
would be materially lessened in the light of an endorsement by
such an undoubted scientific authority as W—.

"I guess I left ye, gen'lmen, where we was plantin' Mister Ince
in the sand," continued the captain, when W— had done talking;
"that was the fifteenth o' December, the same day he died, for it
warn't no use keepin' the corpse any longer in that hot climate.
Well, them prep'rations as I was a tellin' ye about was kep' up till
the twenty-first o' December, which, as ye know, is the longest
day in the year south o' the line. But on the mornin' o' that day
I could see that suthin' onusual was goin' to happen, an' I kep'
my eyes skinned, case I might get roped into suthin' as warn't
in the game, for I tell ye there's no trustin' them savages when
they gets to celebratin', even if they is purty rash'nal at or'nary
times. 'Bout a' hour arter sun-up the high priest comes for'ard,
outen his hut, to where the balance o' the blacks was a-stan'in',
howlin' an' beatin' their drums an' things, an' he makes them a
sorter speech, an' forms 'em into a percession like, with twelve

or fifteen young girls in the front, an' then the hull gang begins to march to where there was a big grove o' cocoanut-trees, an' orange, an' iron-wood trees a-stan'in', 'bout a quarter o' a mile off. Now I must tell ye that me, an' Ben Baxter, an' Mister Ince had often been curious for to see what was inside o' that there grove, 'case it was guarded day an' night, all round, by a troop o' savages with weepons, but they never would allow nary one of us to get past the outside; an' wunst when Ben Baxter offered to go through the trees they actooally showed fight, an' Ben was so s'prised that he concluded he didn't care to go nohow. Arter that we all kep' a-wonderin' an' spekylatin' what sort o' a secret there was in that grove; but, 's far's we could see, there was never one o' them savages as went into it—not even the guards as stood outside. Well, gen'lmen, when the percession begun to form, an' marched in the direction o' the grove, Ben was stan'in' alongside o' me, an' he says, says he:

"'Jim,' says he, 'I'm a goin' for to foller up them blacks. I kin see there's suthin' goin' to be done inside that there grove, an' bust my toplights if I don't find out what it is.'

"An' I says: 'Don't ye do it, Ben, if they ain't willin', 'case no good can come o' counterin' 'em.'

"But Ben didn't mind me, but goes an' jines in, goin' hand-an'-hand with his wife, an' as I didn't keer to be left behind all alone, I followed up the march a little ways off. When we comes to the grove, the high-priest—a' old man, painted so's to make him look like a devil—calls a lot o' big, strong blacks, an' they drives the young girls as was a-walkin' in front right into the grove among them trees. An' afore they got 'em in the girls screeched, an' screamed, an' fell on their knees, an' cried enough to break anybody's heart; but them blacks pushed, an' rolled, an' hustled 'em in with their clubs an' the p'ints o' their spears, an' the rest o' the crowd kep' up a howlin', an' beatin' drums, so's you'd ha' thought all hell had broke loose.

"Well, gen'lmen, in course I didn't like to see this bizness goin' on, but what could I do? Why, if I had made a move to do anythin' I'd ha' bin chawed up into mince-meat too quick. In a minute or two they druv an' pushed all them girls inside the grove, an' as a lot o' the savages stood guard afore it, in course we couldn't see nothin' more, though the screechin' and yellin' went on wuss nor ever. In about a quarter of a hour the screechin' quieted down, an' arter a minute or two the priest an' the savages comed out, an' I could see blood on their hands an' their legs, as if they had been butcherin' sheep. Then all hands went back to the village except the guards as stayed constant at the grove, an' they had feastin', an' singin', an' dancin', an' kep' it up till mornin'. I didn't keer to jine in, arter what I seen, an' I jest lay in my hut a-thinkin' 'bout strikin' out an' leavin' the durned place anyway, when Ben Baxter comed into the hut, an', says he:

"'Jim,' says he, 'atween you an' me, they've been a-slaughterin' all them young girls as was druv into the grove to-day, Now, sure's my name's Ben Baxter, I'se a-goin' what's in that there grove, an' if it's some idol, as I guess it is, I'm a-goin' to smash the durn thing up, an' put a stopper on them purceedin's wunst for all.'

"'Well, Ben,' says I, for I sees his mind was set on it, an' it warn't no use counterin' him, 'be keerful, an' don't take no more risks nor ne'ss'ry. But if ye *are* bound to go, why, I'm with ye. A feller mout jest as well git killed at wunst as stay in this hell-hole, anyway.'

"So, when it got to be dark, and all the savages was feastin' an singin', me an' Ben slips quiet out o' the hut an' makes for the grove. Now, I must tell ye that this grove covered about four acres o' ground, an' the north side of it was backed by as funny a cliff as ever ye see. It was about two hunderd feet high, an' the top o' it leaned over the grove so that the sun couldn't never shine upon them trees as were under its lee, not even on the longest day when he was south o' the line. Me an' Ben made a kind o' circle like around the grove so's not to let the guards see us comin', an' then we sneaked along the bottom o' the cliff till we reached the trees. I guess them guards thought, mebbe, it wasn't much use a-stayin' 'round in the cold when the fun was a-goin' on in the village. Anyways, me an' Ben crawled in, an' wunst under cover o' the trees we knowed we was all right, perwidin' we didn't make no noise so's to 'tract attention. Well, we crawled along through the grass till we come to a clear place in the middle, 'bout a quarter of a acre, as far as I could jedge, an' in the middle o' the space was a sandy mound-like about twenty foot high. There was a half moon jest a-risin' in the east, an' we walked up to the mound, an' what do ye think we seen? As I'm a livin' man, the bodies o' all them girls as was druv into the grove that mornin' was a-lyin' butchered, with their throats cut, around an' all over that mound, an' the sand was red with the poor things' blood. 'Bout five or six lazy vultures flapped their wings an' flew away over the trees as we comed nigh, an' as we was afeared o' diskivery we got back among the trees in a jiffy, and waited.

"'Jim,' says Ben, arter awhile, 'there's some mist'ry in that there mound. 'Spose you go down to the hut, an' bring up them iron-wood shovels. I'm a goin' to find out what's under that heap.'

"So I crawls mighty keerful out o' the grove, gets the shovels, an' brings 'em back to Ben. Then we each takes a shovel and goes back to the mound, an' as we was goin' back over the open space the sand crackled like under foot, an' Ben stooped down an' 'xamined it, an' scooped out a hole with his shovel.

"'Jim,' says he, feelin' down, 'as I hope to die, if this here place ain't made o' nothin' else but human bones strike me blind.'

"An' I looked down too, an' dug down, an' found nothin' but bones, small an' big. An' jedgin' from the arey o' the clear place, an' the depth o' the bones, though we cuddent find no bottom to them so far's we dug, I should calk'late there must ha' bin thousands an' thousands o' people killed right in that spot, an' I says to Ben:

"'Ben,' says I, 'it's enuff to make a man shudder when he thinks how many poor critters must ha' bin slaughtered here to make all them bones.'

"An' Ben says, 'Yes, that's so; let's hurry up or else them savages 'll ketch us, and there'll be hell to pay.'

"So we went to the mound, an' fust we cleared away the bodies o' the twelve young girls as was layin' around dead, and we lays 'em side by side, orderly like, an' then we takes our shovels an' begins to shovel away the sand o' the mound, beginnin' at one side o' the bottom. It was purty stiff work, 'case the sand was more like clay, an' a dark, dingy color, 'pearin' to have been soaked with blood through an' through. Well, we shovels on for mebbe ten minutes, an' had got three or four foot into the stuff when I hears suthin' rattle like iron, an' Ben says:

"'Jim,' says he, 'I struck suthin' hard,' an' he jabs his shovel in agin, an' says, 'yes, whatever it is, it's almighty hard.'

"An' then I gives the thing a dig with my shovel, an' it seemed like as if I was hittin' a piece o' gutty-perky, for the iron-wood bounded back off of it, an' it guv a little.

"Then Ben says: 'That there thing is big. Let's get to the top o' the heap, an' shovel the sand off of it till we gets down to the durned thing, whatever it is.'

"So we both climbs to the top o' the mound, an' starts in to shovel like good fellows. Arter 'bout half a hour's work we got about six foot o' sand throwed off, an' struck our shovels on to that hard stuff agin.

"'This is the top of it,' says Ben, 'an' I guess that there fust hole's at the bottom. I'm a-goin' to clear every grain o' sand off of it afore I stop, if it takes a month, an' find out what the durn thing is.'

"So we both starts in ag'in, sayin' nothin', but workin' steady. We must ha' worked purty quiet, too, for them sentries never heerd us, though they warn't more'n a hundred yards off. The moon was 'bout a' hour high when we began the job, an' 'bout five hours high when we got through an' got the thing clear, an' day was beginnin' to break in the east. An' what d'ye think it was? Well, gen'lmen, I'm blest if I ever seen a funnier thing in my life. It looked like a round ball 'bout twelve or fourteen foot through, but flattened out where it was layin' on the sand. Its color was a sorter yaller brown, an' the thing was wrinkled all over like the hides o' them rinosserys I wunst seen in Afrikay. We struck it with our shovels all over, but cuddent make nary mark nowheres, the stuff was so thick an' solid.

"'Well,' says Ben, wipin' his forrid, 'here's a go. I wonder what them savages 'll say when they finds out what we done. That's a purty sort o' a god for to kill girls to,' an he hits the thing another lick with the shovel, so hard that it sounded all over the grove, an' next minute 'bout fifty savages come runnin' in with their clubs an' spears, an' makin' sech a hullabaloo as ye never heerd in all yer life."

Part 2. The Hatching of the Iguanodon
A Primeval Monster Now in New Guinea

"Well, when they seen what was done, an' the big round ball a-stan'in' where there had on'y bin a heap o' sand afore, they stood dazed like, lookin' at each other, an' at me an' Ben, who was stan'in' there leanin' on his shovel, onconsarned like. It was easy to see they didn't know what to do, 'case the hull thing was out o' their 'xper'ence, an' so we jest waited to see what would turn up. Arter a few minutes the high priest comes in with a gang o' blacks from the village, an' then the hull o' them stood jabberin' their lingo, an' p'intin' to me an' Ben an' the big ball. Presen'ly the high priest goes to one side with some o' the savages, an' begins talkin', an' I reckoned they was holdin' a council o' war or suthin' o' that sort. When they got through jabberin' to themselfs they turned round, an' the priest made a sign, an' the balance o' the savages formed a circle around us, an' stood threatenin' like. Then Ben says to me:

"'Jim, them blacks means mischief, but the fust one as comes at me I mean jest to let him have it good. There's one got to fly up ahead o' me,' an' he took a tight hold o' the iron-wood shovel, an' I seen he meant bizness.

"'All right,' says I, 'I guess we kin die jest as hard as the nex' one if it comes to the p'int.'

"An' jest at that moment Ben's wife come a-runnin' in through the trees, an' breaks through the circle, an' stands alongside Ben, an' begins jabberin' like mad. I didn't know what she was a-sayin', but Ben did, an' as I found it all out arterwards I'll give ye the jist of it now. The rules o' the place was that no one should enter that there grove on pain o' death, and the high priest had said that we was to die. When Ben's wife come a-runnin' in, an' seen what was up, she told Ben his on'y chance was to do suthin' that the high priest cuddent do. Ben looked at me sorrowful, an' said:

"'What in blazes kin I do, Jim, that them savages will respeck, an' that they can't do themselfs? The high priest says that there thing's a god, an' if I'm a god I must pe'form a merricle to prove it,' for, mind ye, them savages had still some ling'rin' idee that Ben was more nor a or'nery man.

"Then I thought a minute, an' I says: 'What did ye do with that can o' tar that was lyin' in the boat when we was wrecked?'

"Ben says: 'I guess it's lyin' there yet.'

"'Hold on till I fetch it,' says I. 'I guess we kin pe'form a merricle with that tar.'

"So arter some purlaver they 'lowed me to leave the grove, half a dozen o' the savages goin' with me to see I wasn't playin' to escape. When I got down to the shore, sure enuff there was the tar-can a-layin' in the bottom o' the boat, an' arter I got it I dug up a lot o' them mangrove roots as grows in the water, and when I got enuff, I starts up back for the grove, an' the savages with me. An' on the way up I smears four o' the wet roots with the tar that was in the can, on the sly, an' unbeknownst to the savages, that hedn't no idee what tar was anyways. When we gets back, I hands the roots to Ben, and tells him what to do. Then I waits quiet to see what would happen. Then Ben, an' his wife, an' the high priest got a jabberin', an' Ben hands the wet mangrove roots as hedn't no tar on 'em to the high priest, and axes him if he could burn 'em, at the same time tellin' him that he could burn his'n. I could see that Ben's move staggered the priest, for you bet he warn't no fool for a savage; but he put a good face on it, an' sent some o' the blacks down to the camp for firebrands. Bimeby they comes back with the firebrands, an' builds a big fire on the sand, an' the priest he takes his wet mangrove roots and makes passes over 'em, an' mumbles an' prays as nat'ral as any real priest ever I see, an' then he takes the biggest flamin' brand he could see out o' the fire, an' the littlest mangrove root he could find in the bunch, an' holds it steady in the flame; but it on'y fizzed and spluttered, an' though he kep' on holdin' it in the flame, there was nary burn in it; an' at last it put out the fire in the brand, and the blacks as was stan'in' round looked on solemn, as much as to say: 'What are ye tryin' to do, old man? Haven't ye lived long enuff to know that them wet mangrove roots won't burn?' An' the old priest looked kinder 'shamed of hisself for showin' the people there was suthin' he couldn't do. Then Ben comes for'ard, smilin', with his mangrove foots as had the tar smeared over 'em, an' bows to the comp'ny, an' takes one o' the roots and holds it to a blaze, the same's the priest did, an' in course the tar that was on it caught fire to wunst, an' blazed up like tinder. An' you jist bet them savages seen the p'int right away, an' every mother's son o' them downed upon his marrow bones, and slammed his forehead into the sand afore Ben, an' the high priest downed hisself too, an' crawled upon his knees to where Ben was a stan'in', an' kissed his toes.

"'Now,' says Ben, to me, 'we got them savages jest where we want 'em, an' I'm a-goin' to spile this god bizness right now.' Then he hollers out in their lingo, an' commands 'em all to rise. An' they riz to their feet, an' stood with their hands crossed on their breasts like mummies, the hull gang o' them. Then he sent some o' them down to the village for ropes, for they made tidy strong rope out o' cocoanut fibre, them savages did. An' while they was gone Ben says to me: 'I guess the best way to stop this murd'rin' bizness is to take that there ball out o' this grove, and cut down the trees.'

"'Well, Ben,' says I, 'you are the boss god now, an' I reckon ye better do it.'

"So, when the savages come back with the ropes, Ben set the whole crowd to work a-tearin' up an' knockin' down the trees with their iron-wood axes. It was purty heavy work, 'case the trees was old an' thick, but soon there was a lane cleared wide en-uff to drag the ball through into the open. There was one thing, gen'lmen, that I noticed pertikler, an' that was that at high noon that there ball laid jest on the edge o' the shade o' the cliff, an' this bein' the longest day in the year, an' the sun at its furthest p'int south o' the line, it was easy to see that the sunlight hadn't never shone on the ball so long as it laid in that there place. I didn't think nothin' o' the suckumstance jest then, but arter-wards when I seen what happened, I called to mind that very fack for a explanation o' the mist'ry.

"Well, as I was a-goin' to say, when night comed on me an' Ben Baxter an' the savages lef' the grove, an' went down to the huts to sleep, but a lot o' them stayed in the grove around that ball, I s'pose through habit. An' next mornin' we all goes back to the grove, an' Ben an' me twists a lot o' them ropes into a three-strand hawser, for we cuddent tell how heavy the durned thing might be, an' we didn't want for to break the ropes with too heavy a strain. So, arter we got the hawser made, we throws a hitch around the ball, bringin' the two ends inter a slip-noose, leavin' about a hunderd feet o' cable for pullin' at. Then we gets about fifty o' the strongest savages an' stations 'em all along the rope, an' Ben gives 'em the word to pull. Jest then the high priest an' a lot o' the old gray-headed men kneeled down afore Ben, who was a-standin' right in front o' the ball, and began talkin' their lingo. I didn't know what they was drivin' at, but I heerd arterwards that they was prayin' an' beseechin' Ben not to move the ball, as suthin' fearful would happen them, sayin' as how no-body knowed how long it had laid there, but there was a mound in one corner o' the grove made o' pebbles, an' each year, when the young girls was sacrificed, the high priest put another pebble on the mound. Fust o' all, me an' Ben went an' looked at the heap o' pebbles, which was a sort o' pyramid 'bout ten foot high, an' as far's I could calk'late, must ha' held more nor a million pebbles.

"'Why,' says Ben, when he seen that mound o' pebbles, 'that there ball must ha' laid there thousands o' years afore Adam an' Eve, or else that high priest is the durndest liar I ever see. Any-ways, I reckon the last pebble has been throwed on that heap, an' that ball's a-goin' out o' this here grove this very hour, or my name ain't Ben Baxter.'

"So we goes back to the ball, an' Ben he shoves the priest an' the old men out o' the way, an' gives the word to pull; but the durned thing stuck so fast to the sand that there was nary pull to it, till all of a sudden it tilts up, 'case me an' Ben an' about twenty more savages was givin' it a h'ist from behind, an' so it made a roll over, an', in course, the hawser slipped over the top.

"'Ye might ha' knowed that, Ben,' says I; 'we kin git that there ball out a durn sight easier rollin' it than draggin' it.' So we all gits behind it, an' jest rolled it over an' over, like a big snow-ball, till we got it clear o' the grove, an' right out on the open flat in front o' the village. An', although the thing was about fourteen foot through, it didn't weigh no more nor about five ton, noways.

"Then Ben says to me: 'Jim, I guess we've settled this biz-ness now; but the idee's got to be kep' up, an' I'm a-goin' to show them blacks the diff'rence atween a real livin' god an' a big, round, horny ball. Jest fetch up that stool that I made when we fust comed here.'

"So I brung the stool up from the hut; an' Ben takes out his jack-knife, an' cuts steps in the side o' the ball, to climb up to the top o' it, 'case he said it would look ondignified for a god to go sprawlin' an' scramblin' up the smooth side of a ball, a-holdin' on by his teeth an' eyebrows. When he was wunst up I throws up the stool to him, an' then he digs four holes in the top for to steady the stool's legs, an' then wipes his forrid, an' sets down. An' when the savages seen Ben a-sittin' on the top o' the ball what they used to think was their god, when it was a-layin' in the grove covered up with sand, an' nobody knowed what it was, they sets up sech a whoopin', an' a hollerin', an' beatin' o' drums as ye never heerd in all yer born days. Arter that they builds Ben a big hut, with four ply o' cocoanut mattin', an' twice as big as any o' the other huts, an' they brings him the best o' the fruits an' sich other grub as there was, an' he hedn't nothin' to do but jest take it easy. An' the high-priest knuckled to him, 'case the folks all knowed how bad he was beat a-burnin' them mangrove roots, an' he seen it warn't no use buckin' agin popylar opinion. Every mornin' an' evenin', bein' the coolest time o' the day, Ben used to climb the ball, an' set down on the stool, an' smoke his pipe—for there was a weed on the island suthin' like 'baccy—an' he laid down the law to them savages if they got quarrelin' or stealin', an' guv 'em fifty or a hunderd strokes with a bamboo if they got onruly.

"Well, gen'lmen, things goes on jest the same as ever for the next five or six months, an' nary sign of a ship to be seen in the offin'. We begun to git 'customed to the kind o' life, an' gradooally got to speak the lingo purty free, an' last o' all, I gets married myself to a purty nice young gal, I tells ye, take her all-in-all. It was the twenty-second o' December when we rolled the ball out o' the grove where, as I said afore, the sun hadn't never shined upon it, 'case it was layin' jest in the shadder o' the cliff; but arter we rolled it out on to the open flat in course the sun kep' a shinin' onto it all the time, exceptin' night times. Ben used to say to me when he comed down from the top of an evenin':

"'Jim, no man could go for to mount that there ball durin' the heat o' the day. The horn, or whatever stuff it's made on, gets red hot in the sun, an' burns ye as bad as red-hot iron'—which was a fack, for I felt it many a time.

"Well, it comed on to July or August, which is the winter season there, though the sun's jist near as high in the north as at any time o' the year, for there ain't much diff'rence nohow in the tropics, and though I hain't partic'lar sure 'bout the 'xack date, still you kin jist bet I remember what happened then jist as clear as if it was yesterday. It was a stiflin' day; not a breath o' wind stirrin'; an' I kep' in doors all day 'case o' the heat. 'Bout sundown I takes a turn as usual, and when I gets out I seen Ben a-makin' for the ball with his pipe in his mouth, the same's usual. He clumb up to the top by the steps cut in the side, an' sat down, the savages a-stan'in' round, an' talkin' to Ben the same as to a jedge in the court. I was strollin' around, smokin', and not pertiklerly keerin' for what was a-goin' on, havin' seen the same thing ev'ry evenin' for months, when suddenly I hears one o' the savages givin' a yell, an' lookin' round, I seen that there ball a-movin' an' swayin' this-a-way an' that-a-way, an' Ben Baxter a-sittin' on the stool a-top with his pipe in his mouth, an' lookin' as white's a sheet, and his eyes a-rollin', and his hull body stiff like. I was parilyzed myself, and cuddent move a muscle, I was so s'prised, an' so was the savages, an' for about five seconds, I guess, though at the time it seemed more like a month, that there ball kep' a-shakin' an' swayin', an' everybody stan'in' lookin' at it, onable to speak or move through s'prise. Then all to wunst one side of it cracked and bust wide open, an' a head looked out, and it was the most hijousest head I ever seen or expeck to see. It was flat like a lizard, an' 'bout four foot long, an' two big eyes, like soup-plates, stood 'bout half a foot out from its forrid, an' it had a tusk comin' out from the top of its nose, 'bout a foot long. An' a second arter I hears r-r-rip, an' that there ball or shell bust right in two, an' a tremenjous beast comed out and stood upon the sand. Its body was 'bout twelve foot long, dark-brown in the color, an' scaly like a crocodile. Its fore-legs was short, an' its hindlegs big and strong, an' it had three sharp claws upon each foot. An' it had a tail like a lizard, 'bout ten foot long, that wiggled an' curled as it walked. An' jest as the ball bust the second time, the stool as Ben Baxter was a-settin' on fell down, an' Ben with it, an' hit the beast on the back o' the neck, an' Ben rolled over, and lay on the ground like dead. An', meanwhile, all the savages as was in the huts had come out when they heerd the fust scream, an' was a-lookin' on, all a-stan'in' still an' onable to move. An' the big beast stood still for about three seconds a-lookin' about him, an' seemin' puzzled like, an' onsartin' how to act, an' then he moved off, makin' straight for the swamps an' mud banks as I told ye was covered with sago-palms, an' cocoa-nuts, an' big thickets o' all kinds o' trees an' brush. An' the fust move he made was acrost Ben's body, though he didn't notice Ben, an' seemed skeered an' afeered like. An' as soon's he moved all them savages, ev'ry mother's son o' them, set up sech a yell o' fear as no man ever heerd afore, an' they made a break for the woods, men, women an' childen, till the last one o' them was out o' sight, an' I was left alone with Ben Baxter an' the ball. It's no use for me to say I warn't skeered, 'case I was, but when I seen that the beast had went away, I knowed there warn't no 'mediate danger, an' I went over to look at Ben Baxter. I stooped down an' turned him over on his back—he was layin' on his face—an' tried to rouse him, but he was stone dead. Nary scratch on him, nuther, for the beast, though I seen him walk acrost his body, hadn't put a foot on to him, or else he would ha' been smashed inter pulp. So I concluded that Ben had jest simply been skeered to death.

"It was three days afore the savages comed back to the village, an' then they was mighty slow an' keerful about it. That's all, gen'lmen, I've got to tell ye about it."

"And did you ever see this monster again?" I inquired.

"Hunderds an' hunderds o' times," replied Captain Sebright. "I lived with them savages for nine years arter that, till a schooner from Australey happened to come up the bay for nutmegs an' spice, an' I got off in her."

"What were the characteristics of the monster?" asked W——. "Did it ever attack the settlement, or make itself obnoxious in any way?"

"I never seen nor hearn tell o' no one bein' hurt by it. It kep' to the swamps and jungles, an' never bothered the folks in the village. It growed very fast, too, for it was on'y 'bout twelve foot long when it was hatched out o' that ball, or egg, or whatever ye may call it, an' the last time I seen it it was 'bout sixty foot long, an' smashin' an' crashin' its way through big forest trees the same as if they was stubble."

"Did you never give the facts of the case to the public before this—I mean, did you never tell the story before just as you have told it to us?" I inquired, after a pause.

"Bless you, yes," returned the captain, smiling, "many an' many a time. But d'ye think they would b'lieve a word o' it? Not much. Some o' them would smile, an' look wise, as much as to say, ye can't come over *me* with yer yarns; an' some would git mad, and call me a old fool, an' I s'pose you gen'lmen is jest like the balance o' them."

"Have you any immediate use for this paper, Captain Sebright?" asked W——, taking up Mr. Ince's manuscript from the table. "If not I should like to borrow it for scientific purposes."

"You kin have it, sir, an' return it when you git ready," replied the sailor, and without further comment we took up our hats, said good-bye, and left.

* * * * *

"THIS IS A MOST extraordinary narrative," observed W—, throwing himself into an easy chair, when he reached his rooms. "My reason refuses to credit it, and yet its internal evidence corroborates it. Had the story been told by a person of intelligence and education, I should have regarded it with very grave suspicion; but it seems scarcely possible that this ignorant sailor should have so arranged his facts as to tally with what would actually happen had the subject of his theme existed. The second-mate's description of the geological characteristics of that region, too, show that the physical conditions were just such as were essential to the production of such a prodigy. But the idea of an egg lying out upon the sand, and coming down to us from the Secondary Period—"

"Hundreds of thousands of years ago," interrupted I.

"And its juices not getting dried up—"

"And not getting hatched out long before by the mere caloric of the atmosphere—"

"Why the thing is preposterous!" And W— went to his bookcase and took down a book.

"Still," I ventured to remark, "the vitality of Nature's germs is almost infinite. To destroy species must be a titanic task. Man, at least, has always failed in doing it, and yet he is at constant war with all. Grain seeds which have lain centuries upon centuries in the buried vaults of Pompeii, and in the Pyramids of Egypt, have sprouted with the same vitality and vigor as those of last year's wheat crop; and shall we say that, under certain conditions, the egg of an animal might not preserve the vital germ for an equally indefinite period? Can you assert that such an instance is physically impossible?"

"No," rejoined W—, thoughtfully; "I have no right to do so. Here," continued he, opening a volume, "is a representation of what the iguanodon, that monstrous dinosaurian of the Secondary Period, would look like, were it reconstructed from the few osseous remains found in the Wealden clays and other cognate formations. Let us see what the article accompanying it says, and

how far it tallies with Captain Sebright's narrative," and W—
turned over the leaves till he found the place. "Now," he continued, "this monster might possibly have been a teleosaurus,
certain species of which, the book informs us, measured as much
as thirty-three feet in length, three of which were occupied by
the animal's head. Its awful jaws, which were well defended beyond the ears, opened as wide as six feet, through which it could
engulf, in the depths of its cavernous palate, 'animals of the size
of an ox.' Or, possibly, a megalosaurus, which measured, we are
told, thirty-eight to forty feet in length, and which is fully and
graphically described in Dr. Buckland's admirable Bridgewater
treatise. Cuvier, however, 'from the dimensions of the coracoid,
(a process of the scapula,) supposes that the *Megalosaurus Buck-
landi* may have been some seventy feet in length.' But neither of
these animals possessed the facial horn, and both were carniv-
orous—two facts which are at variance with Captain Sebright's
description. Ah! here we have it—the iguanodon. 'Of more for-
midable dimensions than the megalosaurus was the *Iguanodon*,
(or "iguana-toothed,") which, so far as our researches have hitherto extended, must be pronounced the most gigantic of the primeval saurians. Professor Owen differs from Dr. Mantell in his
estimate of the animal's length, which the latter makes from fifty
to sixty feet. The comparative dimensions of its bones show that
it stood high on its legs, the hind-limbs being much longer than
the fore, and the feet short and massive. The form and disposition of the feet show that it was a terrestrial, as its dentition
proves it to have been an herbivorous animal. The iguanodon
carried a horn on its muzzle. A skeleton, nearly perfect, was discovered by Mantell in Tilgate Forest.'"

"It would seem, then," I remarked, "that our savants differ
materially in their estimate of the size of these animals, and in
view of the old apothegm, 'who shall decide when doctors dis-
agree?' I suppose the testimony of Captain Sebright, and the
captain of the Australian schooner who sighted the monster, as
reported in the Brisbane *Courier*, both of whom put down the
animal's length at from eighty to a hundred feet, is entitled to

quite as much respect as inferences merely drawn from an examination of bones, though made by authorities however distinguished."

"Well," responded W—, thoughtfully, "unscientific men, and men untrained in forming nice estimates of dimensions in relation to distances, are more prone to err on the side of exaggeration than diminution of facts. The mere assertion of a parcel of sailors on a matter of size of any object seen would carry little weight in my formation of an opinion. But what *does* carry weight is Captain Sebright's account of the dimensions of the egg. If the captain's measurement of the egg's diameter—fourteen feet—is to be accepted, we must necessarily accept his measurement of the egg's depositor—eighty to a hundred feet. *Ex pede Herculem*—from the size of the egg the size of the animal. The captain's testimony is unimpeached, yet it is not corroborated. Its strongest title to belief lies in the internal evidence of the story backed up by the credibility of the narrator. Meanwhile, I shall lay the facts before the Academy of Sciences, and await further accounts in the Australian papers."

THE MONSTER-GOD OF MAMURTH
Edmond Hamilton

Out of the desert night he came to us, stumbling into our little circle of firelight and collapsing at once. Mitchell and I sprang to our feet with startled exclamations, for men who travel alone and on foot are a strange sight in the deserts of North Africa.

For the first few minutes that we worked over him I thought he would die at once, but gradually we brought him back to consciousness. While Mitchell held a cup of water to his cracked lips I looked him over and saw that he was too far gone to live much longer. His clothes were in rags, and his hands and knees literally flayed, from crawling over the sands, I judged. So when he motioned feebly for more water, I gave it to him, knowing that in any case his time was short. Soon he could talk, in a dead, croaking voice.

"I'm alone," he told us, in answer to our first question; "no more out there to look for. What are you two—traders? I thought so. No, I'm an archeologist. A digger-up of the past." His voice broke for a moment. "It's not always good to dig up dead secrets. There are some things the past should be allowed to hide."

He caught the look that passed between Mitchell and me.

"No, I'm not mad," he said. "You will hear, I'll tell you the whole thing. But listen to me, you two," and in his earnestness he raised himself to a sitting position, "keep out of Igidi Desert. Remember that I told you that. I had a warning, too, but I disregarded it. And I went into hell—into hell! But there, I will tell you from the beginning.

"My name—that doesn't matter now. I left Mogador more than a year ago—1923—and came through the foot-hills of the Atlas ranges striking out into the desert in hopes of finding some of the Carthaginian ruins the North African deserts are known to hold.

"I spent months in the search, traveling among the squalid Arab villages, now near an oasis and now far into the black, untracked desert. And as I went farther into that savage country, I found more and more of the ruins I sought, crumbled remnants of temples and fortresses, relics, almost destroyed, of the age when Carthage meant empire and ruled all of North Africa from her walled city. And then, on the side of a massive block of stone, I found that which turned me toward Igidi.

"It was an inscription in the garbled Phoenician of the traders of Carthage, short enough so that I remembered it and can repeat it word for word. It read, literally, as follows:

> Merchants, go not into the city of Mamurth, which lies beyond the mountain pass. For I, San-Drabat of Carthage, entering the city with four companions in the month of Eschmoun, to trade, on the third night of our stay came priests and seized my fellows, I escaping by hiding. My companions they sacrificed to the evil god of the city, who has dwelt there from the beginning of time, and for whom the wise men of Mamurth have built a great temple the like of which is not on earth elsewhere, where the people of Mamurth worship their god. I escaped from the city and set this warning here that others may not turn their steps to Mamurth and to death.

"Perhaps you can imagine the effect that inscription had on me. I was the last trace of a city unknown to the memory of men, a last floating spar of a civilization sunken in the sea of time. That there could have been such a city at all seemed to me quite probable. What do we know of Carthage even, but a few names? No city, no civilization was ever so completely blotted off the earth as Carthage when Roman Scipio ground its temples and palaces into the very dust, and plowed up the ground with salt, and the eagles of conquering Rome flew across a desert where a metropolis had been.

"It was on the outskirts of one of those wretched little Arab villages that I had found the block and its inscription, and I tried to find someone in the village to accompany me, but none would do so. I could plainly see the mountain pass, a mere crack between towering blue cliffs. In reality it was miles and miles away, but the deceptive optical qualities of the desert light made it seem very near. My maps placed that mountain range all right, as a lower branch of the Atlas, and the expanse behind the mountains was marked as 'Igidi Desert', but that was all I got from them. All that I could reckon on as certain was that it was desert that lay on the other side of the pass, and I must carry enough supplies to meet it.

"But the Arabs knew more! Though I offered what must have been fabulous riches to those poor devils, not one would come with me when I let them know what place I was heading for. None had ever been there, they would not even ride far into the desert in that direction; but all had very definite ideas of the place beyond the mountains as a nest of devils, a haunt of evil Jinns.

"Knowing how firmly superstition is implanted in their kind, I tried no longer to persuade them, and started alone, with two scrawny camels carrying my water and supplies. So for three days I forged across the desert under a broiling sun, and on the morning of the fourth I reached the pass.

"It was only a narrow crevice to begin with, and great boulders were strewn so thickly on its floor that it was a long, hard job getting through. And the cliffs on each side towered to such a height that the space between was a place of shadows and whispers and semidarkness. It was late in the afternoon when I finally came through, and for a moment I stood motionless; for from that side of the pass the desert sloped down into a vast basin, and at the basin's center, perhaps two miles from where I stood, gleamed the white ruins of Mamurth.

"I remember that I was very calm as I covered the two miles between myself and the ruins. I had taken the existence of the city as a fact, so much so that if the ruins had not been there I should have been vastly more surprised than at finding them.

"From the pass I had seen only a tangled mass of white fragments, but as I drew nearer, some of these began to take outline as crumbling blocks, and walls, and columns. The sand had drifted, too, and the ruins were completely buried in some sections, while nearly all were half covered.

"And then it was that I made a curious discovery. I had stopped to examine the material of the ruins, a smooth, veinless stone, much like an artificial marble or a superfine concrete. And while I looked about me, intent on this, I noticed that on almost every shaft and block, on broken cornice and column, was carved the same symbol—if it was a symbol. It was a rough picture of a queer, outlandish creature, much like an octopus, with a round, almost shapeless body, and several long tentacles or arms branching out from the body, not supple and boneless, like those of an octopus, but seemingly stiff and jointed, like a spider's legs. In fact, the thing might have been intended to represent a spider, I thought, though some of the details were wrong. I speculated for a moment on the profusion of these creatures carved on the ruins all around me, then gave it up as an enigma that was unsolvable.

"And the riddle of the city about me seemed unsolvable also. What could I find in this half-buried mass of stone fragments to throw light on the past? I could not even superficially explore the place, for the scantiness of my supplies and water would not permit a long stay. It was with a discouraged heart that I went back to the camels and, leading them to an open spot in the ruins, made my camp for the night. And when night had fallen, and I sat beside my little fire, the vast, brooding silence of this place of death was awful. There were no laughing human voices, or cries of animals, or even cries of birds or insects. There was nothing but the darkness and silence that crowded around me, flowed down upon me, beat sullenly against the glowing spears of light my little fire threw out.

"As I sat there musing, I was startled by a slight sound behind me. I turned to see its cause, and then stiffened. As I have mentioned, the space directly around my camp was clear sand, smoothed level by the winds. Well, as I stared at that flat expanse of sand, a hole several inches across suddenly appeared in its surface, yards from where I stood, but clearly visible in the firelight.

"There was nothing whatever to be seen there, not even a shadow, but there it was, one moment the level surface of the sand, the next moment a hole appearing in it, accompanied by a soft, crunching sound. As I stood gazing at it in wonder, that sound was repeated and simultaneously another hole appeared in the sand's surface, five or six feet nearer to me than the other.

"When I saw that, ice-tipped arrows of fear seemed to shoot through me, and then, yielding to a mad impulse, I snatched a blazing piece of fuel from the fire and hurled it, a comet of red flame, at the place where the holes had appeared. There was a slight sound of scurrying and shuffling, and I felt that whatever thing had made those marks had retreated, if a living thing had made them at all. What it had been, I could not imagine, for there had been absolutely nothing in sight, one track and then another appearing magically in the clear sand, if indeed they were really tracks at all.

"The mystery of the thing haunted me. Even in sleep I found no rest, for evil dreams seemed to flow into my brain from the dead city around me. All the dusty sins of ages past, in the forgotten place, seemed to be focused on me in the dreams I had. Strange shapes walked through them, unearthly as the spawn of a distant star, half icon and vanishing again.

"It was little enough sleep I got that night, but when the sun finally came, with its first golden rays, my fears and oppressions dropped from me like a cloak. No wonder the early peoples were sun-worshippers!

"And with my renewed strength and courage, a new thought struck me. In the inscription I have quoted to you, that long-dead merchant-adventurer had mentioned the great temple of the city and dwelt on its grandeur. Where, then, were its ruins? I wondered. I decided that what time I had would be better spent in investigating the ruins of this temple, which should be prominent, if that ancient Carthaginian had been correct as to its size.

"I ascended a near-by hillock and looked about me in all directions, and though I could not perceive any vast pile of ruins that might have been the temple's, I did see for the first time, far away, two great figures of stone that stood out black against the rosy flame of the sunrise. It was a discovery that filled me with excitement, and I broke camp at once, starting in the direction of those two shapes.

"They were on the very edge of the farther side of the city, and it was noon before I finally stood before them. And now I saw clearly their nature: two great, sitting figures, carved of black stone, all of fifty feet in height, and almost that far apart, facing both toward the city and toward me. They were of human shape and dressed in a queer, scaled armor, but the faces I can not describe, for they were unhuman. The features were human, well-proportioned, even, but the face, the expression, suggested no kinship whatever with humanity as we know it. Were they carved from life? I wondered. If so, it must have been a strange sort of people who had lived in this city and set up these two statues.

"And now I tore my gaze away from them, and looked around. On each side of those shapes, the remains of what must once have been a mighty wall branched out, a long pile of crumbling ruins. But there had been no wall between the statues, that being evidently the gateway through the barrier. I wondered why the two guardians of the gate had survived, apparently entirely unharmed, while the wall and the city behind me had fallen into ruins. They were of a different material, I could see; but what was that material?

"And now I noticed for the first time the long avenue that began on the other side of the statues and stretched away into the desert for a half-mile or more. The sides of this avenue were two rows of smaller stone figures that ran in parallel lines away from the two colossi. So I started down that avenue, passing between the two great shapes that stood at its head. And as I went between them, I noticed for the first time the inscription graven on the inner side of each.

"On the pedestal of each figure, four or five feet from the ground was a raised tablet of the same material, perhaps a yard square, and covered with strange symbols—characters, no doubt, of a lost language, undecipherable, at least to me. One symbol, though, that was especially prominent in the inscription, was not new to me. It was the carven picture of the spider, or octopus, which I have mentioned that I had found everywhere on the ruins of the city. And here it was scattered thickly among the symbols that made up the inscription. The tablet on the other statue was a replica of the first, and I could learn no more from it. So I started down the avenue, turning over in my mind the riddle of that omnipresent symbol, and then forgetting it, as I observed the things about me.

"That long street was like the avenue of sphinxes at Kamak, down which Pharaoh swung in his litter, borne to his temple on the necks of men. But the statues that made up its sides were not sphinx-shaped. They were carved in strange forms, shapes of animals unknown to us, as far removed from anything we can imagine as the beasts of another world. I can not describe them, any more than you could describe a dragon to a man who had been blind all his life. Yet they were of evil, reptilian shapes; they tore at my nerves as I looked at them.

"Down between the two rows of them I went, until I came to the end of the avenue. Standing there between the last two figures, I could see nothing before me but the yellow sands of the desert, as far as the eye could reach. I was puzzled. What had been the object of all the pains that had been taken, the wall, the two great statues, and this long avenue, if it but led into the desert?

"Gradually I began to see that there was something queer about the part of the desert that lay directly before me. It was *flat*. For an area, seemingly round in shape, that must have covered several acres the surface of the desert seemed absolutely level. It was as though the sands within that great circle had been packed down with tremendous force, leaving not even the littlest ridge of dune on its surface. Beyond this flat area, and all around it, the desert was broken up by small hills and valleys, and traversed by whirling sand-clouds, but nothing stirred on the flat surface of the circle.

"Interested at once, I strode forward to the edge of the circle, only a few yards away. I had just reached that edge when an invisible hand seemed to strike me a great blow on the face and chest, knocking me backward in the sand.

"It was minutes before I advanced again, but I did advance, for all my curiosity was now aroused. I crawled toward the circle's edge, holding my pistol before me, pushing slowly forward.

"When the automatic in my outstretched hand reached the line of the circle, it struck against something hard, and I could push it no farther. It was exactly as if it had struck against the side of a wall, but no wall or anything else was to be seen. Reaching out my hand, I touched the same hard barrier, and in a moment I was on my feet.

"For I knew now that it was solid matter I had run into, not force. When I thrust out my hands, the edge of the circle was as far as they would go, for there they met a smooth wall, totally invisible, yet at the same time quite material. And the phenomenon was one which even I could partly understand. Somehow, in the dead past, the scientists of the city behind me, the 'wise men' mentioned in the inscription, had discovered the secret of making solid matter invisible, and had applied it to the work that I was now examining. Such a thing was far from impossible. Even our own scientists can make matter partly invisible, with the X-ray. Evidently these people had known the whole process, a secret that had been lost in the succeeding ages, like the secret of hard gold, and malleable glass, and others that we find mentioned in ancient writings. Yet I wondered how they had done this, so that, ages after those who had built the thing were wind-driven dust, it remained as invisible as ever.

"I stood back and threw pebbles into the air, toward the circle. No matter how high I threw them, when they reached the line of the circle's edge they rebounded with a clicking sound; so I knew that the wall must tower to a great height above me. I was on fire to get inside the wall, and examine the place from the inside, but how to do it? There must be an entrance, but where? And I suddenly remembered the two guardian statues at the head of the great avenue, with their carven tablets, and wondered what connection they had with this place.

"Suddenly the strangeness of the whole thing struck me like a blow. The great, unseen wall before me, the circle of sand, flat and unchanging, and myself, standing there and wondering, wondering. A voice from out the dead city behind me seemed to sound in my heart, bidding me to turn and flee, to get away. I remembered the warning of the inscription, '*Go not to Mamurth.*' And as I thought of the inscription, I had no doubt that this was the great temple described by San-Drabat. Surely he was right: the like of it was not on earth elsewhere.

"But I would not go, I could not go, until I had examined the wall from the inside. Calmly reasoning the matter, I decided that the logical place for the gateway through the wall would be at the end of the avenue, so that those who came down the street could pass directly through the wall. And my reasoning was good, for it was at that spot that I found the entrance: an opening in the barrier, several yards wide, and running higher than I could reach, how high I had no means of telling.

"I felt my way through the gate, and stepped at once upon a floor of hard material, not as smooth as the wall's surface, but equally invisible. Inside the entrance lay a corridor of equal width, leading into the center of the circle, and I felt my way forward.

"I must have made a strange picture, had there been any there to observe it. For while I knew that all around me were the towering, invisible walls, and I knew not what else, yet all my eyes could see was the great flat circle of sand beneath me, carpeted with the afternoon sunshine. Only, I seemed to be walking a foot above the ground, in thin air. That was the thickness of the floor beneath me, and it was the weight of this great floor, I knew, that held the circle of sand under it forever flat and unchanging.

"I walked slowly down the passageway, with hands outstretched before me, and had gone but a short distance when I brought up against another smooth wall that lay directly across the corridor, seemingly making it a blind alley. But I was not discouraged now, for I knew that there must be a door somewhere, and began to feel around me in search of it.

"I found the door. In groping about the sides of the corridor my hands encountered a smoothly rounded knob set in the wall, and as I laid my hand on this, the door opened. There was a sighing, as of a little wind, and when I again felt my way forward, the wall that had lain across the passageway was gone, and I was free to go forward. But I dared not go through at once. I went back to the knob on the wall, and found that no amount of pressing or twisting of it would close the door that had opened. Some subtle mechanism within the knob had operated, that needed only a touch of the hand to work it, and the whole end of the corridor had moved out of the way, sliding up in grooves, I *think*, like a portcullis, though of this I am not sure.

"But the door was safely opened, and I passed through it. Moving about, like a blind man in a strange place, I found that I was in a vast inner court, the walls of which sloped away in a great curve. When I discovered this, I came back to the spot where the corridor opened into the court, and then walked straight out into the court itself.

"It was steps that I encountered: the first broad steps of what was evidently a staircase of titanic proportions. And I went up, slowly, carefully, feeling before me every foot of the way. It was only the feel of the staircase under me that gave reality to it, for as far as I could see, I was simply climbing up into empty space. It was weird beyond telling.

"Up and up I went, until I was all of a hundred feet above the ground, and then the staircase narrowed, the sides drew together. A few more steps, and I came out on a flat floor again, which, after some groping about, I found to be a broad landing, with high, railed edges. I crawled across this landing on hands and knees, and then struck against another wall, and in it, another door. I went through this too, still crawling, and though everything about me was still invisible, I sensed that I was no longer in the open air, but in a great room.

"I stopped short, and then, as I crouched on the floor, I felt a sudden prescience of evil, of some malignant, menacing entity that was native here. Nothing I could see, or hear, but strong upon my brain beat the thought of something infinitely ancient, infinitely evil, that was a part of this place. Was it a consciousness, I wonder, of the horror that had filled the place in ages long dead? Whatever caused it, I could go no farther in the face of the terror that possessed me; so I drew back and walked to the edge of the landing, leaning over its high, invisible railing and surveying the scene below.

"The setting sun hung like a great ball of red-hot iron in the western sky, and in its lurid rays the two great statues cast long shadows on the yellow sands. Not far away, my two camels, hobbled, moved restlessly about. To all appearances I was standing on thin air, a hundred feet or more above the ground, but in my mind's eye I had a picture of the great courts and corridors below me, through which I had felt my way.

"As I mused there in the red light, it was clear to me that this was the great temple of the city. What a sight it must have been, in the time of the city's life! I could imagine the long procession of priests and people, in somber and gorgeous robes, coming out from the city, between the great statues and down the long avenue, dragging with them, perhaps, an unhappy prisoner to sacrifice to their god in this, his temple.

"The sun was now dipping beneath the horizon, and I turned to go, but before ever I moved, I became rigid and my heart seemed to stand still. For on the farther edge of the clear stretch of sand that lay beneath the temple and the city, a hole suddenly appeared in the sand, springing into being on the desert's face exactly like the one I had seen at my campfire the night before. I watched, as fascinated as by the eyes of a snake. And before my eyes, another and another appeared, not in a straight line, but in

a zigzag fashion. Two such holes would be punched down on one
side, then two more on the other side, then one in the middle,
making a series of tracks, perhaps two yards in width from side
to side, and advancing straight toward the temple and myself.
And I could see nothing!

"It was like—the comparison suddenly struck me—like the
tracks a many-legged insect might make in the sand, only magnified to un-heard-of proportions. And with that thought, the
truth rushed on me, for I remembered the spider carved on the
ruins and on the statues, and I knew now what it had signified
to the dwellers in the city. What was it the inscription had said?
'*The evil god of the city, who has dwelt there from the beginning
of time.*' And as I saw those tracks advancing toward me, I knew
that the city's ancient evil god still dwelt here, and that I was in
his temple, alone and unarmed.

"What strange creatures might there not have been in the
dawn of time? And this one, this gigantic monster in a spider's
form—had not those who built the city found it here when they
came, and, in awe, taken it as the city's god, and built for it the
mighty temple in which I now stood? And they, who had the
wisdom and art to make this vast fane invisible, not to be seen
by human eyes, had they done the same to their god, and made
of him almost a true god, invisible, powerful, undying? Undying!
Almost it must have been, to survive the ages as it had done. Yet I
knew that even some kinds of parrots live for centuries, and what
could I know of this monstrous relic of dead ages? And when the
city died and crumbled, and the victims were no longer brought
to its lair in the temple, did it not live, as I thought, by ranging
the desert? No wonder the Arabs had feared the country in this
direction! It would be death for anything that came even within
view of such a horror, that could clutch and spring and chase,
and yet remain always unseen. And was it death for me?

"Such were some of the thoughts that pounded through my
brain, as I watched death approach, with those steadily advancing tracks in the sand. And now the paralysis of terror that had
gripped me was broken, and I ran down the great staircase, and

into the court. I could think of no place in that great hall where I might hide. Imagine hiding in a place where all is invisible! But I must go some place, and finally I dashed past the foot of the great staircase until I reached a wall directly under the landing on which I had stood, and against this I crouched, praying that the deepening shadows of dusk might hide me from the gaze of the creature whose lair this was.

"I knew instantly when the thing entered the gate through which I too had come. Pad, pad, pad—that was the soft, cushioned sound of its passage. I heard the feet stop for a moment by the opened door at the end of the corridor. Perhaps it was in surprise that the door was open, I thought, for how could I know how great or little intelligence lay in that unseen creature's brain? Then, pad, pad—across the court it came, and I heard the soft sound of its passing as it ascended the staircase. Had I not been afraid to breathe, I would have almost screamed with relief.

"Yet still fear held me, and I remained crouched against the wall while the thing went up the great stairs. Imagine that scene! All around me was absolutely nothing visible, nothing but the great flat circle of sand that lay a foot below me; yet I saw the place with my mind's eye, and knew of the walls and courts that lay about me, and the thing above me, in fear of which I was crouching there in the gathering darkness.

"The sound of feet above me had ceased, and I judged that the thing had gone into the great room above, which I had feared to enter. Now, if ever, was the time to make my escape in the darkness; so I rose, with infinite carefulness, and softly walked across the court to the door that led into the corridor. But when I had walked only half of the distance, as I thought, I crashed squarely into another invisible wall across my path, and fell backward, the metal handle of the sheath-knife at my belt striking the flooring with a loud clang. God help me, I had misjudged the position of the door, and had walked straight into the wall, instead!

"I lay there, motionless, with cold fear flooding every part of my being. Then, pad, pad—the soft steps of the thing across the landing and then silence for a moment. Could it see me from the landing? I wondered. Could it? For a moment, hope warmed me, as no sound came, but the next instant I knew that death had me by the throat, for pad, pad—down the stairs it came.

"With that sound my last vestige of self-control fled and I scrambled to my feet and made another mad dash in the direction of the door. Crash!—into another wall I went, and rose to my feet trembling. There was no sound of footsteps now, and as quietly as I could, I walked into the great court still farther, as I thought, for all my ideas of direction were hopelessly confused. God, what a weird game it was we played there on that darkened circle of sand!

"No sound whatever came from the thing that hunted me, and my hope flickered up again. And with a dreadful irony, it was at that exact moment that I walked straight into the thing. My outstretched hand touched and grasped what must have been one of its limbs, thick and cold and hairy, which was instantly torn from my grasp and then seized me again, while another and another clutched me also. The thing had stood quite still, leaving me to walk directly into its grasp—the drama of the spider and the fly!

"A moment only it held me, for that cold grasp filled me with such deep, shuddering abhorrence that I wrenched myself loose and I fled madly across the court, stumbling again on the first step of the great staircase. I raced up the stairs, and even as I ran I heard the thing in pursuit.

"Up I went, and across the landing, and grasped the edge of the railing, for I meant to throw myself down from there, to a clean death on the floor below. But under my hands, the top of the railing moved, one of the great blocks that evidently made up its top was loosened and rocked toward me. In a flash I grasped the great block and staggered across the landing with it in my arms, to the head of the staircase. Two men could hardly have lifted it, I think, yet I did more, in a sudden access of mad strength; for as I heard that monster coming swiftly up the great stairs, I raised the block, invisible as ever, above my head, and sent it crashing down the staircase upon the place where I thought the thing was at that moment.

"For an instant after the crash there was silence, and then a low humming sound began, that waxed into a loud droning. And at the same time, at a spot half-way down the staircase where the block had crashed, a thin, purple liquid seemed to well out of the empty air, giving form to a few of the invisible steps as it flowed over them, and outlining, too, the block I had thrown, and a great hairy limb that lay crushed beneath it, and from which the fluid that was the monster's blood was oozing. I had not killed the thing, but had chained it down with the block that held it prisoner.

"There was a thrashing sound on the staircase, and the purple stream ran more freely, and by the outline of its splashes, I saw, dimly, the monstrous god that had been known in Mamurth in ages past. It was like a giant spider, with angled limbs that were yards long, and a hairy, repellent body. Even as I stood there, I wondered that the thing, invisible as it was, was yet visible by the life-blood in it, when that blood was spilled. Yet so it was, nor can I even suggest a reason. But one glimpse I got of its half-visible, purple-splashed outline, and then, hugging the farther side of the stairs, I descended. When I passed the thing, the intolerable odor of a crushed insect almost smothered me, and the monster itself made frantic efforts to loosen itself and spring at me. But it could not, and I got safely down, shuddering and hardly able to walk.

"Straight across the great court I went, and ran shakily through the corridor, and down the long avenue, and out between the two great statues. The moonlight shone on them, and the tablets of inscriptions stood out clearly on the sides of the statues, with their strange symbols and carved spider forms. But I knew now what their message was!

"It was well that my camels had wandered into the ruins, for such was the fear that struck through me that I would never have returned for them had they lingered by the invisible wall. All that night I rode to the north, and when morning came I did not stop, but still pushed north. And as I went through the mountain pass, one camel stumbled and fell, and in falling burst open all my water supplies that were lashed on its back.

"No water at all was left, but I still held north, killing the other camel by my constant speed, and then staggered on, afoot. On hands and knees I crawled forward, when my legs gave out, always north, away from that temple of evil and its evil god. And tonight, I had been crawling, how many miles I do not know, and I saw your fire. And that is all."

He lay back exhausted, and Mitchell and I looked at each other's faces in the firelight. Then, rising, Mitchell strode to the edge of our camp and looked for a long time at the moonlit desert, which lay toward the south. What his thoughts were, I do not know. I was nursing my own, as I watched the man who lay beside our fire.

It was early the next morning that he died, muttering about great walls around him. We wrapped his body securely, and bearing it with us held our way across the desert.

In Algiers we cabled to the friends whose address we found in his moneybelt, and arranged to ship the body to them, for such had been his only request. Later they wrote that he had been buried in the little churchyard of the New England village that had been his childhood home. I do not think that his sleep there will be troubled by dreams of that place of evil from which he fled. I pray that it will not.

Often and often have Mitchell and I discussed the thing, over lonely campfires and in the inns of the seaport towns. Did he kill the invisible monster he spoke of, and is it lying now, a withered remnant, under the block on the great staircase? Or did it gnaw its way loose; does it still roam the desert and make its lair in the vast, ancient temple, as unseen as itself?

Or, different still, was the man simply crazed by the heat and thirst of the desert, and his tale but the product of a maddened mind? I do not think that this is so. I think that he told truth, yet I do not know. Nor shall I ever know, for never, Mitchell and I have decided, shall we be the ones to venture into the place of hell on earth where that ancient god of evil may still be living, amid the invisible courts and towers, beyond the unseen wall.

THE BELLS OF OCEANA
Arthur J. Burks

IT WAS ON A HEAVILY LADEN TROOPSHIP, westward heading. Hours before, the sun had gone down toward China, trailing ebon night behind her. For a full week, since dropping the California coast behind us, there had been nothing in all the wild waste of waters for us to see save ourselves. No ship's funnels broke the lowering horizon, no sign of land, for our skipper had chosen a passage lying somewhere in between the usual steamer lanes. The nearest land, save that which stretched in eternal darkness some three miles below us, was more than a thousand miles beyond the southern horizon. We were just a single ship, burdened with a precious freight of souls, upon an ocean that seemed endless. The first day out had been squally, and everyone had been sick, save those of us who had gone down to the sea in ships before. But with the dawning of the second morning the sea had calmed down, and our vessel rode through the blue, toward the horizon bowl which ever crept before us, in the golden wake of the setting sun. The voyage, if the old salts spoke truly, would be uneventful; but, with that strange premonitory feeling which comes to all of us at times, I did not believe them.

Something, from the very first, warned me that our voyage was ill-fated. I couldn't explain my feeling. It wasn't a feeling of dread, exactly, nor of fear. Just a strange feeling of unease, much like that which comes to people on their first voyage, when a ship is rolling slightly under their feet, and everything, until they get their sea-legs, seems strangely out of focus. That doesn't explain it, I know; but it is as near as I can put my feeling into words.

I knew, when the sun went down ahead of us, with the hundred and eightieth meridian less than twenty-four hours ahead, that we were on the eve of strange, momentous happenings. To add to my feeling of unease, and as though it had been all planned out by some invisible *something* or *somebody*, in the vague beginning, the officer who should have had the watch that night fell suddenly ill, and I was called upon to take his place. I knew, as I donned my belt, holster and pistol, that I but obeyed the will of some invisible prompter—a prompter without a name.

We had seven sentries out at various important places about the ship, and I made the routine inspections before turning in, less than an hour before midnight. When I entered my stateroom and turned on the light, that feeling of unease was more pronounced than it had been at any time previously. I had the feeling, though I had locked my door when I had last quitted my stateroom, that I had entered again immediately *after* someone had left it. Yet that was impossible. I had carried the key in my pocket all the time, and my cabin-boy was not provided with one. There was no way that anyone, or anything, could have entered my stateroom in my absence, save—

Still as though my every move had been ordered by some invisible prompter, my eyes darted to the port-hole beside my bed. It was quite too small for the passage of a human body, and even to think of such a thing were the utmost folly. If anyone had gone out through the port-hole, that one had fallen, or plunged into the sea, for had the port-hole been ever so big, there was absolutely no way one could have left my stateroom by that way and still remained upon the ship—unless that one had gone out and were even now hanging by his hands along the ship's side. So strongly had the feeling of an alien presence obtruded itself upon me that, in spite of knowing myself an utter fool for entertaining any doubt whatsoever, I strode to the port-hole and looked out. There was nothing, of course, save water, now black and forbidding, stretching away to the south, to a horizon that, since night had fallen, seemed to have crept quite close to us to watch our passing.

Still unsatisfied, in spite of arguing with myself, condemning myself for a fool, I deliberately closed the glass which masked the port, took my seat in a chair beside the bunk, facing the round glass—which resembled, to an imagination suddenly fevered, the eye of a huge one-eyed giant—of the port-hole, and began to undress. Mechanically I lifted first one foot and then the other, removing shoes and stockings.

But I kept my eyes upon the closed port-hole—and that feeling of an unseen presence in the room was stronger as the moments fled. My undressing completed, I stood erect to turn out the lights, and paused in the very act, a cry of terror smothered in my throat by a sheer act of will.

For, for the most fleeting of seconds, I had seen a dead-white face outside the glass which covered the port-hole! It was the face of a person who had drowned, I told myself wildly, and the dripping hair wore a coronet of fluttering seaweed. The eyes of this strange outsider stared straight into mine, devoid of expression, totally unwinking, and the lips, which seemed blue as though with icy cold long endured, smiled a thin and ironic smile. It took all the courage I possessed, which is little enough in the face of the unknown, to hurl myself across the bed, right hand extended toward the heavy screw which held the circular piece of glass in place. In the instant my hand would have touched the glass, the ship rode into the edge of the storm that was to fill the remainder of the night, and the stern of the steamer rose dizzily on the crest of a mighty wave, dragging all the vessel with it—and the face slid slowly out of sight below the port-hole, the bluish lips still smiling ironically!

I admit that I was trembling, that my fingers were unsteady as I fumbled with the screw to unloose the glass. When the port-hole was open once more, and the cold breeze of this latitude came in to fan my fevered face, I thrust my head out of the port and gazed right and left, and up and down, along the curving side of the ship. But there was nothing—save straight ahead, on our port side. And even there, there was nothing but black water, huge mountainous waves, touched with whitecaps at their crests, like flying shrouds, or like lacy streamers created as a fringe for the mantle of night.

I watched several of the waves sweep under the vessel, which rose and fell sluggishly. The waves seemed to be traveling in no certain direction, but broke into a veritable welter of warring forces, roaring as they came together with the roaring of maddened, deep-throated bulls. Valleys with darkness on their floors, mountain-tops touched with snow that shifted eerily in the breeze.

I was about to close the port when, many yards away from the ship, as though born of the womb of old ocean, I heard the bells!

Like the tiny bells which the bellwether wears to signal the ewes and the lambs, was the tinkling of the bells—like those bells, yet not like them, totally out of place in mid-ocean, and I felt a strange prickling of the scalp as I listened. Hurriedly, driven by a fear I could not have explained then, nor can I now explain, I closed the port-hole again. And whirled about with another scream, which this time came forth from my quivering lips in spite of all I could do to prevent.

Just inside my stateroom door stood my sergeant of the guard, and his lips were trembling more wildly than my own, his eyes protruded horribly, his face was chalk-white, and he was striving with all his power to speak! As I watched his manful struggle, I dreaded for him to speak—for I knew that what he had come to tell me would be something strange and terrible, something hitherto entirely outside my experience.

"Sir," he managed at last, when I stiffly nodded permission for him to speak, "I just made the rounds of the sentries!"

Here the poor fellow stopped, unable to go on, and his knees knocked together audibly.

"Yes, sergeant," I managed to mutter, "you went the usual rounds of the sentries, and then?"

"The sentry who should be on duty on the main deck, forward of the bridge, is missing!"

Of course I knew on the instant that there might be many reasons for the failure of the sergeant of the guard to find the sentry, many logical reasons. The sentry might have quitted his post (a violation of regulations, true) for a quiet cigarette in the lee of a lifeboat; he might have been walking his post in the direction taken by the sergeant, so that the latter had not overtaken him, even with a complete circling of the main deck; he might—oh, there were many logical explanations; but I guessed instinctively that none of these reasons fitted the case. For one thing, the sergeant of the guard was an old-timer, had spent many years of his life at sea—yet he was frightened half out of his wits, and I knew he held as many decorations for bravery as any other officer or man in the marine corps. There was something terrible, something—if you will—uncanny behind this disappearance of the sentry.

I muttered an oath, more to prod my own flagging courage than for any other reason, and started toward the door, motioning the sergeant to precede me. But he shook his head stubbornly and barred my way. I halted, for it was evident that he had not completed his report.

"You'll maybe think me daft," he said; "but I couldn't let you go out there, sir, without telling you everything. The corporal on watch at the head of the promenade gangway told me a strange story just before I made my rounds. He opened the door leading onto the starboard promenade, for a look at the weather outside, and just as he was about to close it again, the ship lifted on the crest of a huge wave—and out beyond the wave, many yards away from the ship, he heard something which he likened to the tinkling of little bells!"

"Good God!" I exclaimed.

"And," the sergeant continued, "all the time I was looking for the missing sentry, I had the idea there was someone behind me, following me every step of the way; yet when I whirled to look, the deck behind me was empty!"

"And you found no sign of the sentry?" I said stupidly.

The sergeant shook his head.

"Nothing," he said, "except—except—well, sir, you'll maybe think me daft, as I said before; but on the spot where the sentry had stood to wait for me on my last round, I found wet marks on the deck floor—the marks, as near as I could tell with my flashlight, of bare feet!"

Mechanically, as the sergeant spoke, I had been donning my clothes, leaving my shoes, however, unlaced. I felt an icy chill along my spine as the sergeant continued, and I dreaded, as I had never dreaded anything before, to ask him further about those wet footprints on the deck.

"The wet footprints," he went on, and he was talking wildly now, his words tripping over one another, so rapidly were they uttered, as though he wished to finish his report before I could interrupt again, "led away where the sentry should have been standing, straight to the starboard rail! Right at the rail I stooped to examine the prints more closely. They were the footprints of a human being, I was sure, and the marks of the toes were blurred, and very wide, as though whoever—or *whatever*—had made them, had been carrying a burden in his arms!"

"Good God, sergeant!" I said again; "what are you driving at?"

"Just this, sir. There's something terribly wrong with this ship! *Something took that sentry bodily over the side!*"

I believe that putting a name, however meaningless, to what was in my own mind, caused a little of my courage to return, for I did not find it difficult now to bring myself to leave the state-room. The sergeant almost trod on my heels as I hurried to the main deck, starboard side, where the wind wrapped icy fingers around me, chilling me to the bone on the instant.

As I hurried forward I looked over the side, into the welter of waters—and stopped short!

Behind me the sergeant groaned—hollowly, like a man who has been mortally wounded. For out of the waters, away to starboard, came the sound of tinkling bells! I darted to the rail and leaned far outboard, striving to pierce the gloom. But there was nothing save the watery wastes, mountains and valleys—and two spots of greenish phosphorescence, far out, like serpent's eyes which watched the passing ship. But when I looked at them closely, straining my eyes, seeking the form below the eyes, the twin balls of eery flame vanished, a wall of water obtruding itself between!

Well, we found the sentry, sprawled on his face, where the sergeant should have found him on his rounds. I turned the body over, and it was quite cold—with excellent reason! The corpse was dripping wet, entirely nude, and the lips and cheeks as coldly blue as though the corpse had been dragged for hours on a line in the wake of the ship!

No matter how secluded one's life may have been, no matter how carefully one may have been guarded during one's lifetime, there come into the lives of most of us certain inexplicable happenings which may never be forgotten. This matter of the dead sentry was one of these for me, and I shall go to my grave with the memory of his cold cheeks and bluish lips limned upon the retina of my very soul. So many strange circumstances—thank God that, at the moment, I could not look into the two hours or more of terror, which even then stretched before me, else I should most surely have gone entirely mad!—were there connected with this matter that, taken altogether, it is little wonder that I have been unable to forget, or ever shall forget. The roaring of the wind which was lashing all the ocean into fury, a maelstrom in mid-ocean, ghostly whitecaps stretching away into darkness, into seeming infinity; the frightened sergeant behind me, his teeth chattering with fear; the dead sentry at my feet, his body blue with cold, entirely nude as I have said; the marks on the deck of huge bare feet, wet as though the feet had come up out of the sea; the eery sound of bells between our vessel and the lowering horizon—and that dead-white face which I had seen beyond the port-hole of my own cabin a half-hour before.

What was the explanation of it all? What was the cause of the bells, if bells there were? What had come up out of the sea to stride barefooted across the promenade deck of the slumbering troopship? Had my sentry seen whatever had come for him before he had been taken?

Add to all these circumstances the fact that all hell was loose in the watery wastes, that it was now after midnight, and you will understand a little of my feelings. Never before or since have I been as frightened as I was then. I don't regard myself as a coward, nor am I ordinarily superstitious; but show me the man who is without fear in the presence of the unknown, the utterly uncanny, and I will show you a man who has no soul.

I whirled, bumping into the sergeant, who manfully muffled a scream at my unexpected movement, and started, almost blindly, toward the stern of the troopship. As I strode along, with the sergeant at my heels once more, strange images fled across my mind. I remembered the tale of *Die Lorelei*, the maiden who lured sailors to their death with her eery singing, and strained my eyes through the gloom, seeking shapes I feared to see. Then my mind went farther back, to the years before I could read, years in which, thirsty for knowledge, I studied pictures out of old histories to satisfy my longings for wisdom. One of these pictures came back to my mind as I hurried aft: a picture of a hideous monster of unbelievable proportions, who had come up from behind the ocean's horizon, blotting out the sunlight, long arms extended into the picture's foreground, the right hand holding aloft a medieval sailing vessel which had been lifted bodily from the ocean. A fantastic picture, I knew now, drawn to prove the existence of terrible monsters beyond the horizon to which, as yet, no caravel or galleon had dared travel. I wondered, as I strode aft, why this old picture should return to my mind at this time, and fear was at my throat again as I walked.

"I am coming, oh, my beloved!"

The words, high-pitched with ecstasy, came from straight ahead of me, and out of the heavy shadow cast by a huge funnel stepped one of my sentries. Just for a second, as he strode toward the starboard rail, I could see his face—and the face was transfigured, as though the man gazed into the very soul of the Perfect Sweetheart somewhere beyond the rail. Slowly, step by step, as though he would prolong the joy of anticipation, the sentry, who had hurled his rifle aside, approached the rail, still with his eyes fixed on the welter of waters overside, while I halted spellbound to watch what he would do. From out of the waters there came once more the tinkling of bells! And with the sound, as though the sound had been a signal, a huge shadow detached itself from the shadow whence the sentry had stepped but a moment ago, and loomed high above the luckless youth. At the same time the ship climbed high upon a monster wave, so that her starboard side went down, down, until white water came over the side— and when she straightened again, shuddering through all of her, the sentry had vanished! From well rearward of where the man had disappeared, from out of the smother of waters, there came a single long-drawn cry—and it was not a cry of terror, not a cry of pain; but a scream of ecstasy!

"He's gone, sergeant," I said stupidly, "but what took him? Not the wave: he had but to seize the rail to save himself."

"Did you see the shadow, Lieutenant?" the sergeant replied.

I did not answer. He knew I had seen it.

We strode on again, heading toward the stern of the ship— and all about us now, over the ship, on either side of her—but never on her—there tinkled the eery, unexplainable bells!

We stood at last in the very stern of the troopship, gazing into the ghostly wake far below our coign of vantage, and with certain care, I followed the wake rearward with my eyes. But one could not follow it far! That was the circumstance which impressed itself upon me almost at once. The wake died away, short off, within less than a dozen yards of the ship's stern—as though, at the very moment of birth, it had been ignominiously smothered!

In a trice I understood the reason, and thought I understood many things besides. For, like a monster raft, stretching away rearward as far as I could see, and into the darkness beyond my vision to right and left, there followed us, close to, an undulating mass of odorless seaweed! Acres and acres of it there were, rising and falling sluggishly, but keeping pace with the troopship through the night and the storm! Came again that sound of bells, and my hair stiffened at the base of my skull when I saw, watching the seaweed, the result of the tinkling of the bells. The seaweed, when the bells sounded, seemed imbued suddenly with life that was utterly and completely rampant. Long tendrils of the stuff drew away, to right and left below us, as though endowed with will of their own, and these tendrils, countless thousands of them, collided with other tendrils in the mass, and slithered over them so that all the mass of the seaweed writhed as though in torment, resembling countless hordes of serpents gathered together from all the evil places of the earth—and where the tendrils had drawn aside I could see black water in the rift as though the tendrils had drawn aside so that I *might* see. Some terrible fascination held me, my eyes fixed on that space of black water, for several moments after the tendrils of seaweed had drawn away to right and left—and up from the depths, into the opening, came two who filled all my being with abject terror—and something else.

One of the two was dead, I knew on the instant, for I could see his face, all white and drawn, yet with the blue lips smiling, of the ill-fated sentry who had gone over the side before my very eyes! And he had been brought up from the depths in the arms of—I hesitate to give the creature a name. A woman? I scarcely know; yet this I do know: in the instant I looked into her eyes, raised to mine for a full minute, I understood the ecstasy which I had read in the face of the sentry whom she now held in her arms. Her breasts, nude and unashamed, were the breasts of a buxom woman, her lips as red as full-blown roses, her hair as black as the wings of a crow, a mantle of loveliness all about her wondrous body, whipping this way and that in the storm.

Her eyes swerved away from mine, and one arm, shapely and snowy, raised aloft from the water—and to my ears came again the sound of tinkling bells! Once more the sea-weed writhed and twisted, pressed forward about the ship; but a single mass of it detached itself from the larger mass, pressed close to the—should I call her "woman"—and swerved away again; and the arms of the beautiful creature were empty. Instinctively I whirled about, knowing somehow that I must move my head before I met this creature's eyes again, and stared forward to the shadowy portion of the promenade whence the sentry had emerged before his plunge over the side. Up the starboard side of the ship crept a veritable wall of seaweed; up to the rail, pausing there for a moment, then to the deck, where it writhed for a moment or two, taking a weird distorted shape that made me think of a man, yet which I knew was not a man, before it strode into the center of the promenade. From out of the heart of this monstrosity there dropped soggily a white, cold figure! The second sentry had returned, as the first had done!

Why? Why? Why? What did all this unbelievable terror mean?

I knew, as I searched through all my experience, seeking the key to this uncanny enigma, that we were heading westward outside the usually traveled sea-lanes; that ships seldom, if ever, came this way; that in seven days we had seen not one vessel, nor even the smoke of one upon the horizon. Why did not vessels come this way?

But I could not answer my many questions. I could only ask them, and hope within me that they be not answered, ever. Nauseated by the return of the dead sentry, nude as the first had been, I closed my eyes for a moment, and when I opened them again, there was no seaweed, no monstrous shape, upon the promenade; but even from where I stood I could see the wet footprints—and wondered whom next the creature of the deep would claim from aboard our ill-fated vessel.

Resolutely I drew my pistol and returned once more toward the stern of the vessel. This creature of the depths, whatever it was, had taken life—twice. Whatever it was, it was mortal, and whatever is mortal a bullet will slay. But, in the very act of whirling, I stopped short—for between me and the stern of the vessel, smiling dreamily, water rippling over her nude and glorious body to splash upon the deck, stood the creature who had come up from the depths in the wake of the ship, bearing the dead man in her arms! My arm fell to my side, my weapon clattered to the deck, and as I moved forward once more, slowly, a step at a time as the sentry had done, the wondrous creature held out her dripping arms, and my eyes drank in all the glorious wonder of her—from head to—but she had no feet!

Where the feet should have been, and the legs, there were neither legs nor feet; but a scaly column, wet and dripping, like a serpent with a woman's body; I screamed in terror and unbelief; but it was too late, and her arms were about me, preventing all escape! But, with the touch of those arms, I did not wish to struggle. I knew what had happened to the two sentries; knew the same was in prospect for me; yet at the moment there seemed nothing in all the world more worthwhile than to slip over the side, into the depths, with the arms of this wondrous creature about me.

"Lieutenant! Lieutenant! For the love of God what is happening to you?"

It was the voice of the sergeant of the guard, freighted with abysmal terror; but I did not care. The shapely, strangely warm arms of the sea-creature were about me, and the sound of the bells, unbelievably sweet now, was in my ears. For me the world had ceased to exist, save for knowledge that these two things were true. I was carried to the rail, and went over slowly, without commotion, as comfortably as though I had been riding on a couch of eiderdown—and came to myself to know myself lost indeed!

I was deep down, whirling over and over behind the whirling screws of the ship, holding my breath until my lungs were nigh to bursting, swimming with all my might, striving to reach the surface, and life-giving air, when I hadn't the slightest idea which way was upward. With all my power I fought toward the surface; but my progress was slow and dragging, for there was a weight about my knees, as though arms were clasped about them, striving to hold me down. A wordless voice was in my ears—begging, beseeching, and there was something in the voice which made my struggles seem foolish and unnecessary, so that I desired never to reach the air I needed. I closed my eyes, which I had opened instinctively upon striking the water, and two lips pressed firmly against my own—and those lips saved my life, and my reason; for they were the cold lips of a corpse, with neither love nor challenge in them. I flailed out once more, and my hand caught in the line which the steamer dragged over her stern to measure the knots she traveled. All about me as I was hurled forward, now under water, now with nostrils out for a brief breathing space, the mass of seaweed rose and fell on the heavy seas.

GOD KNOWS how I ever got back aboard the troopship; but I awoke at mess-call in the morning, and sent immediately for the sergeant of the guard.

"What happened after I came back aboard last night, sergeant?" I asked abruptly.

The sergeant of the guard stared at me as though he thought me insane.

"I don't understand you," he managed finally.

"Have we finally passed through the area of seaweed?"

"Seaweed? Is the lieutenant making sport of me? We're two thousand miles from any land, save the ocean bottom, and there ain't any seaweed anywhere! I don't understand you!"

"Let it pass," I said. "When did you last visit the sentries last night?"

"Just before midnight, sir."

"And were all of them at their post of duty?"

"Yes, sir."

"And what about the bells?"

Again the sergeant's puzzlement was so genuine that I knew he did not understand my meaning. How much of my experience had been real, how much fantasy? I tried another tack.

"Did you make a round of the sentries after midnight?"

The sergeant shook his head sheepishly—it is one of the rules of guard duty that one visit to all sentries must take place between midnight and morning.

"Then the guard hasn't been mustered this morning? Is everyone present? You don't know? Then go at once and find out!"

Ten minutes later the sergeant returned, chalk-white of face, to report that two of the guard were missing, and could not be found anywhere aboard. He told me their names—and instantly my mind went back to the night of uncanny happenings just past, and the two nude bodies brought back from the deep in the arms of—whom? Or what?

I never knew, and to this day the questions I have propounded have never been answered.

But this I know: there are strange things, and sounds, in the sea near the hundred and eightieth meridian, a thousand miles north of Honolulu—and this is the strangest incident in my night of terror: the clothing which I donned next morning was entirely dry; but my hair was stiff with salt water, and there was the tang of sea-weed in my room when I awoke!

I looked, too, at the glass which covered the port-hole beside my bed—

Outside that glass were the smudged prints of thin lips, the blur above them which told of a face pressed against the glass from outside—as though somebody, or *something*, had tried to peer in, between nightfall and morning!

And the bells? I still can hear them, in memory, when sometimes I waken at sea after midnight, and the rolling and the plunging of the ship tell me that a storm is making.

THE FLYING DEATH
B. WALLIS

"SAY, WHAT WAS THAT, BILL?" exclaimed the taller and thinner of the two men staring at the thick bush that for some way lined each side of the dusty lane.

"Hanged if I know, Joe—thunderbolt, maybe," replied his companion, eyeing blankly the dense scrub.

"Thunderbolt! But there ain't no clouds," objected Joe, turning his gaze to the evening sky. "Least nothing to speak of," he amended his assertion as he solemnly surveyed a few dwindling remnants of what an hour ago had been a mass of gray vapor that all day had veiled the glare and tempered the scorching rays of a July sun.

Though there had been a promise of rain in the low-lying shroud, yet toward evening it had thinned and rapidly dispersed, so that shortly only a few wisps flushed with the setting sun were left. Most certainly the mighty Thor stored no shaft of his in such flimsy housing. Yet something—they had no idea what—from out the nowhere had suddenly plunged through the bush with a frightful crash. Close beside them, apparently not a dozen paces from the lane, it had entered the fringing wood with terrific force and its short transit from the topmost boughs to the ground was but a rending smash of splintered wood punctuated by the dull impact that wound up its volcanic career.

"Well, if it ain't a thunderbolt, what is it?" queried Bill. "It come from way up, anyway, whatever it is," he added with conviction.

"How about a flying-machine, then?" observed his friend hopefully.

"This wasn't all that size," countered Bill, still slightly nettled by the summary rejection of his thunderbolt.

"But say! it might be a guy—a birdman—dropped out of his machine. Gee! maybe come down miles and miles! Gosh!" and he ceased as the profundity of that presumed descent gripped him.

"Flying-men don't fall out—they're strapped in, ain't they?" said Joe diffidently, his temperamental skepticism more than a little shaken by the nerve-racking phenomenon. "But—Lord! if it is a guy come down, he'll be a sight!" he added in an awestruck mutter.

The two men stared at each other in sudden fear. They realized that the terrible final thud had been sickeningly suggestive of something limp, inert, and compressible; imagination completed the picture and speculation abruptly ceased.

"Say, Bill!" said the tall man hoarsely. "We got to go in there." He nodded toward the fringing bush.

"Yep, I guess so; I ain't stuck on it, though," replied Bill with a catch in his voice. "Come on!" he added with querulous impatience.

Now that the matter had assumed such a significant aspect, their course, distasteful though it might be, was quite clear. And it augurs well for the future of our race that two very ordinary individuals such as these, whose lives from boyhood had been devoted to a pursuit of the slippery dollar rolling between the purchase and disposal of second-hand furniture and personal effects, should so instantly and simply obey the dictates of our common humanity. Naturally their vocation carried them far afield, and to this fact—and a lately deceased farmer—they owed their introduction to the little fishing-village of Lytham, Maine, and the after-supper stroll that had been interrupted so rudely.

At once the two men entered the scrub, and for a little they cast about like a couple of sedate retrievers in search of their objective. Then they came upon it, resting in a little open space tunneled by the shattering of stems and the stripping of limbs from a stouter and taller growth that chanced here to rear a spearlike crest as though to mark the horror at its base.

"My God, Joe! What's this? Reckon he's dead—don't you?" exclaimed Bill in an awed whisper.

"Yep, it's awful! I ain't going no closer," said Joe hastily, then paused and admitted reluctantly, "though I guess we should make certain."

ASSUREDLY DEATH had come in no gracious mood to the poor broken thing they gazed upon. For the man's body was smashed and twisted most horribly and lay in a huddled heap amid the splintered boughs of the tall tree and the crushed shrubbery. Limbs were hinged strangely and repulsively at places where joints are normally absent, and the face was merely a mass of shapeless pulp through which the jagged end of a shattered bough projected. Apart from total disintegration it was hard to conceive of a human frame more completely devastated; it was only too visibly obvious that every bone in the dead man's body was broken and the flesh either gashed, or stripped, or perforated in a score of places.

For a moment the two men stood staring in awed and commiserating silence at the terrible thing, and no further word was uttered concerning a closer investigation. Then the taller man shivered a little and said harshly, "Say, we'd better beat it back and tell the folks in the village."

And at once, stepping softly as though they would conceal their presence from something feared, they turned and made their way back to the dusty road.

"Say, Bill, this poor guy now," said Joe as they hastened on their mission; "there ain't no doubt but he dropped out of a flying-machine, so high up we never heard it, but it's queer—he's dressed all wrong. It ain't the front of a birdman—or even a passenger—no coat, no mitts or helmet, not even goggles, and him all that way up!"

"That's so," said his companion slowly. "And ain't these flyers strapped in their seats, case of accidents?"

"Sure!" confirmed Joe with the easy assurance that another's ignorance often begets. "Though maybe this guy's straps went back on him, or—by Jiminy!—now I wonder!"

"Wonder what?" queried his companion briefly, the unwonted pace having told on him.

"Well—I dunno. But maybe this guy done it himself—jumped out, went bugs or something!" replied Joe hesitatingly.

"Meanin' suicide? I never heard of a birdman taken that way—they being sure to smash some day," said Bill, voicing the pessimistic popular conception of the fate awaiting such intrepid adventurers.

"But Lord, what a nerve! if he done it—miles and miles of dropping through nothing!" mused Joe, loth to relinquish the horrific pictured descent.

"What would he strip his working-rags for, anyway? There ain't no sense to it," objected his companion with an innate love of debate.

"I dunno—it's a mystery," avowed Joe frankly.

And that was the verdict accorded the occurrence by a coroner's jury and the expert investigators who at once were engaged to elucidate the strange and tragic enigma. For immediately the poor, shattered thing had been identified as one James Symington, a youth in his early twenties, and son of a wealthy shoe manufacturer—a young man of exemplary habit and pleasing personality; quiet, unassuming, and devoted to his parents, his business, and the hobby of photography: in short, a level-headed, estimable young American, and certainly the last one his friends would consider to be afflicted with the insanity of self-destruction—though a most cursory survey of the known facts banished effectually the incipient rumor that possibly the discoverers had thoughtlessly originated.

It appeared that the boy had never ascended a foot save by the aid of his legs or an elevator, and had a natural antipathy to aeronautics. Moreover, on the morning of the tragedy he had left his home for a few days' vacation, and had taken his car and camera out for a ramble along the picturesque Maine coastline, with no particular objective in view but merely to wander as fancy dictated. And the car was found ten miles from the fatal spot, overturned in a ditch bordering a lonely stretch of by-road that there for a space closely parallels the cliffs which for many miles tower a hundred feet or more above the surf-lashed sands.

By what possible means had the victim been transferred from his car, conveyed ten miles, ascended to an unguessable height and there been launched in that terrible descent? It was all inconceivable, both in the mode of its execution and in its object. One might as well endeavor to formulate a plausible explanation of the sudden materialization of a prehistoric monster in the trim flowerbeds of a city park! And each detail as it was brought to light but further meshed the affair in a net of mystery.

The little clock in the overturned car had stopped at 6 p.m., and this might reasonably be taken to indicate the moment of capsizing, and James Symington's translation; but what had at that moment happened? If for some incomprehensible motive the youth had been taken captive and transferred to a flying-machine, where had it alighted, and how arisen? Not a sign of such a happening was visible amid the fields of tall grass ripe for mowing, that lay on the landward side, while to the seaward lay a narrow strip of broken, boulder-strewn waste bounded by a sheer hundred-foot drop; the road itself was much too narrow to accommodate the smallest plane man has ever flown in. Yet by what other means had been effected that rapid migration? For less than half an hour later his body had ended its terrible flight—the taller of the two discoverers, with an eye to future questioning, had glanced at his watch as he emerged from the shrubbery.

Two planes had indeed some hours earlier passed over the neighborhood and been noted by several persons, but both had flown high over the water and quickly vanished into the cloud-weighted horizon; and on inquiry they proved to be a couple of military "busses" used by instructors and their pupils. So there lay not a single shred of tangible evidence to connect the tragedy with the only possible means of its consummation, with an assailant of any nature whatsoever.

The wrecked car was itself inexplicable, the road affording no reasonable excuse for an accident, or any evidence of its nature.

The youth's camera was discovered about fifty feet distant, immersed in the scummy seepage that lay in festering pools over the ditch bottom. And though the tracks were barely decipherable because of a stiff breeze that had stirred the fine dust and almost smoothed the indentations, yet there was sufficient evidence to hazard the presumption that the car had been stopped and the owner had alighted and wandered slowly ahead and stood a little while, probably taking pictures of the lonely scenery. Then, more uncertainly, he had returned rapidly, and midway had broken into a run. Ten feet from the car his hat was discovered, in the ditch also; there the steps had ceased, at least no trace of them remained.

From all evidence of the wrecked engine the car had been standing motionless at the moment of its capsizal, and no trace of deep-gashed ruts of swerving wheels was visible. It had simply capsized as though a huge lever had been applied to its side and heaved it over.

There all logical deductions and reasonable surmises ceased; other tracks were obviously more recent and probably left by the wondering farm-hands who early the next morning had passed that way. All that was certain was a car overturned and an owner who had vanished as though snatched aloft by the fabled jinn.

But the medical profession had further and equally astounding testimony to offer. The inquest revealed the startling fact that almost certainly the poor boy had died before that frightful landing, and been done to death in a most abominable manner. The doctors stated that by some strange means every drop of blood had been extracted from the veins and what they examined was but an arid shell as devoid of moisture as a dry sponge. No known wound would account for such complete extravasation; for normally there always remained a residue imprisoned in a network of the lesser conduits by the rapid caving in of the main channels. But this shattered thing was absolutely devoid of the least drop of its life's fluid.

Then more abstrusely the medical evidence spoke of some small areas of skin and tissue still intact about the throat, face and hands; areas that exhibited a most peculiar condition, being

pitted with innumerable minute excrescences which under micro-
scopical examination were found to be of craterlike construction
whose vents were in reality but pores greatly distended and rup-
tured so badly beneath the surface that in their bursting they had
lacerated the mesh of tiny veins about them so completely that
to the naked eye the tissues appeared merely as a puffed, disor-
ganized mass of macerated pulp. Whether this condition was the
result of immense pressures experienced in such a stupendous fall
was a matter they lacked the data to affirm or deny, but save for
this purely speculative supposition they had no other solution
to offer—a pronouncement quite in accord with the cherished
traditions of scientific reserve and caution.

As usual, public imagination seized on the sensational, and
promptly garbled, misquoted, and maltreated the hesitant speculation, and spoke knowingly of strains and stresses, and vascu-
lar tissue, and felt exalted by their perspicacity, and justified in
spoiling reams of good paper informing weary editors of absurd
and weird conclusions the writers had evolved to account for
an impossible, objectless translation to an invisible, untraceable
flying-machine.

And there the matter rested; money and brains had collaborated and utterly failed to unearth a single fact upon which
to base any rational theory of mode or motive of the killing of
James Symington; who being but one man among many millions,
each with his bread to earn and his niche to fill in a busy world,
it is not surprising that the millions shortly shelved the tragedy
in the dim subconscious vaults where side by side lie every shred
of emotion, every fact, everything felt, seen, or heard in a lifetime, be it junk or treasure.

A MONTH LATER the body of one Harriet Conroy was discovered, face down, on the lonely sands of Ladner Bay, barely three
miles distant from the spot where poor Symington's car had capsized.

Again the public thrilled with horror as it learned the strange
and gruesome facts connected with the grim tragedy; and with
the odd, illogical intuition of the mass mind in moments of high

emotion immediately the two fatalities were associated, though save in one particular there lay no resemblance between the manner of the victims' slaying.

Harriet Conroy, only daughter of a retired sea captain, a widower with a modest competence, was school mistress in her home village of Shaldon. Just turned twenty, healthy, cheerful and level-headed, she was liked and respected by all in the little community. The fact of that solitary stroll to Ladner sands was due to no morbid love of lonely self-commune, but merely the result of a persistent headache. For on that tragic day, after tea with her father, she had remarked that probably a brisk walk along the cliffs to the sands would be better than any medicine; and mentioning that on her return she would likely spend a few minutes at a neighbor's, with a smile of affectionate reassurance to her parent she had gone on her way.

That was the last time her father ever watched the trim figure unlatch the little garden gate. At dusk she had not returned, nor an hour later, when, mindful of her words, the lonely old man had smiled and grumbled fondly, "These women! and their minutes—it seems but yesterday she was snug in bed and hours sleeping by this time." Then, thinking a little sadly that a day might come when another home would claim her, he slipped from reverie to slumber; and awoke to find the clock hands were nearly laid together and the house as lonely as ever. Then, with a sudden black fear clutching at his heart, the lost fire of his seafaring youth returned to him, and hatless he ran into the darkness, and pounded fiercely at the doors of sleeping neighbors.

Shortly two friends and the distracted man set off with lanterns the way she had taken—and found her, face downward, cold and dead, in the soft, dry sand above high water. With dreading touch they sought for evidence of foul murder, but failed to discover wound or mark of evil clutch upon her. Then by the yellow light of a lantern they searched the vicinity for trace of assailant; for it was evident there had been a struggle, or rather a defense against something that had overtaken her.

The crooked, rigid fingers, the outthrust arms, and the deep depression in which the victim lay spoke eloquently and horribly of the short, desperate struggle she had waged to protect herself against a merciless antagonist who had leaped and hurled her headlong. While the frenzied old man bent over his darling, moaning and calling piteously to the cold, unhearing ears, his two companions tramped the vicinity and examined closely the soft, shifting sand. Though so loose that the imprint of their steps was at once half-filled and blurred behind identification, nevertheless it was plain enough that the poor girl had come from the steep descent in the ravine at the head of the bay and strolled toward the firm, smooth floor left by the receding tide. Half-way to it she had halted, then apparently returned a few paces, and there suddenly turned and run for the line of great boulders that strewed the foot of the sheer cliff, the nearest of the two giant black arms enclosing her.

This absurd turning and haste was so apparent that it was obvious something had intercepted her return and she had madly raced for the only shelter at hand. But not a third of the distance had been covered when a most astounding thing had happened, for the tracks vanished! Not a trace of her step was visible in the space of at least a dozen feet that lay between the last deep slurred indentation and the dead girl.

But for these two searchers the strange fact would have escaped notice, for at dawn the feet of many shocked friends had quite obliterated every trace of her movements. At the inquest the affair was sworn to by the discoverers, but excited little comment, for other even stranger matters occupied the attention of the astounded and baffled inquiry; yet to the two witnesses that void space, the visible evidence of a thing unknown and inconceivable, was the most appalling memory they retained. And for many a night they pondered over it and spoke darkly of things evil and malignant that of old they had heard their fathers' fathers declare roamed such desolate places; and the cheery lamplight within seemed more comforting than ever they had known it.

But men of learning and those skilled in the murky labyrinths of evil vainly sought to elucidate the matter; even a great surgeon from the city had willingly found time to assist at the autopsy, summoned by a wire from an humble country medico, who nevertheless in college had ranked higher than his famous chum. And in terms unintelligible to the lay mind the two had agreed and wrangled throughout one whole night, until the gray of dawn had sent the visitor hastening back to waiting patients. His last words as he pressed the starter were, "Thanks, Slater; the most amazing case I ever encountered—most interesting. But what the deuce caused it I haven't a notion."

As with an earlier verdict, those few curt words summed the facts the strictest probing had elicited. Well they might, for never a bruise or the least abrasion lay upon the poor body, yet of blood not a drop remained within it; and as in the case of young Symington the staggering completeness of the extravasation was an anomaly to science, the tissues being disrupted in the self-same violent manner, and every exposed surface of epidermis betraying a like eruptive disfigurement. Though the body was otherwise not mutilated, the examination was unhindered by the shocking maceration that Symington's corpse had suffered. In spite of this the verdict was identical: "Murder! but no evidence of how, or by whom committed."

AGAIN THE GREAT PRESSES roared in their pangs of conceiving columns that dripped with adjectives and horror; and staider prints admitted frankly that the tragedy had really happened, and in them learned men penned articles that meandered through the dictionary, and seemed very wise and conclusive, but left the reader wondering what it was all about, yet oddly comforted that such men lived to deal with these ghastly enigmas as coolly and confidently as though the solution were concealed in tomes of algebra or differential calculus.

But the great public, whose emotions feed on simpler diet, just wondered, and thrilled with the horror of that strange, piti-less slaying, and throbbed with pity for an old, brokenhearted man mourning his only child; yet, lacking fuel to keep alight the gracious fire of sympathy, it shortly expired, just as reports of vast calamities in foreign lands flame dazzlingly for a moment in our mental firmament, then flicker and vanish as another star leaps above the horizon and outlives its predecessor.

Probably sooner or later there would have been other victims, and by chance some terror-stricken witness to afford humanity the first inkling of the gravest peril that has ever beset it. But it so happened that Philip Daimler, the talented painter, and his friend Richard Messinger, the well-known curator of the geological section of the Jackson Institute, were the first to solve the mystery of the two terrible slayings, and in detail render an account of the fearful assailant—a relation that left humanity gasping and bewildered as we realized our impotence to combat the menace that now must be reckoned with. In a twinkling it had thrust our species back a hundred thousand years, to days when the survival of our hirsute ancestors trembled in the balance and only by a miracle escaped from the chaos of ravening monsters to become the dominant masters of their destiny. But now as well, or better, might we plan to clear the black depths of the oceans of the monstrous octopi that lurk a hundred fathoms below the surface invincible in their murky kingdom and calmly awaiting the diving leviathans or foundered floating palaces to appease their gargantuan appetites.

It might have been better had we never learnt the truth, never awakened to the fact that after all our thousands of years of striving, ceaseless war with ruthless creatures, pride of victory and attainment, after all we are not the lords of creation, and though in no danger of a world-wide catastrophe, yet neither science, police, nor politics can guarantee protection in the future to the individual. Now the serene cerulean dome has lost its divinity, for we know that merciless malignancy is hidden in its profundity; and the seductive peace of the green country, the charm of solitude, must forever be haunted by the dread of impending tragedy. Only surrounded by our fellows or with walls enclosing us can we know the security that once we lightly deemed our heritage.

The relation of their terrible experience is perhaps more vitally descriptive in the simple words of Messinger rather than the later careful summaries by the learned of the mere facts shorn of their emotional reactions; just as a first impression often more truly portrays a scene than does a photograph.

"Daimler and I," said Messinger to the press representatives who rushed to the village early the following morning, "came here by car yesterday. As you know, Daimler's art is highly imaginative, though in detail truth itself; and for a canvas he desired to obtain some studies of the massive rock formations in this locality. I had been working rather strenuously of late—a little brochure on the sedimentaries—and feeling a trifle stale, came with him for a few days of rest and a mouthful of ozone.

"Naturally we were not ignorant of the tragic happenings that had occurred so recently in the neighborhood; but the victims being total strangers, and neither Daimler nor I of hypersensitive disposition, we hardly gave the matter a thought.

"Last evening, about two hours before sunset—my friend particularly desired to observe the evening effects —we set out for Ladner Bay; and though the road above would have been much the quicker route, yet the sloping shingle beach was preferable for Daimler's purpose.

"Daimler carried a small sketching-outfit and a light folding easel, while I had my old friend, a short-hafted prospector's pick which invariably accompanies me on these outings. Probably you know the tool—the head is shaped much like a small pick, but one prong has a flat hammer head. I think it weighs about five pounds, but in a practiced hand a surprisingly powerful blow can be dealt with it.

"To this simple tool my friend owes his life; for, lacking it, I would have been quite powerless to aid him. As a matter of fact it was, I think, probably the best weapon that could have been devised for the purpose—the finest rifle would have been no more effective than a pea-shooter against that frightful thing.

"My friend had so frequently halted to admire some wild outline of crag or boulder that by the time we arrived at the bay the sun had dipped behind the western crest of the enclosing cliffs and that side lay in a fast-extending and deepening shade.

"The bay, I may remark, is a singularly picturesque one. It is about half a mile wide across its mouth and almost as much from low tide to the steep trail in the ravine where the great walls come together. In the bay the cliffs are higher than elsewhere and the strata more contorted; as though the spot had been the center of a violence that had thrown up miles of towering rock like a feather. Of course really the process was an infinitely prolonged one, the effect of vast strains and adjustments of the earth's envelope; nevertheless one can not avoid the impression of wrathful titanic forces unleashed and working instantaneously.

"High water seldom comes more than half-way over the smooth sands, and the huge, sheltering arms afford ample protection from the northerly gales that sometimes ravage this coast; therefore fishermen occasionally put in and wait until the blow is past. I believe the fine sands sometimes attract picnic parties, but otherwise it is as lonely a spot as can be found in a hundred miles of this coastline. The nearest house is more than a mile away and of course quite hidden from the beach; the road above is merely a rough country track and used only by a few farmers as a means of access to their widely separated neighbors. I believe one could camp for weeks in that lonely cove and never a soul be the wiser.

"Daimler was delighted with the wild grandeur of the spot—it was through my advice he had come—and for a little he flitted about from one point to another until the spirit moved him to set to work, while I made for the foot of the near-by massive wall and commenced busily with my pick to remove slabs from the face of it; for in this formation not infrequently were to be found small fossils of mosses, lichens, and diminutive crustaceans.

"Some measure of success attending my labor, I became interested and immersed in the quest, and save for the waning light hardly noticed the passing of time until I found myself climbing the steep ascent that leads to the crest.

"This trail is merely the bottom of a great V-shaped gash that in the course of years has become partly filled with fallen fragments, and likely some day will be completely blocked by them. The way is extremely narrow, and not far from the beach it is for many yards a mere slit where two could hardly walk abreast; though for a sheer wall, maybe twenty feet high, on each side, the ramparts fall back and ascend in a series of giant steps.

"It was here that Daimler's cries first reached me, though he states that he had shouted several times before he heard my response; a fact for which a turn of the passage just below me and his rapid approach may be held accountable. At once I answered with a loud 'Halloo' and commenced quickly to retrace my steps. The only thought I held at the moment was that he had completed his sketch, and not seeing me about had called to inform me that it was time to return. We had previously agreed to return by the road, for in the dark the shingle would be rough walking.

"So intent had I been on my chipping that the gathering dusk had gone almost unnoticed. But now I realized that some time must have elapsed since I had left him; for as I turned the corner and the bay opened before me I saw that the scarlet and crimson of the horizon were fading, and though not a hundred yards distant his figure was blurred and only just recognizable.

"He was coming toward me quickly, in fact faster than I ever remembered seeing him move; for Daimler, though not grossly corpulent, is a big, heavy-built man, averse to rapid motion.

"At that second he called again, though I do not think he had yet seen me. He seemed to be walking in a crouching position, and his bent head was foreshortened to half its normal height above his broad shoulders. Although, as I have stated, his hastening form was somewhat blurred in the gathering dusk, yet his outline in the main was fairly well defined by the lighter-hued sands and sea that lay behind him.

"'What's the matter?' I cried sharply. The tone of his cry had surprised and startled me, it was so undeniably a cry of warning and agitation. But as I called back to him I was staring at something many feet away, a something that lay a hundred feet above him.

"I had perceived it directly I turned the bend in the trail, for it was quite impossible to miss its huge bulk. Yet one may perceive a strange and incomprehensible object without instantly grasping the enormity of its presence; we have lain so long in the rut of the known that our perceptions do not lightly rise out of it. Doubtless in the days of King Arthur they were quicker to accept and instantly tabulate the fantastic things they were taught quite commonly might be encountered; things which we dismiss with a smile as mere chimeras of ignorance and auto-suggestion. Yet now it occurs to me to wonder whether there is not a base of fact somewhere or other at the back of these dragons and ogres, centaurs and satyrs that they so often engaged in combat. For I feel certain that I, too, have seen a thing utterly opposed to sane credence, something abnormal, unknown and very horrible, yet as truly a fact as your presence at this moment.

"What I stared at was strange beyond imagining. Above him hovered—no other word quite conveys the instant impression I received of conscious movement—a something more resembling an appalling thundercloud condensed, or compressed, to an undreamt-of solidity, if such a phenomenon was possible, than anything else I can call to mind. In conveying to you a mental picture of this thing I am handicapped by having to describe something that has no counterpart in human experience and benumbs the brain with its staggering incomprehensibility.

"Viewed as a living entity it was enormous; I should judge fully thirty or forty feet in diameter, though its circumference was irregular and its outline so ragged that in many directions it might be much more than this figure. It seemed to rise from its edge to a dome center considerably higher than the stature of the hastening man beneath it; while underneath it appeared slightly hollowed.

"You understand I am giving you the sum of the impressions I retained after the encounter, and not merely my first instinctive observations; for it would be tedious, if not impossible, to separate my earlier impressions from later surety.

"At the moment my only emotion was amazement; though intertwined with my amazement there lay a shrinking, a loathing, of its abominable hue, which, save at the murky edges, was blacker than ink, or coal, or night—the black I should imagine we mean when in the phrase 'Black as Death itself' we endeavor to convey a profundity beyond all art to picture.

"Daimler of course heard me; in that quiet enclosed spot my voice seemed swollen unnaturally.

"'Look out, Messinger! The thing is alive—it's going to attack. I think!' he cried hurriedly and breathlessly.

"'Alive!' I exclaimed; and although instinctively I knew that it was indeed a living thing, yet the spoken word shocked me exceedingly. 'Nonsense! It's queer, but—quick, Daimler, run! It's dropping!' I shouted in a panic of sudden fear that strangely contradicted my curt refutation of his assertion.

"An instant realization of his great peril had come upon me as I saw the outlandish hovering thing that kept pace with his steps—by what means it moved I have no notion—abruptly fall for at least a third of the space between them. It fell just like a stone! No planing, or slanting swoop like a hawk at its quarry, but in a flash it was thirty feet lower, and the soughing swish of its passage was very audible.

"As I called, Daimler leapt forward and commenced a frantic dash toward me, and at the same second I rushed to meet him. Exactly how I expected to aid him I cannot say, or indeed what manner of offensive I could summon in the slightest way effective against such a monstrous creature. The action was merely a blind impulse, the age-old urge of combination—the human species versus all comers.

"What this thing was dumfounded me, but I was convinced it was utterly malignant; for so close was it now that I glimpsed the sinuous rippling that agitated its ragged edge. The thing was visibly throbbing with vital life; even through the dusky pall I had seen that every inch of its surface was swelling, subsiding, and again heaving tumultuously with the apparently aimless convulsions of a gigantic bunch of knotted worms. Possibly part of this perception arose in a later impression; I can not be certain, for everything passed in a whirl in those tense seconds. But one detail I can state with certainty occurred in its rightful sequence: the sound that was emitted coincidently with its abrupt descent. A thin, piping sighing filled the air around me, and though so thin and quavery, yet its volume seemed to saturate the vicinity like the whine of a horde of tiny mosquitoes. I can not recall that thereafter it ceased for a moment.

"Daimler when he started to run had not more than fifty yards to cross to gain whatever shelter the narrow trail could offer; yet before we met it happened. As I ran, my eyes never left the appalling thing, and I saw it quite clearly lessen in its area. There was no warning or any preliminary adjusting; it simply shrank, or rather contracted, as a length of slightly stretched elastic on release diminishes; and like it, this thing also thickened. Or perhaps in view of its concavity I might better liken the action to the half shutting of a huge umbrella.

"Then its huge mass had fallen and it lay exactly where Daimler had been running. For an instant I halted and stood staring blankly at the monstrous thing, just as one stares at an apparition—palsied with fear, mute and motionless. Then the enormity of the catastrophe that had overtaken Daimler flooded upon me and I hurled myself forward, frantically calling him by name.

"It seemed like circling a hill, for its summit rose many feet above me, and its height, I should judge, would be less than a third of the diameter. And all the time that queer piping sound was ceaselessly welling from it, only now in volume immensely greater and the note much shriller and more like the escaping of innumerable little jets of high-pressure steam.

"Behind that huge palpitating bulk lay Daimler on his back; head, arms and shoulders alone were visible; below this his form was missing, being covered by his assailant.

"He says that something impelled him at that critical second to hurl himself backward; likely it was an impulse, an emergence from the subconscious, the mysterious self that gains its knowledge from unknown channels. At any rate he hurtled backward, and instead of engulfing him the vast hood caught him a slanting blow and still further expedited his effort. Had it not been for this action, beyond any doubt he would have been instantly and most horribly smothered.

"'I can't get clear—and it's moving up!' he gasped hoarsely as I rushed to him and slipping my hands beneath his armpits sought to snatch him from the loathsome thing. But with all my might, and with Daimler thrusting desperately at the sands, I could not by an inch release him, and beyond the slight natural flexion permitted to the human shoulders I failed to raise him appreciably.

"I stared at the monstrous thing as the cold sweat of terror poured profusely from me; but Daimler though white and haggard, was, I think, much the cooler and more collected.

"'I can't gain an inch! What shall I do?' I exclaimed hoarsely as I, too, saw that the revolting, glutinous-looking edge was extending farther over him. It seemed to flow with a rippling motion outward—the smooth creeping of a tide of festering slime more solid than liquid.

"Now the light was very dim but, the sky being cloudless, I could distinguish in a blurred, unreal fashion that the substance of the thing was still in a state of ceaseless pulsing fluxion; swelling into ridges and bosses, sinking in grooves and craters everywhere over a surface as coarsely wrinkled as the withered skin on the hands of age.

"'For God's sake, Messinger, do something! It will be all over with me in a minute!' said Daimler tensely but quietly—I can not too highly rate his courage.

"In a frenzy of despair, my eyes swept the vicinity for anything—a piece of driftwood, a boulder even—to batter this nightmare with. But the sands here were far above high water and bare of a single splinter, and the loose debris fringing the nearest cliff at least fifty feet distant; and at any second that ghastly living tide might sweep over its victim.

"Then my eye alighted on a weapon that somehow I had forgotten—the pick at my feet, where I had dropped it. These simple tools are marvels of efficiency and in a practiced hand produce results; I do not doubt but with a single blow I could split the skull of an ox. In a second I had swung it aloft and at the extreme limit of my reach dealt the brute a savage stroke. It was indeed fortunate that I had not hit closer to the edge, for I might easily have seriously wounded if not slain my friend. The eight-inch prong went through the substance as though it were butter, and haft and hand were deeply pressed into a soft resilience.

"It was as flimsy as a sponge, or rather like hitting a cushion that would give but not rend before the mightiest fist, yet a child could drive a pin through it. At once there arose a series of little explosions such as might be made by the bursting of small air-filled paper bags or toy balloons.

"Astonished but elated by this unexpected vulnerability, instantly without raising the weapon I raked it down toward me. Thus attacked, it was more resistant, and I had to exert some force as if opposed by the strands of a half-rotten net. But I rent it to where the prong bit into the sand close beside Daimler. The deep laceration closed behind the steel like molten tar, and a line of grayish scum, greasy and frothy, welled out to mark the ravage.

"'All right, Daimler, I'll have you clear in a moment!' I cried. 'It's as soft as a jelly-fish!' I cried exultingly as I feverishly plied my pick and with blow after blow roughly raked a great V-shaped wedge of it to tatters.

"Nevertheless, though I had spoken so assuredly, I was still in a state of panic. For the bulk of the thing was so appalling that my efforts seemed those of a pigmy assailing a whale with a bodkin: every second I expected to see some vast movement convulse it, some gigantic offensive that would erase us both as simply as my hand would crush a mosquito. Moreover each blow was meeting with a greater resistance, and if my attack was to be confined merely to stabbing the prong into it, then my friend was doomed to a certainty. For if I could not weaken it by scoring the portion that lay above him, I realized that there was no hope of saving him. So rigidly did this nightmare confine him that it seemed as if they were cemented together, or welded by suction like a glutinous limpet to a rock; and of course, in spite of its loose construction, this stupendous brute must have weighed tons.

"FROM START TO FINISH, the whole experience could only have been a matter of moments, but to me the time seemed infinite.

"I ceased to attack the inner mass and confined my blows to the edge about the prisoner. It was much tougher, but I tore it to pieces for a couple of feet inward.

"'Quick, Daimler! Put all your strength to it!' I cried, as, dropping the pick again, I caught him under the shoulders and strove to pull him from under. Whether unaided we would have been successful I can not say, but aid came from a most unexpected quarter.

"I suppose even that unnatural monster possessed the rudiments of feeling and its wounding reached some center of sensation; for suddenly it shook—one might better say 'shuddered'—violently, and there came a shrinking, a sort of retrogression of the wounded portion into itself; and a wavelike shaking and rippling agitated the entire monster.

"'It's loosening! Put every ounce of strength into it!' I gasped as I heaved desperately at the broad shoulders—and moved them! Swaying him from side to side, inch by inch I drew him clear to the waist; then abruptly resistance ceased and I went sprawling. He was free, and groaning and attempting to rise as I picked myself up and leapt to his side.

"'Lean on me! We've got to reach the trail—it's the only shelter about here!' I panted, winded by my efforts and the fall.

"Somehow I got him standing, and with my arm about him we started, at a tangent to clear the throbbing horror, and made with all speed we could summon for the trail. Lurching and stumbling—for as I have said, Daimler is a big, heavy man, and now was badly shaken and benumbed by the pressure he had borne—we circled the brute; and though in the blurring dusk I had but a hasty glimpse of its black immensity, yet at once I saw that it had become even larger than a moment back and the throbbing had changed to a swaying motion that went from side to side. At once I guessed the truth.

"'My God! Daimler, the brute is rising—we must go quicker!' I hoarsely whispered, somehow fearing that even a whisper would precipitate another attack.

"I heard the staggering man's breath indrawn with terror, and felt his form stiffen and strain to further effort, but a shambling amble was the utmost we could manage. My spirit fairly crawled within me as every step of that slow passage I felt that escape was impossible; and any second we might be dashed headlong with the blackness of unimaginable night and tons of living pulp smothering us.

"But at last, unharmed, we reached the ascent and staggered up until the walls closed in and we neared the narrow slit where I had been chipping and which now offered our only refuge. Here we halted for a moment.

"'I think we are fairly safe now, thank heaven!' said I fervently as I peered back into the blur of the bay. Only a toneless pearly gray remained of the many-hued sunset. But one could distinguish quite well the cliffs, and the sands, and the darker band of sea beyond; and all that colorless expanse was solitary and nothing met the eye but the natural and the explainable.

"'Why, it's gone!' I exclaimed in surprise and relief.

"'No! Look up there, Messinger,' said Daimler in a shaking whisper as he clutched at my arm.

"I suppose by recent association of space and horror instinctively he had sought the quarter from which that horror had been born. I followed his lifted, pointing arm, and there floated the beast, level with the cliff crest and directly above us; and as I fearfully stared, it dropped a little lower and lay between the upper outflung sides of the gorge.

"'It's coming down! Quick! into the shelter ahead!' I urged in a panic.

"'Shelter! Where!' asked Daimler eagerly.

"'Just above—the passage is so narrow, it couldn't reach us there,' I replied, regaining some confidence as I thought of the deep narrow cleft ahead.

"In a moment we had stumbled up the steep slope and stood between the sheer walls that for thirty or forty feet lay so close together that we could only just stand abreast and stare up at the thing that loomed so menacingly against the infinite gray behind it. But now I had less fear, for I felt it was impossible that such a huge mass could ever penetrate into our shelter; and probably the brute was of the same opinion, for it made no further attempt to attack us but lay motionless for a few minutes as though gloomily pondering over the matter.

"Then in a flash it had gone; I had just an impression of a huge expansion like a roller-blind snatched across the sky, and then it was thousands of feet above us and appeared no larger

than a tablecloth, and as harmless. In the flick of an eyelid followed another extension and instant diminution to a mere
smudge that for an instant floated in profundity. And after that
all trace of it vanished, and for a moment I was left awed by the
imagination of prodigious heights and a lone monster fearlessly
navigating the silent infinite void beyond.

"'It's gone this time, anyway,' I heard Daimler mutter; and
at his voice I returned to solid earth and things understandable.

"'Yes, I hope forever to the hell it came from,' said I, savagely.
'But we'd better move before they cast it out with other stunts
to try on us.'

"At once we climbed the steep ascent, and on the crest stood
for an instant to ease the distress that now acutely beset Daimler.
No longer spurred by imminent danger, he complained of pain
and weakness in his limbs, faintness and dizziness, and would
have lain on the rocks and coarse grass; but fearing the relaxation
might incapacitate him I sternly refused to allow it.

"While we stood resting, my gaze wandered with loathing
over the somber solitude that lay below us, and unbidden there
came to me a thought of the poor girl who found death awaiting
her in this treacherous loneliness—a tragedy which, as I now
recalled, had never been solved, even as Daimler's fate if he had
been solitary.

"'My God! Of course—that nightmare from space!' I muttered, aghast at the thought of that horror. For I knew beyond a
shadow of doubt that I had solved the mystery of Harriet Conroy's slaying.

"'Come on, Daimler!' I urged hoarsely.

"The rest of the story, gentlemen, is of no moment. Even-
tually we reached a farmhouse and secured a conveyance to this
inn. Today my friend is confined to his bed, so bruised in limb and
racked with nausea that I do not anticipate he will be fit to leave
it for several days. The local man—Dr. Slater—assures me that
save for shock and this severe bruising my friend is as sound as
ever. But he awaits a friend of his, a famous specialist, with much

impatience to learn his opinion. It seems that they collaborated in the examination of certain extraordinary phases at the poor girl's inquest recently; and with this new evidence on the matter he is anxious that I should meet him and relate our astounding and terrible experience. Moreover I understand that still another tragedy is linked with this locality. I mean the fate of young Symington—you know I am but little interested in such matters, being, I suppose, of skeptical temperament and completely immersed in my profession, and having no time to waste on the merely sensational; though I have some recollection of the affair, but very fragmentary and certainly nothing on which to found any conclusion of resemblance. Yet Dr. Slater assures me that our encounter with this unique assailant has forged the key to an otherwise inexplicable tragedy. Doubtless the whole matter will receive the closest official attention, even not improbably a world-wide investigation, and some definite conclusions and co-operation of offensive—if possible—be arrived at. For I can not conceive of a greater catastrophe to humanity than the existence in numbers of such monstrous, malignant creatures. One shrinks appalled at the thought of their size, their powers and their immunity from detection.

"This new science of aviation? Why, one of those brutes could overwhelm a Zeppelin, and in a moment cast it a flaming heap of junk to destruction; and a dozen could clear the skies of every flying-machine the world could gather together, and make of aviation just another term for certain suicide. For how can one combat a creature that with the speed of a falling stone comes out of nothingness invisible until the darkness of death is smothering you?

"What this creature is I have no notion, whether a single survival of our planet's early abortions, or a type evolved in comparatively recent times, along a line and in an environment we, from inability to explore, have never thought of; these are enigmas that only research and further evidence can elucidate. All I know to a certainty is that my sense of peace and security has vanished forever; the nature I have been wedded to, the lonely loveliness I have loved, now all is profitless—it is abhorrent! For what I have seen will dog my memory to my last day."

Such, deleting a few repetitions, was the narrative of Richard Messinger, and in the main is the extent of our knowledge today of the creature that popular misconception has christened "The Flying Death." For as yet no fresh witness has arisen to affirm or deny the particulars he has given.

Speculations, learned treatises, and discursive theories exist by the dozen, proving that the monster is mentioned allegorically in the Bible, or was known to the Chinese before Confucius, or has no existence—are there not persons who affirm that the world is flat and ignore the certain evidence to the contrary?

But the world has no doubt that this thing exists—a nightmare that can prey on humanity with the ease and impunity of a cat catching mice. For, immersed in alcohol in a glass jar in the great Metropolitan Museum, there lies one item of incontrovertible evidence of the creature's unique and terrorizing ability to destroy as it will and when it lists. And marveling crowds daily read the inscription beneath it.

Thus preserved for perpetuity lies a fragment, a mere strip—though originally somewhat larger, the vandals of science having wrought on it—the size of one's middle finger, that Messinger's pick had torn from the monster. In this liquid it looks exactly like a greasy, saturated sponge, of the coarse, dark-hued variety used in garages and for window cleaning. It was salvaged by a farmhand, who early on the spot the following morning had disturbed a horde of gulls which were screaming and squabbling on the sands above high water. Just in the nick of time he arrived to secure this morsel, the last of a banquet the feasters had been enjoying; consumed with the glory of his discovery he had straightway sought the authorities and turned it over, and finding his name mispelt in the papers had felt amply rewarded.

Lengthy and exhaustive examination of this fragment has resulted in some startling conclusions about the interior economy of its former owner, and its marvelous adaptation to altitudes so vast that the most daring aviator has never more than touched their fringe. We know for a certainty that its substance is as light and strong as a feather, elastic, and permeated by innumerable tiny cells, miniature bladders void of contents, connecting one with another by a network of small channels.

Primarily it was conceived that as with some species of fish these empty containers might be used for the storage of air to render the brute buoyant, but this would in no way account for its superb powers of levitation in a like medium. Then under chemical analysis distinct traces of the gas hydrogen were found to be present. At once the secret was revealed. For this gas is the lightest of all the vapors and was used in all our great airships until helium, though heavier, was found to be safer, being non-inflammable. Undoubtedly this monster possesses the ability to separate the gas from the humid vapor always more or less present in our atmosphere. The process is probably of chemico-electric nature and instantaneous in action; which, though very astounding, is no more so than the extraction of oxygen from water with every inflating of the lungs of a fish.

Such an inflation of a tenuous elastic fabric would result in just such an instantaneous levitation as Messinger described; and when the hydrogen was expelled and the structure contracted, a falling stone would hardly drop quicker. The miracle lies really in the amazing control and nicety of manipulation of its medium of locomotion; but then all living creatures, save man, control their movements with a like perfection of accuracy.

By a little shrewd reasoning it has been deduced that its natural habitat is probably within the tropics where the humidity is greater than our latitudes; and for some unknown motive we have been visited by a lone strayer from its fellows: possibly the moment of the odd chance in a million that has peopled continents has dawned for their species.

It certainly is strange that all wild tribes dwelling near the equator are ridden by the fear of monstrous, shapeless, evil things that assail the night wanderer who at dawn is found lifeless and withered with the terror of that encounter. We have deemed these stories superstition; but the fear is a living force and must be based on something, to dominate millions as it does.

No explanation of the extraordinary mutilation of each of its victims has yet been advanced. All we can conceive is an organism endowed with a means of imbibing sustenance, much as a vastly magnified reproduction of the apparatus of the common mosquito—a lower surface with an infinite number of hairlike filaments, each the counterpart of that insect's proboscis and similarly provided with an irritant poison that draws the blood of a victim to the inserted borers.

But this is mere theory and may be right, or may be wrong, and well it will be for us if the truth is never known, and this the brute's last appearance; though several inexplicable disappearances have recently occurred among our flying men—craft and men have vanished from our world as though they had found another and been unable to return. And yet the daring adventurers fly still higher seeking the thing that dwells in the unknown beyond; and these missing craft may have encountered it.

LEFT BY THE TIDE

Edward E. Schiff

WERE IT NOT for that four-inch scar upon my forehead, I would have thought it a nightmare—some ghastly hallucination, even though it happened in broad daylight. But there is that scar, which mars my features for life, tangible and terrible evidence to prove that I did not dream it.

I had gone down to the beach with the rising sun, but I was the only one there. None of the other guests from the hotel had yet come down to take their early morning plunge. A charity affair that did not break up till 3 o'clock that morning kept them abed. So I was alone upon that sun-drenched stretch of sand.

The tide was low and I had to walk some hundred yards before I was waist-deep and breasting the invigorating waters of old ocean. I swam out at once to a pile of rocks, a good quarter of a mile from the shore, and climbed out upon them. Now, at low tide, they formed a nearly circular, barnacle- and weed-covered island, about fifty feet in diameter and rising only a few feet above the waters. After resting a few minutes I clambered over the jagged stones toward the center, where there was a depression about six or seven feet deep and about the same width, and where the retreating waters sometimes left strange denizens of the deep which could be observed under ideal conditions.

Just before I reached the little pool, I thrilled to the sound of a splash of a heavy body. The tide had left something there with a vengeance, I thought gleefully, and I hastened forward to see what it was.

I stared, sickened by what I saw—a dead man, with shriveled, shrunken skin, hollow cheeks, and hideous in apparently the last stages of putrefaction. There he was floating on his back a bare few inches below the surface. His hands were under him, and at first I thought he was naked. Then, as I overcame my first horror, I noted that he had a sort of apron about his loins—an apron made of what appeared to be the scales of a large fish. It was a curious garment and covered with green algae or sea moss. The man must have been dead a long time to have allowed for the formation of that slime. I puzzled over this, wondering how it was he remained whole and not half devoured by the scavengers of the sea. Then suddenly I remembered the splash I had heard. Who had made it? Not the dead man. Closely I searched the pool for some other sign of life, but except for a sea crab or two there was none.

Turning my attention to the body again, I scrutinized it closely and felt my scalp twitch when I thought I detected a barely perceptible rising and falling of the chest. The more I stared the more certain I was that I was not mistaken. But drowned men do not breathe, I told myself; I must be laboring under a hallucination. I turned my eyes away and gazed out over the sea and sky to rest them, and when I turned them back again I was shocked into an exclamation. The body had moved toward me. I could still see the faint traces of the eddy it had made to reach me. But dead men cannot move and there was no wave or tide or any breath of wind that could propel it within that enclosed space.

Now I was certain it was breathing. The slight but definitely regular expansion and contraction of the chest were caused by respiration. I could not be mistaken.

Then suddenly the lids flashed open and I was staring into its eyes. And they were the eyes of a living creature, sea-green and evil, that probed through mine into the very recesses of my brain with satanic curiosity. Then, still holding me with its baleful gaze, the thing reached for the brink with huge hands that were webbed like the feet of some aquatic bird, and started to pull itself up.

Somehow I broke the spell by which the thing held me, and, half mad with loathing and horror, I kicked him with my bare foot back into the pool.

I think I stumbled half back to the open water before I recovered my courage and paused to look back. It had come out of the pool and was dragging its slimy length over the rocks toward me. I realized at once it could not walk upright and that I would have no difficulty in evading it. With unmitigated loathing I watched it crawl until it approached to within a few feet of me. Then I backed away from it, taking care to avoid being crowded into the sea where it could easily outmaneuver me with its finlike appendages.

Again it tried to hold me with its hypnotic stare, but I avoided its eyes, and, stooping down, picked up a fragment of rock and tried to threaten it back. Suddenly it, too, reached out and picked up a stone, and we both threw at the same moment. But I was completely beside myself with horror and missed him by inches, while he caught me fairly on the chest—a blow that knocked the breath out of me and dropped me to my knees. The next moment he was upon me, his powerful hands closing about my throat, his cold, slimy body against my cringing, warm flesh, his fetid breath in my nostrils.

But I fought, fought in a stark, frenzied madness that promised to rid me of his clinging, hateful weight, when suddenly he released one of his hands from my throat, and I could feel him fumble around his waist. The next moment I would have been free of him, but his hand came up again wielding a stone or coral knife.

I screamed and tried to evade the blow, but while I spoiled his aim for my throat he managed to inflict that awful gash on my forehead.

When I came back to consciousness it was with a cry of terror, in the arms of two men who were lifting me into a skiff; and for some minutes I struggled with them, before I realized they were my rescuers.

Their story is briefly told. They had observed me from the beach apparently trying to avoid some creature which they thought was a seal. They quickly got into a skiff and rowed to the rocks, shouting to frighten off the creature when they saw me struggling with it. Then for a minute or two I was out of their sight, hidden by a projecting rock, and when they again saw me I was alone and lying flat on my back, though a moment before they had heard the thing splash into the sea.

That is their story. Mine they would not believe. In fact, they tried to stop me in the telling of it, and attempted to soothe me as if I were a terror-stricken child, or crazy. They said I had injured my forehead by falling on a jagged stone.

But that day two bathers were pulled down to their death by some creature of the sea. Sharks, they all said. But I know better.

THE NET OF SHAMLEGH
Lieutenant Edgar Gardiner

Billy Singleton stood just inside the high gate of the Kashmir Serai and cursed—cursed as fluently and efficiently as any native, which is something that few of the ruling white race can do.

All his long trip up from the coast through the sweltering, enervating heat of the Punjab at summertime had been in vain; the time he could so ill spare and the expense account that would doubtless set the Kimball line's auditors about his ears again, all wasted—wasted because of the absence of one man. And because that man was a "black man" to boot—a native—well, that was the crowning insult.

A camel caravan creaked into the serai through the hot black night, coming almost magically under the blazing lights from out the velvety darkness. Perhaps this was he at last; perhaps Mahbub Ali, the Afghan, had but been delayed.

Apathetically he watched the ill-tempered, snapping beasts loom up out of that furnace of the night, laden with bundles and bales; almost mechanically his eyes swept the shrieking, cursing Balti camel-drivers' faces, looking for that of the Pathan horse-trader.

The caravan passed and melted into the steaming, milling crowd that filled the serai with a riot of color and a pandemonium of sound, and Singleton cursed his ill luck again.

This was the romance and the glamor of the East; this was the wonder and the mystery of the Orient, that had so thrilled him when he was first offered that odd position with the mighty Kimball steamship lines! In his ignorance he had thought that as their confidential agent he would enjoy a palatial suite of offices with a retinue of native clerks and servants, perhaps in Singapore, or maybe Calcutta. Instead, he had been rushed hither and yon, now to see an obscure Hill raja in some out-of-the-way part of India; now up some sluggish, stinking river in the F. M. S. to confer with an equally obscure princelet whose dignity was in inverse ratio to his importance; or, like the present occasion, when the man he sought was not even so important, but merely a wandering horse-trader. What possible cargo could accrue from such a one!

No wonder Billy Singleton stood just within the high gate of the Kashmir serai under the blazing lights and cursed the dilatory, careless Afghan, root and branch, with the thoroughness of the native, even unto the fifth and sixth generation. For Billy was that rarest of all men, the English-born European who thoroughly understood the native mind, who "when he was in Rome did as the Romans" with a vengeance, even thinking native. Some there are who will tell you that there is no such animal; they will shout that even the country-born European, brought up by native servants, playing with native children, can not do that. But Billy could and did.

A great and absorbing game, this, matching wits with the white men from competing steamship lines, matching them with the infinite varied traits and habits of yellow, brown and black, and winning, too, far more often than he lost.

Billy never knew the esteem in which he was held by his employers; he never knew the regard in which the natives held him—those who were his friends, and they were legion; but he did know the hatred engendered in his enemies. For he made these last, even as any other who does things, whether in the Orient or the Occident. It is only the man who does nothing who makes no enemies in this world, and sometimes I am not so sure about even that.

Romance, mystery—bah! Dirt and delay, double-dealing and derision—*that* was the Orient, he thought, as he turned away for his hotel in the European quarter of Lahore.

He turned his back on the swarming, colorful hive that was the Kashmir Serai as evening passed into night, and threaded his way through the crowds of the narrow streets that reminded him of nothing so much as a heap of working maggots on a dung-hill; he pushed his way absent-mindedly through the hot, crowded Motee Bazar where every race in the Asiatic world rubbed elbows—screaming, cursing, chaffing, dickering; past the Lahore Museum, the "Agaib-Gher" of the natives—the "wonder-house"; past the brick platform opposite where stood the great gun "Zam Zammeh," the "fire-breathing dragon." Tradition has it that whoso holds that holds the Punjab, and the great obsolete green-bronze piece of ordnance has ever been the coveted bit of the conqueror's loot.

It was too hot to hurry; besides, why hurry in this land where even Time stands still? Billy passed from the crowded, garish way into a narrow, tortuous alley that made more directly for his ultimate destination than the better-lighted, thronging thoroughfares. A foolhardy thing for any white man to do, especially when he is alone; but Billy was never one to think of risks. He came and went as he pleased, took appalling risks with the utmost sang-froid, and turned up debonair and smiling at the end. Billy passed into the narrow, tortuous alley and met his Kismet.

HALF-WAY DOWN THAT DARK WAY his inattentive ears heard the thud of blows on flesh, caught the whisper of a voice begging for mercy—a child's voice—or a woman's. Billy stopped. A moment or two he listened in indecision; his reason told him not to interfere—no native would, even had that beating occurred in the open street instead of behind the high wall. Native or white, either knew better than to interfere openly with other's private affairs in this swarming land of vice and crime and intrigue.

"*Chûp*," ordered a gruff voice; "*Chûp*—be still—or I break thy head." Followed the soft whimpering of a child, then the sound of blows again.

A red mist swam before Billy's eyes. In a flash he leaped upward and grasped the coping of the wall, heedless of the broken glass that might be imbedded thickly along its top, drew himself lithely up and dropped softly into the blackness on the other side. A little way before him, in the yellow rectangle of light streaming from an open door, stood a turbaned, bearded figure with upraised bamboo cane above a crouching, whimpering child—a boy it was, a boy of twelve or thirteen, certainly not more, who raised a tear-stained, terrorized face at this incredible apparition from out the inky night.

"Let be," Billy growled in Urdu. The tall native made a swift move toward his deep embroidered Bokhariot belt, and like a flash Billy's hard brown fist flashed up to land square on the point of the bearded chin. The native dropped like a poleaxed Brahminee bull and his turban rolled to Billy's feet.

Mechanically Billy picked it up; just as automatically he lifted the shrieking *Kunjiri* child to his feet. He clapped the turban on the child's head, still more or less thoughtlessly.

"Come thou," he said in the vernacular, as he slipped back to the wall. Swiftly he swung the slight form to its top; quickly he hauled himself over. Both dropped lightly into the black alley and Billy strode quickly to its farther end, the urchin at his heels.

Why under the sun had he acted so? What damnable impulse had prompted him to act in this quixotic fashion? Where would he take the lad—or what would he do with him when he got there? Mechanically he strode to his hotel and, still buried in thought, went up to his room, the lad hard at his heels.

"Thy name, *Kunjiri* (low caste)?" as the boy squatted on the floor.

"Chota Lal, oh Lion of the Helpless, Defender of the Weak."

"And he that beat thee?"

"Was Sikhandar Khan, oh, great Maharaja of the *Feringhi*."

Billy pondered. Doubtless the boy was lying; all natives do when a white man questions them—or any other for that matter.

"Why did he beat thee?" he asked suddenly.

"Because I saw that which he had done to Mahbub Ali, the horse-trader," whispered the little Hindoo, and in his eyes dawned a growing terror,

"What!" shouted Billy, thoroughly aroused.

"Oh, do not beat me, master," wailed the lad, throwing himself at Billy's feet while his hands fluttered at Billy's ankles.

"What talk is this of beating?" growled Billy, "*I* do not beat beggar brats—if their talk is true. What talk is this of Mahbub the Afghan?"

"Last night it was, ere the first cockcrow, in the black night beside the train. Sikhandar Khan and one other"—the boy's face worked pitifully—"Sikhandar Khan and that other—" Wordlessly he pantomimed what he feared to tell.

"Dead?" whispered Billy.

The lad nodded solemnly.

So *this* explained Mahbub Ali's failure to appear! Dead! Waylaid beyond the railroad station that shouldered the Kashmir Serai at its other end. Waylaid and robbed, no doubt, in the darkness of the railroad yards. But why? Why? Billy's dazed mind ran in circles. Something tremendously important it must be to force Sikhandar Khan and his confederate to such a step in Lahore, of all cities. On the road beyond the border—there dead men are a commonplace that excites little or no comment. But here, right under the nose of the police, under the long arm of the British Raj—. A soundless whistle of amazement came from his lips. Meditatively he stared at the lad unrolling Sikhandar Khan's turban from about his head.

"But why, little Friend of All the Stars?" he asked.

The lad flashed him a smile at the endearment.

"I think because of this," and he held out what he had found secreted in the folds of the soiled cloth.

Billy took the foot-long silken rope and fingered it curiously. Silk? Yes—no—was it after all? More attentively he examined it. Silk-like the cord surely was, but no silk such as he had ever seen before. A solid rope, finger-thick, incredibly strong as he found out by tugging on the ends with might and main. But silk! In all the world there was no worm that could spin such a monster thread as this! Artificial? It must be. Yet no! Billy would stake all his knowledge of silk—and that was considerable—that this was no artificial substitute. His mind took another turn as he considered the importance of this thing. No wonder Mahbub Ali had bid him come in haste! No wonder that imperturbable Afghan had been wildly excited! A cordage such as this—why, it was priceless! A fortune for some lucky one, this stuff he held in his grasp! His mind raced on in a maze of speculation as he pictured the upheaval in the industrial world that this new material would produce. For it was new—never had he seen or heard of such a thing! If he could get it for the Kimball lines—he was made! And so was Mahbub Ali!

His face clouded as he remembered. Mahbub Ali was dead. He had perished and the secret of this wonder had perished with him. Had it, indeed? Or had the dastardly Sikhandar Khan and his helper Thug forced from Mahbub the precious secret? Probably not; else they would not be still in Lahore. Had they known, they must assuredly have gone post-haste after it. Or, wait—perhaps they were hiding from the long arm of the police for that cowardly murder. What a way to die! By strangulation with the deadly silken coil thrown about the neck from behind! He died by the silken cord of Thuggee that another might possess his one treasure; another silken cord—but such a cord!

A long time Billy pondered, thinking of ways and means, weighing the evidence pro and con, sitting in rapt meditation, while the little Hindoo lad crouched at his feet like a graven image.

At last Billy saw his way clear, through those peculiar thought-processes that he employed so successfully. He rose to his feet.

"Come, my little Prince of Troubles, thou Son of Shaitan," he grinned good-humoredly at the lad. "It is our Kismet—thine and mine. And our star, it is the red one of War." He pointed out the open windows at red Mars lying low in the heavens. "Wilt thou come with me?" he asked banteringly in the vernacular.

"Thou art my father and my mother. Didst thou not save me from Sikhandar Khan when he would have slain me?" asked the *Kunjiri* lad.

Billy started. He had not expected such plain words as these; such devotion from a mere baby for the slight service he had rendered. As for Sikhandar Khan slaying the lad—nonsense! And yet—child though he was, he knew far too much about that rascally rogue.

As he turned to go, Billy bethought himself of that precious thing, the silken cord, and as he tucked it within his bosom he slipped his flat automatic into his pocket as an afterthought. If these rogues had killed Mahbub Ali for this, surely they would do no less for him in their determination to repossess themselves of it.

HE STRODE BACK the way he had come, through the Motee Bazar to the still noisy Kashmir Serai, as active all night long as by daylight—more so, even—for the Oriental turns day into night or night into day, imperturbably. But it is noteworthy that he kept to the wide, well-lighted thoroughfares and avoided that short cut through the alleys as he would the plague. And his eyes roved incessantly about, never still a moment, while Chota Lal dogged his footsteps, a faithful little shadow.

Billy had decided on his course of action. He had determined to retrace Mahbub Ali's footsteps as best he might. Though he could ill spare the time, he would make the weary trip, for he was playing, he realized, for millions. That these millions would flow into the Kimball line's coffers were he successful troubled him not a whit. His was the joy of the game, the pitting of his wits against those other's, the winning, all alone, against he knew not what, nor cared.

He remembered that Mahbub Ali had a partner who was a cousin of sorts, and that partner he found after a long weary search in that maggotlike Oriental crowd, but trying to make him talk was a more difficult thing; for he had all the native's version against truth-telling and there was, besides, such a pitiful bit to be found out.

From the few of Mahbub's caravan train that had not gone to seek employment elsewhere, he found out that Mahbub Ali had come through Mussoorie Pahar from Rampur, and before that from Chini. Beyond that the trail was blank, nor would they talk overmuch of Chini, that valley in the High Hills. Was it not a place of Shaitans, where stalked Murrah and Awan, the Companion of Kings, and other devils and djinns without number? They were all *Jullalee*, those devils—all terrible; that much was certain.

That was the sum total of information that Billy carried back to his hotel in the early morning after cursing them all heartily as children of the devil Mushoot, the Lord of Liars. Nor was he surprised to find that during his absence the place had been searched and ransacked most thoroughly. He had expected that. But he had not expected them to *bukk* (bungle) the job as they had done. His opinion of Sikhandar Khan dropped distinctly as he surveyed the disorder. Small matter. There was nothing they could have found there that mattered.

He grinned at Chota Lal, who was stuffing himself with more delicacies than he had ever before eaten at one time, then winced as a movement of the young body showed the raised bamboo welts of the beating of the night before. Sikhandar Khan would have to pay through the nose for that night's work. In the fullness of time there would be a bitter bill for him to foot.

"As soon as may be," he said in the vernacular, "we go upon the road, thou and I. A long trail, a weary trail, perhaps even a trail of death, oh my son. What matter? Art thou minded even yet to follow me?"

"If I eat thy bread how shall I forget thee, oh Father of All the Friendless?"

"Well said, little one," and for the waif there welled a great affection in his heart, a friendship, a love that was to endure for longer than either of them realized. A thousand times we have heard of love at first sight between the sexes. A thousand and one tales have been woven about it. Can that happen only between man and woman? Perhaps so; I do not know. But between the Englishman and the little half-starved, beaten, low-caste lad there sprang up then a bond that was to lead to—but that is another story.

Two DAYS LATER found the pair at Simla, the summer capital of India, among the hills, where each house looks down upon the roof-pots of its neighbors on the terrace below; and that same week found the two attached to the hunting-party of one of Billy's English friends who was bound for the High Hills. Ostensibly Billy was going to hunt, a carefree adventurer with no thought in the world other than sport. And Chota Lal, re-sourceful little devil that he was, was one of the hangers-on who followed them, subsisting on the careless bounty of the sahibs.

But a very different Chota Lal this, from that one who had pattered through the Motee Bazar living on his wits and the charity of those minded to acquire merit. That one had been a beggar brat in soiled and ragged clothing; this one was an Afghan lad from the top of his clean blue turban to the tips of his long upcurled slippers; impudent, and likable withal, but a total stranger to Billy—a stranger lad who mingled with the shikaris and the syees—the hunters and the grooms—or the personal ser-vants in the swarm that always attends the Anglesi on such a trip, but he mingled not with the lordly sahibs; though of a night, had he been watched, he might have been seen to wriggle as softly as a snake into Sahib Singleton's tent to retail to him the varied gossip of the day that he had picked up.

It was his strong young voice that roused the camp to inef-fectual uproar one night when he found a greased and slippery devotee of Thuggee bound for the same place. The Thug had vanished into the thin black night, easily evading the clutching hands and clumsy efforts of the sleepy servants, scarce roused from their first heavy slumber; he had gone from there, but he had left behind him that dread cord of his office: it lay in Billy Sahib's hand as Chota Lal whispered of the events of the day.

But by now their wandering road led no longer climbing, dipping, sweeping about the spurs and the stony hillsides where sounded the voices of a thousand and one watercourses, with the solemn deodars climbing one after the other with down-droop-ing branches. The vista of the far-rolled-out plains beneath them was done; the Sewaliks and the half-tropical Doon were behind them along with Mussoorie.

The deodars had given place to oak and birch, holly and pine, gay with rhododendrons and ferns; the bare hillsides were

slippery with sunburnt grass, to merge again with the cool wood-
lands, while above them flamed Kedemath and Badjunath in the
sunrise and sunset, true kings of the wilderness. And the gentle
breezes that had blown cool in those early marches now bit deeply at heat-accustomed flesh and tugged with fierce clutching fingers at wholly inadequate garments.

Billy Singleton grinned cheerfully at these things and at
the steep, breath-taking short cuts that the hillmen insisted on
making, but it was no laughing matter to poor Chota Lal, who
had never been so high in the diamond-clear air in all these, his
twelve years. And too, Chota Lal had all the plainsman's love for
a beaten trail though it wound its six-foot width as tortuously as
any snake over all the country.

Along the track lay the occasional villages of the hill folk—
rude huts of mud and earth and now and then a rare, crudely
ax-carved timber, like swallows' nests against the steep pitches,
or huddled on tiny flats midway on a four-thousand-foot slide,
or jammed, perhaps, into a tiny crevice of the cliffs that funneled
and focused every wandering blast.

And the villagers! Greasy, sallow, duffle-clad; bare-legged,
short, squat, yellow-faced—truly this was indeed a land of Shaitans and Djinns!

Here it was that Billy slipped away from the rest of the party
after a short earnest chat with Foster Sahib the day that Chota
Lal had retailed to him a bit of gossip he had picked up regarding
a red-bearded stranger of two months gone who had come from
Shamlegh Midden, where few men have trod, where even the
Hillmen will not go. He had pushed away from this somber land
as though all the sons of Eblis were indeed after him. Mahbub
Ali beyond all reasonable doubt! Billy's heart sang within him as
he followed the plain lead.

How he and Chota Lal ever got down those awe-inspiring
cliffs only Allah the Merciful and the Compassionate knows—
surely it was His hand that led them on.

How Sikhandar Khan and that other followed—truly that
was the work of a *jumalee* (well-wishing) Shaitan—none other!
For follow they did less than eight hours after the others.

And on those great boulder-strewn slopes, cut up by narrow abysses that yawned to unguessed depths, weird and horrible even under the bright sun that scarce burned the bitterest of the chill from the cold air, Billy came upon the rope again. Fifty feet long it must have been, stretching over the cliff edge to a projecting ledge below—and it was glued to the rocks! Billy's cheeks were blanched as he faced the terrified boy.

"It is truly the work of the djinns!" panted Chota Lal. "Let us go—and quickly."

"Hast thou fear for a djinn," teased Billy, "thou Babe of Small Courage?"

Chota flushed and wriggled uncomfortably but stood his ground.

"Then, too, oh my master, there is that matter of the two specks that I saw this morning behind us."

Billy's face grew grave. "Why didst thou not tell me ere this, little Prince of the Plains?"

Sikhandar Khan and his confederate that must be, following the plain trail they had left. Well, let them come. Billy felt himself more than a match for both of them as he looked at his Mannlicher and patted the flat automatic lovingly. If it came to a fight, he was more than willing, he and Chota Lal. If they two lost out—and then his thoughts turned to the faithful little bazar imp beside him. After what he had seen of Sikhandar Khan's treatment of Chota—he shut his teeth with a snap. He must not fail.

They ate from the canned provisions that they had brought; ate in a cranny of sheltering boulders with the declining sun scarce warming the chill air of these high places; then Billy half dozed against a solid rock as he watched and Chota Lal slept fitfully under his thin blanket until Billy wrapped his own about the sleeping child while the cold stars looked down on the unbroken solitude.

THE MOON SANK SLOWLY to rest; dawn was not far off when they heard that first hoarse shout of terror. It was followed by another and another, until the hills echoed and re-echoed to the clamor.

Billy flashed to his feet. "Come," he said authoritatively to the wide-eyed boy as he played his flashlight about. Cautiously they moved through the gloom in the direction of the din, their flashlight picking out their path, while Billy's revolver swung free in his other hand.

What a sight met their eyes! Sikhandar Khan it was, indeed; a pitiful, terrorized wreck of that bearded ruffian, straining and struggling desperately against more of those odd ropes. Rayed from a common center these were, like the spokes of a wheel, and fastened tightly to the rocks at waist height, while across them in concentric circles that began at that common center was another.

As Sikhandar Khan saw them in the lightening dawn he stretched an imploring arm to them and straggled anew while the network of ropes shook under the fury of his struggles.

Gingerly Billy felt of the nearest strand of that odd net before he set his weight upon it. His hand stuck tenaciously to its glistening, viscous surface. So that was how Sikhandar Khan was being held, was it? And in his every struggle, whenever he touched it anew, that net but clung the tighter to the new hold.

What the devil was it, anyway? And whose the hand that had stretched it there? Billy dropped on all fours to crawl along under it after shouting to the frenzied man to cease straggling; but it was doubtful if that fear-maddened one even heard him.

Billy had no desire to have that sticky thing catch him helplessly by the back. He jammed his automatic into his pocket and brought out his knife, intending to cut the man free; then he crawled carefully inward, glancing ever and anon at the brightening sky. The false dawn was done; the day had come.

Again came Sikhandar's frenzied thrashing, though he was now almost helplessly fastened to that dreadful net. Billy lay flat on the stony ground while those viscous ropes vibrated dangerously close to his body. As the struggles ceased he crawled on again toward that helpless unfortunate. The first rays of the newly risen sun shone upon him and turned that net to gold, gilding that colorful human fly in this gigantic spiderweb.

That was what the damnable thing reminded him of: a monster spiderweb—admitting for the moment that such a thing could be. Billy had seen spiders in his travels that snared and killed small birds—with their webs a few feet across. Horrid, saucer-shaped things those spiders were, whose bite was poisonous, producing sickness that lasted for days, that might even cause death if not cared for; but this—no, this was something entirely beyond his knowledge. He was under Sikhandar Khan now, and he rolled over on his back.

"Be still, dog," he ordered as he raised his knife. At the sound of his voice Sikhandar Khan thrashed more wildly than ever and his hoarse voice called upon all the gods of Hind for succor.

"Be still, *bût-parast* (idol-worshiper)," growled Billy in disgust.

"Ohé Billee Sahib, beware! The djinn! Behold, it comes!" screamed Chota Lal in accents of such terror that Billy's upraised arm dropped paralyzed. The net above him vibrated with a curious trembling motion, Billy screwed his head around and lay stupefied with horror. Shades of all the Sons of Eblis! By the Thousand and One Shaitans of the deeper and nethermost Hells! What was this terrible monster? Was it in very truth one of those devils that the Hillmen swore inhabited these wilds?

Huge, leggy, bristly, it flashed toward them. Its legs covered a fifteen-foot circle; its body was a globular bag, gleaming iridescently with blues and greens and blacks, mottled with vivid red splotches the size of a man's head. In a sort of spiny plate on its front were set six gleaming black eyes that glinted redly in the golden haze. The plate and bag were borne on those huge spiky legs four feet or more above the net.

It flashed onto the helpless man above him swifter than the eye could follow and paused there an instant while a lancet-like arm flashed into Sikhandar Khan's upturned stomach.

Sikhandar Khan gave a convulsive shudder and hung limply below the hellish monster, while Billy in a daze of horror lay just below it, so close that he could almost touch the damnable thing.

A spider! It *couldn't* be—but it was—a spider greater than any that the world had ever seen! And it stood there on its net above him sucking out the juices from that lifeless body that a moment before had been a man! He heard Chota Lal sobbing and screaming in terror where he had left him.

In a curious, detached sort of way Billy slowly and carefully drew his automatic, moving almost imperceptibly. To his dazed faculties it seemed as though his mind stood apart from his body and watched those actions which were his own as though they were those of a stranger. The gun flashed—once—twice—thrice—as Billy shot pointblank into that terrible thing just above him. The acrid fumes choked and blinded him, and when he could open his eyes again the Thing was gone, but Sikhandar Khan's body still sagged limply above him. The man was dead! Billy knew that from the drawn, pinched features. That hideous Thing had sucked every drop of blood from out the body. But the Thing was gone!

IT SEEMED AGES before Billy retraced his slow, crawling way back to the shrinking, hysterical lad, and he himself was shaking as with nervous ague.

"Whence came the—the Shaitan?" Billy whispered. "And whither went it, oh my son?"

Chota Lal clung wildly to him and pressed his shaking little body tightly against him. Billy could feel the furious, frightened beating of his heart in the little breast that pressed so close against his own.

"Oh my master, let us fly. Quickly, ere it follow and leap upon us as it did upon that—that—"

"There, there, lad," Billy soothed, forcing himself to speak English. "It's only a spider—but the biggest thing I ever saw or heard of. It's no devil, though it looks like one. Come, lad, where did it go?" He repeated the question in Urdu.

Chota Lal's only answer was to clutch him the tighter.

"No! No! Billee Sahib! Let us go! Do not seek the djinn! It will but take thee as it took that other," he wailed.

Gently Billy disengaged the lad's arms from about his neck and picked up his Mannlicher. "Fear not for me, little one. I shall slay this Thing. Tell me but whither it went."

Slowly he paced the wide circumference of the net, seeking the vanished monster. On the opposite side he paused. Was that not one of the Thing's legs projecting between those boulders?

"Heave thou a stone, my son," he whispered to Chota Lal, who kept light by his side. The lad demurred. Billy insisted. At last Chota tossed a stone the size of a baseball in that direction.

There was no movement, but Billy was more convinced than ever that it was one of the creature's legs that he saw. He inched nearer and nearer until he had a glimpse of that brilliantly colored horrible body. Slowly the rifle raised, flashed, and the hills thundered to its sharp report. Still no movement.

"Seest thou? It is as I said. The Thing is dead."

He drew nearer until he could see the horrid Thing in its entirety. It was surely dead. When he had satisfied himself on that point he crawled under the net once more and succeeded in hacking down Sikhandar Khan's body and then in dragging it out.

"First we bury this," he said as Chota Lal begged him to leave.

A shallow grave was dug at last and stones heaped above the miserable wretch before Billy Singleton with a sigh set his face back along the way he had come.

He had won through, but at what a cost! Had won through and reaped only a disappointment. "It's all in the game," he grunted to himself as he and Chota Lal were climbing back along that dizzy way they had come. He had hoped—with a start he realized that he had come wholly without hopes or plans. He had come for the love of the game alone.

A thousand feet they climbed in a little over a mile, and above them they could see the hillside where wound the path.

"Be brave, thou Little Lion of the Plains," Billy encouraged as they breasted that last steep boulder-strewn slope.

The noise of a rifle sounded above that of the wind; Chota Lal gave an agonized yelp, spun round, and would have slipped down that dizzy slope had Billy not caught him by the arm and dragged him to the shelter of some boulders close at hand.

"What the devil—why, you're hurt, kid," he exclaimed in surprise as he stared at his bloody hand. A flesh wound only, through the upper arm, he found out as he cut away the cloth. Luckily no bones had been broken and no artery severed; the wound, though it bled freely, and was painful, was not dangerous.

"There to the left, he is, behind those bushes, Billee Sahib," whispered Chota Lal, grimacing with pain as Billy tore his own shirt to strips for bandages. "I saw the smoke as I fell."

"Why, you nervy little beggar," grinned Billy in delighted surprise.

"Beggar will I never be again, Billee Sahib, lest I bring dishonor to thee," and Chota Lal smiled faintly.

"So be it. By the bullet that laid thee low, beggar shall thou never be again, but mine own son forevermore, Chota Lal."

He picked up the rifle again and peered round the edge of the protecting boulder. Again the report and the angry scream of the bullet as it ricocheted from the stone.

"That devil can really shoot," Billy whispered softly to himself as he crawled swiftly downward to another boulder, keeping carefully out of sight of the unknown marksman.

Then ensued a tedious game of stalking between the two. An hour went by. Billy could see Chota Lal lying where he had left him, but glimpse that other he could not. He cursed softly as the sun dropped slowly toward the west. Something must be done. But what?

Chota Lal solved the problem by standing up suddenly with a shout. Billy caught the gleam of the other's rifle, saw him half rise, and then Billy shot swiftly in a panic of fear. Suppose that fellow got Chota Lal! The other's gun exploded, but the bullet went wild, for the brain behind it was done. Billy's steel-jacketed bullet had found its mark. The unknown rifleman half straightened, toppled over slowly and went slithering down the slope head foremost, to drop off that tremendous cliff, his rifle clattering after him as it dropped from his nerveless fingers.

"Hast thou lost thy little grain of sense, thou Son of Eblis?" Billy scolded as he helped Chota Lal up those last steep reaches. Chota Lal grinned—the impudent, carefree grin that had so endeared him to Billy.

"Thou art my father and my mother, oh Billee Sahib. I have eaten thy bread and thy salt. Shall I then forget it? I stood up in sight so that one might show himself to thee. What matter though I died, so thou wert freed?"

GHOULS OF THE SEA

J. B. S. Fullilove

MOST READERS OF THE DAILY PAPERS, and especially those persons who follow with interest those accounts relating to the men of the sea, will recall the strange disappearance of the freighter *Kay Marie* some seven months ago. They will recall the brief flurry of excitement attending her reported foundering with all hands aboard. Desperately storm-ridden and swept far off her course, she sent forlorn appeals for aid, reporting that her rudder had been swept away and her engines seriously damaged. Nearby ships immediately put out to her aid, but her wireless signals suddenly ceased. Apparently she had drifted far, for no trace of her was ever found.

In common with most others, I accepted as the most plausible explanation the theory that, in her crippled condition, she had either been swamped by the mountainous waves or driven to her doom upon some uncharted reef in unknown waters.

But today, with the *Kay Marie* farthest from my mind and all but forgotten, I chanced upon something else. As is often my habit, I had risen before the sun and gone down to a favorite stretch of beach to cast in the surf for bass. As I walked along the shore I stumbled upon a large glass jug lying amid a pile of driftwood and debris. Even before I smashed it with my heavy sand-pike I knew that it contained some message from the sea, for through its salt-caked sides I had seen a flash of white.

And message indeed it was! Part of the manuscript was missing, but the remainder comprises a bizarre and incredible tale which I set down here precisely as I found it. The true account of the *Kay Marie* disaster? That is for the reader to decide.

Here is the account:

". . . calm, and immediate danger is past. But we are completely cut off from the rest of the world and there is nothing to do but wait and hope that some ship picked up our S. O. S. and will find us before our food and water become exhausted.

"There are many sharks about, and to relieve the monotony of waiting, the crew for a time engaged in fishing for them. Two were caught, and then the fishing suddenly stopped. Here is something very strange, something which arouses superstitious fears in the men. Until now I have been unable to ascertain exactly what it is, because the men are all strangely reticent concerning the whole affair. All I have been able to get out of them is that the sharks they caught were dead.

"Svensen, the big Swedish mate, however, tells me that there were curious gobs of pinkish jelly covering their heads. He says that Doctor Curey took samples of the stuff to his cabin for examination.

"It is indeed surprising that men like Svensen, who can laugh in the teeth of a storm, should exhibit fear at sight of a few dead fish.

"I HAVE JUST LEFT Doctor Curey in his makeshift laboratory busily engaged in working on the specimen he took from the head of the shark. It somewhat resembles a huge, pink jelly-fish. It has the same disgusting feel, and is without definite form. Still, there are differences. This thing is continually in motion; shimmering at all times as though someone were shaking the table upon which it is placed. A mephitic odor hovers about it, and an indefinable something about it fills me with a kind of loathing and a queer feeling almost of fear. At times I felt as if it were alive and possessed some uncanny power of sight and were watching me.

"Doctor Curey is very much excited. He says that it is an entirely new form of parasitic growth secreting a powerful, bone-dissolving acid which enables it to get at the flesh and blood of its victims. But he, too, is at a loss to explain their immediate and deadly effect when the sharks were taken from the water.

"Captain Wilkes picked up a trail of smoke on the horizon this morning; but they passed us by. We are far from shipping-lanes, and it is good to know that someone is looking for us.

"God is indeed merciful! Had the ship we sighted picked us up, what a ghastly horror might have been loosed upon the world! My fear of the strange specimen of Doctor Curey was well founded. It is a spawn of the nethermost depths of some hell of the sea.

"I was engaged in working on my hopelessly damaged apparatus when suddenly a scream echoed through the ship. It was a scream of paralyzing horror and fraught with agony, but through its terror I recognized it as the voice of Doctor Curey.

"Perhaps no one else knew wherefrom the scream had come, for I was the first to reach the cabin of the stricken man. As I rushed in, I saw the doctor seated in a darkened corner, where, I judged, he must have fallen asleep. Only the pale rays of the moon lighted the room, and I could not see plainly, but there was something peculiar about the way he sat. He seemed strangely stiff and as straight as a statue. Apoplexy! instantly flashed through my mind. I shouted to him and stepped closer.

"At the sound of my voice, he half turned and rose slowly from his chair. Something about his movements abruptly checked my rush toward him. The peculiar, frightful *stiffness* of his actions is impossible to describe. They were the movements of a reawakened corpse who tries to force worm-eaten muscles into the forgotten movements of life.

"With my heart still, I stood motionless and watched him as he painfully arose. Once again I called to him in a voice hoarsened by strange fear. As if in answer, he turned. At the same time my hand darted swiftly to my pocket, and with trembling fingers I lighted a match against the wall. As it flared up, I looked into his face and sank to my knees with a low gasping cry. The flickering light of the match was dim, but, even so, that first view of the horror was so indelibly stamped upon my brain that even now—days later—as I write, I can still see it vividly, frightfully.

"The face staring sightlessly into mine was a white, drawn mask of insupportable agony. The blackened tongue, grown sickeningly to astounding length, protruded from half-open lips. He seemed to be trying to scream. His eyes were leaping from their sockets, and already there was forming over them a cold and ghastly glaze. . . . *The man walking stiffly toward me was plainly dead!*

"And then as the last flickering rays of the match burned out between my fingers, I saw. . . .

"Until now, I had not thought of any connection between the doctor's experiments and *this*. I had unconsciously supposed him to have fallen victim to some new and horrible disease. But with the last dimming ray of the match, a glimmering of the incredible truth burst upon me with terrible clearness. Even then my dazed and weakened mind refused to grasp the full significance of what I saw in all its ghastliness.

"The top of his head was a shimmering mask of dark red jelly, and from it I could see a long tongue of the same unspeakable stuff slithering down the back of his neck. The whole loathsome mass seemed to swell and grow from his skull with unbelievable rapidity. Despite the awful dazedness of my mind, I still noted the significant change in the color of the mass . . . and that mingled with its grisly red, there were flecks of white and gray.

"As in a dream I heard excited voices and knew that the room had filled with men. I saw the captain, with a curious glance at me, dart forward and catch the swaying doctor in his arms. Frozen with horror, I could only stare—and wait.

"As swiftly as the movement of a striking snake—too swiftly for the eye to follow—a tongue of the dribbling mass hanging nearly to the doctor's shoulders licked out and spattered upon the captain's head. He clawed madly at his hair for a moment, gave vent to a single agonized scream, then slumped forward. He stiffened almost before he struck the floor; then with the same frightful rigidity that the doctor had shown, he slowly sat up, then rose to his feet.

"The horror upon his head had sunk in, disappearing beneath his matted hair. Now it reappeared, growing, swelling like a toy balloon—a shuddersome mass of quivering, sensate jelly, whose soul-chilling scarlet was thickly dotted with white and gray. . . .

"Miraculously then my power of movement returned. Gasping weakly, I stumbled toward the door. I saw the thing that had been the doctor move also, and a ghastly hint of its intention thrust itself into my stunned consciousness, lending speed to my laggard limbs. Close behind me, it circled the milling, craning crowd, who still could not understand; or having seen, stood rooted, held powerless to move by sheer ecstasy of horror. I staggered through the door and sank exhausted to the deck. Behind me the door slammed shut, and there came the sound of a heavy body falling against it.

"For some moments, then, there was silence; then from behind the door there came the ghastly sound of scream after scream of mortal agony and horror, the sound of thudding bodies and of madly stamping feet; but now and then above this hellish din I could hear with terrible distinctness a faint *splat, splat,* like the sound of wet rags falling upon the floor.

"Only a short time I lay thus. Then I remember somewhat vaguely running madly and mingling my screams with the screams of the imprisoned men. For the madness of terror that had descended upon me was now complete. *Just in time I had risen, warned by reflected moonbeams shining into my eyes, and seen the faintly luminous, slithering rill of the jelly that was flowing out toward me from under the door. . . .*

"WHEN I REGAINED CONSCIOUSNESS later—whether days or weeks I do not know—I found that I had bolted myself within my own cabin. In the fever of madness I had stuffed up every crack and hole in the walls and door. Still there is everywhere the indescribable stench of the things. I am now certain that I must have been insane much longer than I at first believed, for now I can detect another odor. But upon that I dare not dwell. The picture it brings is too unutterably horrible for contemplation in my weakened state . . . rotting corpses, animated by hellish creatures who supplant their brains, walking in ghastly parades across the decks! . . .

"Am I alone? Outside I can hear the slow tramping of feet. Whether they are the feet of living men or of the horror I dare not look to see. I shout, but never is there an answer. The things I hear outside number many.

"But there is a way out if I am swift. There is powder in the hold. If I can reach it, a match will save me through quick death from the other end I face. Besides, the *Kay Marie* must never be found or allowed to drift too near to land.

"If the things are waiting when I step outside the door, at least I shall have tried to send them back to where they belong— at the bottom of the sea."

DEATH IN THE STRATOSPHERE

Henry J. Kostkos

THE GROUND CREW at the landing field of the Inter-Continental Air Service, Ltd., on Long Island looked up and after one awe-stricken glance they began to run for the nearest hangar. For directly above them, at an elevation of about twelve thousand feet a large silver stratoplane was plunging down toward the earth in what might have been taken for a power dive were it not for the fact that the ship was spinning on its vertical axis like a high-speed twist drill boring into some soft substance.

"Call the ambulance and fire crew!" Dacy shouted breathlessly to a mechanic. "She's going to crash! Looks like Atwell's plane coming in from Paris—Hurry, you fool!" he roared at the mechanic who stood transfixed with horror as he watched.

The wail of a siren rent the air as the emergency crew responded with an ambulance and fire trucks. From the comparative safety of a hangar Airport Superintendent J. R. Dacy and his men watched the "ICA-1" plunge with sickening speed toward inevitable destruction.

"Look! He's caught her!" one of the men shouted.

The plane, after dropping to within a half mile of the earth suddenly came out of the dive with a sharp swerve of its bow. The ship fluttered uncertainly like a falling leaf in swirling air currents. It shuddered as if with horror at the thought of what it had gone through in the short seconds that had just passed, and circling round and round struck the ground with its landing-gear which crumpled under the impact.

When the emergency crew and Dacy reached the "ICA-1" it was lying on its side like a great wounded bird, one wing buried in the ground, the other pointing significantly into the element from which the plane had just fallen.

The men tore open the door, a task made easy since it was battered and twisted out of shape.

"My God!" Dacy exclaimed as he peered into the luxuriously furnished cabin. "It's empty! Look, no one in there!"

Hurriedly he climbed up, then made for the control room.

He focused his eyes on the chair that should have been occupied by Captain Roger Atwell, crack pilot of the Inter-Continental Air Service lines. It required some moments before he could believe the evidence of his senses. He swiveled his massive head on a tree-trunk of a neck as his astonished eyes swept to the positions normally occupied by the first officer, by the navigator, by the radio operator. Finally the voice of a mechanic confirmed what had been an all-too-slowly forming conviction in Dacy's mind: "There's no one in here! The ship flew in by itself."

Dacy nodded an uncertain nod, then forcing himself out of his bewilderment Dacy asked in a hollow voice that sounded like the mere vestige of the loud, angry sound that usually issued from his lips when he spoke: "Have you searched all compartments?"

"Yes," a man replied. "We found nothing."

Then Dace's eyes peered into the far corner of the cabin. Hurrying over, he stooped to examine what proved to be a heap of human bones, picked clean of flesh, yet coated with a thin layer of a slimy substance. Gingerly he poked around among the bones and the shreds of clothing. His hand found something that he hurriedly thrust into his pocket.

"We'll have to search these remains more carefully to find out who this was," he said to his master mechanic.

The master mechanic, Sanford, had been looking over the controls.

"Just as I thought, Mr. Dacy," he exclaimed, "They've set the ship for automatic flying, with this field as the final destination. . . ."

"They?" Dacy asked. "Whom do you mean by they?"

Sanford looked up sharply. "Why Atwell and his officers, of course. Who else could have done it?"

"Then where are they now? How did they leave the ship? What happened to—that in the corner? Who—?"

Dacy's further questions were interrupted by a shout from outside.

"Mr. Dacy! Mr. Sanford! Look at what we've found!"

As THE TWO CLIMBED OUT of the ship the men pointed to the landing gear braces. Clinging to the ironwork were ribbons of bright colored gelatin that quivered and writhed as if alive. Gingerly Sanford touched one, then recoiled as a shred of the substance stiffened and with a lightninglike dart reached toward him. The watching men laughed nervously, but none made any move to step forward. The whiteness of Sanford's face was replaced by a deep red, as he became aware of the significance of the laugh. He wasn't going to be humiliated before his men, even if they themselves lacked the guts to investigate. Undoubtedly, he reasoned, the plane had been forced down, so that it had dragged its landing gear through the water out there in the broad reaches of the Atlantic and had ploughed up a giant jellyfish. Shucks, what was there to be afraid of anyway?

Sanford boldly stepped up to the landing gear and with the forced, jerky motion of an automaton, his hand shot out and grasped the largest shred of quivering gelatine. So quickly that the human eye could not follow it, the ribbon wound around the man's arm. And no longer was it vari-colored, but it had become a deep angry purple, pulsating, living, and with the power of a huge torsion device it bit deeply into the flesh of the forearm until the cold purple mass became dyed with the warm red blood of the man. What might have been a cry of horror was strangled in Sanford's throat even as Dacy leaped to life and with a wrecking bar snatched from a mechanic's hand he dug furiously at the crushing gelatine. With the moan of a man who is weary beyond words, Sanford crumpled up in a heap, with only his right arm, its red-dyed mass of horror wrapped tightly around it, extended imploringly.

"Help me, you fellows," Dacy gasped. Then seeing the ambulance surgeon hurrying toward him, he said: "Never mind, here comes Dr. Lewis."

The young doctor, attempting a nonchalance he was far from feeling, reached toward the mutilated arm.

"Don't touch it!" Dacy warned. "That stuff's alive."

In a few jerky and almost incoherent sentences he explained their findings while the doctor applied a stethoscope to Sanford's heart. The man's face had by now turned a deep shade of purple as if to match the color of the horrible substance that was responsible for his suffering.

"His heart beat is very, very slow, as if he was being strangled," said the doctor. "I'll give him a hypodermic and then we'll have to rush him to the hospital. I'm afraid that I'll have to amputate his arm," he added, keeping his eyes fixed with awed fascination on the quivering gelatin that had by now squeezed the flesh from the bones as if it were soft putty. "I won't want to do anything here without proper equipment," he explained apologetically yet knowing all the while that he most certainly feared to come into contact with the purple mass on the man's arm.

When Sanford had been carried away Dacy directed his men to bring the oxyhydrogen blowpipe equipment from the shops. Then taking the nozzle, he savagely directed the searing flame at the remaining ribbons of gelatine. When the flame struck the substance the shreds sizzled as if in agony and great drops of viscous fluid oozed from it.

Even in its fluid form the substance seemed to cling tenaciously to life; it bubbled angrily on the ground for a full minute then subsided into an oily pool that was gradually absorbed by the dry soil of the landing field.

Sanford never came out of the ether following the amputation. For a while there had been hope. His heart had become stronger, almost normal in fact, but suddenly it faltered and then stopped entirely. The doctors said that he had really died of fright from the effects of the shock of having the living mass of purple slowly squeeze the flesh from his bones like some medieval torture instrument. The amputated arm was placed in a refrigerated cabinet, and doctors and scientists from near and far came to observe it and attempt to determine the composition of the gelatinous mass. Most of them agreed that it was organic, although some maintain that it might be purely chemical—an unknown chemical that had a peculiar, devilish affinity for flesh. Samples carefully cut from the mass were analyzed. The scientists proved beyond question that the substance was protoplasmic and cellular in structure and origin and that it was still very much alive. Yet it did not continue to grow. For want of a more accurate classification, the scientists agreed with Sanford's conviction that the "ICA-1" had torn into the body of some huge sea monster, a jellyfish of an unknown species.

Still, that did not explain the presence of the mangled skeleton or the disappearance of the officers, the crew, and the fifty-nine passengers of the stratoplane. Of course, as in the case of all mysteries, there were countless speculations by experts and laymen alike, by the sensational press and even by the staid scientific journals. Their solutions ranged from cold, clear, unconvincing logic to pink-fringed fantasy that melted away into vapor at the first suspicion of serious consideration. All in all no one was satisfied by anyone else's explanation and in time the disappearance was relegated by the public to the limbo of inexplicable mysteries.

THEN, TWO MONTHS LATER when crusty old Scovill Delray, president of Inter-Continental Air Service, Ltd., no longer felt it obligatory to ease himself by continuous blasphemy of the effect of the loss of the "ICA-1's" passengers, a call on his private radio-phone from his Long Island airport started him off on a fresh stream of vituperation that continued uninterruptedly for fifteen minutes. His secretary who had been taking dictation mumbled some incoherent words and fled from the office, neglecting, in her haste, to close the door. The over-ripe language flowed out into the outer office, effectively silencing the clerks and stenographers either through awe or because they were fascinated into speechlessness by the picturesque expressions that would have been the envy of the most abusive longshoreman.

Buzzers in private offices began to croak as Delray slapped his huge paw of a hand down on an entire row of buttons. Soon an influx of frightened faces filled the large office of the president.

"Sit down, sit down, dang your hides, instead of standing and gaping at me as if I had hydrophobia!" he roared. "I want action, blank blank it! Action!" He brought his hand down hard on his desk, toppling to the floor the ornate desk set that had been presented to him by the Flying Club for blazing new trails, when he had inaugurated commercial stratosphere service four years ago. Delray reached down to retrieve the set and when he came up, in spite of his flushed face, he was calm. Scovill Delray was like that. One moment a stormy petrel, the next a tower of frozen business acumen, unemotional, calculating and courageous. And in spite of his blasphemous tongue his associates and employees all swore by S. D., even while he was busily engaged in swearing at them.

"What happened, Mr. Delray?" Vice-President Thorndyke asked.

"Every blank thing. Here, just as we got through putting the quietus on the loss of the ICA-1's crew and passengers, it's got to come up into the lime-light again. It's unfair, gentlemen, dang dang it." And there followed another torrent of mono- and poly-syllabic expletives that left him exhausted and purple-faced. His staff knew from past experience that the proper procedure was for them to remain silent and wait for S. D. to resume speaking. He did.

"Look," he tapped a powerful index finger on a palm that had not yet lost the roughness acquired in his early machinist days, "we have been flying the stratosphere for years without mishap. Our ships are the safest dang things that ever flew, crawled or wriggled over this old planet. Then all of a sudden Number 1 comes in flying auto, minus crew and passengers. And now—" he paused to gulp a glass of water—"now I get a call from Dacy at the airport and what do you think he tells me?" He looked around, then seeing nothing but bewildered expressions and negative head-shakings, he rose from his chair and punctuating each word with a blow on his desk with his hammer-like fists, he burst out; "Number 7 left London at nine o'clock Greenwich time this morning. That means she should have landed here nine o'clock our time. It is now two-thirty and still there is no sign of her. When Dacy first called me I had him send out a search ship and also ordered one dispatched from London." He paused a moment, and his voice became tinged with hopelessness. "But I didn't expect them to find Number 7," and shaking his head slowly as if to confirm his statement, he repeated, "No, she is lost without a trace."

The vice-president remarked soothingly, "But, Mr. Delray, our ships will float at sea for an indefinite period—"

"Umm, I'm perfectly aware of that, Thorndyke," said S. D. "Number 7 would float if she had the chance. But she never touched the sea, she was carried by some unknown agency high up into the stratosphere, somewhere," and not heeding the gasps of astonishment and the looks of incredulity he snatched up a radiogram and waved it at his staff and continued: "Listen to this. It is the last message from Number 7 before we lost contact with her: " . . . flying at 32 miles above sea level . . . send help . . . rainbow horror . . . the ship is being crushed by . . . carrying us away . . . Mr. Delray, Maureen says . . ."

As he read the last words Delray's voice trembled with an emotion that few of his staff had suspected him of being capable of. He laid the message down very slowly, as if reluctant to relinquish this last contact with the ill-fated ship.

A confused babble of voices began asking questions. The president of the company waved his hand to silence them and said: "You know as much as I do at the present time. But I'm finding out more. I'm going out there and by God I'll stay until I know what has happened! There is something out there in the stratosphere, gentlemen, something devilish. We must find and destroy it so that we shall not have a repetition of these unexplainable disappearances. Carlisle is piloting me, and Dacy will take care of the motors. There will be us three only. Thorndyke, you will remain in charge here. Keep in touch with me by radio-phone—and no one is to know about my leaving; hear me?" He looked around at the group and repeated: "No one."

"But, Mr. Delray," Thorndyke objected, "it might be a decidedly dangerous undertaking. Why risk yourself? Any of us would
gladly go in your place." The others nodded their agreement.

"Thank you, boys," Delray said. "Under ordinary circumstances that might work out. But now I must go. I can't stand the
suspense of waiting. . . . My daughter, Maureen, was on No. 7."

COMMANDER DOUGLAS CARLISLE bent with a preoccupied air
over the charts in the control cabin of the "Stratosphere Scout,"
the smallest of the fleet of the Inter-Continental Air Service,
Ltd. He had set the automatic controls and the ship was now
circling in an ever-widening spiral in the region where No. 7 had
been last heard from.

Douglas' strong young features had become lined with the
tell-tale signs of worry that he tried hard to shake off. Weren't
they doing everything in their power to save the girl—if it were
humanly possible? Yes, and even if it required superhuman effort
he would still find her. But was Maureen Delray alive? That radio
message to her father indicated an unknown horror, something
that in his twenty-six years of living Douglas had never encountered, a something for which there was no precedent, no accepted procedure.

Into his mind flashed images of the hours Maureen and he
had spent together, flying high above the earth's atmosphere,
where there was nothing but the dark purple of the outer world,
nothing but a vast region of silence, that was rendered more
acute by the purr of the impulsor tubes discharging gases at a
tremendous pressure to move their ship in the partial vacuum.
Then he remembered the time when he had driven this very ship
up to an altitude of ninety miles where his instruments no longer registered and he did not know whether he was heading back
toward earth or into the far reaches of outer space. The girl had
seen the expression on his face although he had tried hard to
keep her from knowing.

"I'm not afraid, Doug. Not when I'm here with you," she had
said.

When she said this he forgot about flying, about the ship, about the danger they were in, remembering only that he was young, with the warm love of one who is young. He had taken her in his arms for the first time and she had been contented and happy there. If they returned safely to the earth, they had said, nothing would ever separate them. But now—

With a start he came out of his reverie to realize that Scovill Delray had been addressing him.

"I'm sorry, Mr. Delray. I was so absorbed—" he began.

"I know, boy, I know," the other replied soothingly. "You have checked the position?"

"Yes, we are at latitude 52, longitude 30 west. Dacy has been sitting in the rear observation chamber, watching the sea through his glasses for the last two hours, but he hasn't seen a sign of wreckage or anything that might indicate that No. 7 had fallen into the water."

"Most of the wreckage would have sunk immediately," Delray mused, "but some would float. No, I'm more convinced than ever that she never struck the sea. Take the ship up into the stratosphere, up twenty, thirty, forty, a hundred miles, if you have to. Take her up!" he commanded.

Douglas released the automatic controls and nosed the plane up at an angle of forty degrees, keeping it in a wide circle so as not to lose their position. When the altimeter registered seven miles and the air became rarified Douglas energized two of the nine propulsion tubes to aid the ship in its climb. At twelve miles he turned on four more tubes and shut down the propeller motor. There wasn't enough air here for the screws to bite into. As the temperature outside was dropping steadily he turned on the heating system. The ship had already been made hermetically tight and the oxygen apparatus was functioning to furnish them with fresh air.

Dacy came into the control cabin after checking over the motors and compressors.

"How high are you going, Carlisle?" he asked in a voice that became tinged with alarm as he glanced at the instruments.

"I don't know. It all depends on what we find. As far up as we can go," Douglas replied shortly. He had become not a little annoyed at Dacy's apprehensive manner ever since they had set out on the flight. That the man was reluctant about coming was evident from the first. Douglas thought, "If I had been Mr. Delray I wouldn't have insisted on his coming. A devil of a lot of good he would be in a pinch."

"But we can't fly very much higher," the man insisted. "We'll lose our bearings—the instruments won't register up there." His voice had become whining and an unhealthy pallor had spread over his heavy features. He moved his powerful frame with an uncertain, jerky motion of one who failed fully to co-ordinate his muscles with the impulses sent from his brain.

Scovill Delray turned abruptly from the observation window through which he had been looking.

"What the blank blankety blank are you beefing about now, Dacy?" he thundered. "I gave orders to take this ship up and she's going up as far as the moon if need be. If you don't like it you can bail out any time. Grab a space suit and a life preserver and jump. And if you continue objecting I won't ask you to jump!"

A crafty look came into Dacy's eyes. He had edged slowly toward the far end of the control cabin. Cautiously he opened the door, his eyes fastened upon the two men in the pilots' seats. Douglas did not like what he saw in Dacy's face and he began to rise. In a flash Dacy's hand darted into his jacket pocket and reappeared in a twinkling with a chromium-plated gas pistol in its grasp.

"You're going to throw me out, are you?" he hissed, the blood rushing up from his massive, bull-like neck and displacing the whiteness of his face with an angry, blotchy red. "There's only one place I'm getting out and that's at an airport. And you're heading towards one now, Carlisle, understand? Get going!" he snarled, waving the gun menacingly.

Delray leaped from his seat and made for the man.

"Why, you blankety blank—" he began, but a swish of compressed gas from Dacy's gun cut him short. Delray doubled up, clutching his abdomen, his face turning a ghastly, greenish shade.

With a flick of his hand Douglas threw in the automatic control switch and making a mighty leap that covered the width of the cabin he landed on top of Dacy, knocking the gun from his grasp. Both men struck the hard floor with a thud. Douglas knew at once that he was no match for the man in a physical encounter—not if he was compelled to rely upon brute force. He had seen the man fell, with a single blow of his ham-like fist, a husky laborer at the airport who had refused to do his bidding. And he knew that once the other man got a secure hold upon him it would be the end of that fight. Therefore no sooner had he struck the floor than Douglas began to whip his wiry body around, threshing his arms and legs and swiveling his torso to keep Dacy from pinning him down.

Dacy drew back his arm and aimed a blow at Douglas' head, but so rapidly was the pilot moving that his opponent's fist flew past him and cracked against the hard floor. Dacy loosed a bellow of pain. Then the sheer animalism of the man took complete possession of him. Stripped was the veneer of human polish that had heretofore kept his savage instincts within control. He began to gouge at Douglas with his claw-like fingers, his lips drawn back baring two rows of large, uneven teeth.

Douglas succeeded in landing some heavy blows on the man's face which only served further to enrage him. Now one of Dacy's hands had found Douglas' throat and, as the fingers tightened, the victim's struggles became more and more feeble. As the pressure on his throat increased, Douglas saw the evil red face of the man above become dim as if a heavy mist had gradually enveloped it. Then the mist became an opaque black substance punctuated by tiny pin points of fire through which he seemed to float farther and farther away from himself. Now deeply immersed in darkness, he sensed rather than heard a crunching and tearing sound, followed by the feeling of being shaken violently. With the last feeble spark of consciousness to aid him, Douglas shook himself and attempted to sit upright. To his surprise there was no hand at his throat to restrain him. His head seemed to swirl around as if it were being spun in a centrifuge, then the centrifuge slowed down and he was able to open his eyes.

Not far from him, sprawled on the floor in the same position that he had fallen, was President Delray. Douglas thought that he could see the man's arm moving feebly, his fingers clasping and unclasping spasmodically. Then the pilot's eyes swept past the stricken president's form until they came to rest on something that crouched against the far end of the cabin, a something that moaned in terror. Now Douglas could see what it was. The giant form of Dacy, with his hands pressed over his eyes as if to shield from his sight something that he feared to look upon!

The first clear thought that swept away the confusion in Douglas' mind was that Dacy had indeed gone insane and was now jabbering the fears of a crazed mind. But that thought was dispelled when the crouching man reluctantly drew one of his hands from his face and looked with terror-stricken eyes toward the observation window. The cry that came from his throat was inhuman; it contained all the anguish that a fear-tortured mind could ever conceive in centuries of contact with untold horrors. Involuntarily Douglas looked toward the window and his body jerked spasmodically.

Pressed against the thick glass was a huge eye, fully a yard in diameter, pulsating with red and blue fires that seemed to consume it! And encasing the eye was an indefinable shape, a mass of iridescent, moving, writhing gelatine. The same substance as that which had clung to the landing gear of No. 1!

His gaze held and fascinated by the sight, Douglas rose slowly to his feet. Were it not for the crouching, terror-stricken man, Douglas would have believed that he had passed through a stage of unconsciousness that had left him delirious. He tore his gaze from the living eye and glanced at the instruments. The motors had stopped!

But he could feel movement, a gentle pitching as if the ship were riding on a sea of smooth, rounded swells. And glancing out of the window, on the side opposite to that where the horrible eye was pressed, he could see in the distance what appeared to be cloud formations. But that was unreasonable. Clouds up in the stratosphere? Never. It must be something else, or perhaps the ship had dropped back into the atmosphere. Or gone upward into a region unknown to man. There were all these possibilities, so many in fact that his head again began to reel.

Douglas bent over the body of President Delray and felt his heart. It was beating. Now unheedful of the menace outside, he removed the first-aid cabinet from its holder and breaking an ampoule of aromatic spirits of ammonia, he held it under the man's nose. He noted with relief that the ghastly greenish pigmentation was being displaced by a more natural glow. Apparently Dacy's aim had not been very good, for had Delray received the full charge of the deadly gas in any portion of his body, his blood stream would have instantly frozen in his arteries. The thought of the maniacal airport-superintendent caused Douglas to glance quickly in the direction where the man had been huddling. The corner was empty. And the cabin door was wide open. Dacy had been able to subdue his fright sufficiently to make his way out and now he was somewhere in the main body of the ship.

Douglas laid Delray's head down and hurriedly closed and locked the door. He would deal with Dacy after. First there was S. D. and then the creature outside. A crumpled piece of paper caught his eye, lying near the gas pistol that Dacy had dropped. Douglas thrust the paper into his pocket. Then almost mechanically he picked up the pistol. Might have use for it, he reasoned, but of what avail would such a puny weapon be against a monster that was so enormous that its eye was almost as large as a man's body? He ventured a glance toward the window.

The eye was gone!

BUT SOMETHING ELSE had replaced it in the line of his vision: a mountain of dazzling colors looming up ahead, a mountain that had no definite shape but shifted its formation and coloring with the brilliance of a kaleidoscopic image. And toward this mountain the ship was moving at an incredible pace. Heretofore, sailing through space with nothing tangible to afford an indication of relative movement, Douglas had not realized how swiftly the ship was being borne along by some unknown agency. Far faster, he now realized than any man-made ship had ever been hurled, even through the outer reaches of the stratosphere.

The mountain now appeared larger. Below the peak Douglas could make out a flat stretch of the same iridescent substance of which the mountain was composed. His attention was drawn from the scene outside by a low moan, and he abruptly realized that, with events tumbling on top of one another, he had forgotten about President Delray. The man pushed himself to a sitting position and was looking around in the bewildered manner of a person coming out of a nightmare.

Douglas hurried toward him.

"Where the blank blank are we?" were Delray's first words, uttered in a tone that began in an almost inaudible whisper but which swiftly rose in a crescendo to its former booming volume.

"I don't know, yet, S. D.," Douglas began, "but it won't be long before we find out. Look." He pointed out through the observation window and leaned down to assist the other man to rise. But Delray, disdaining the offer, jerked himself to his feet and stared out ahead.

"Holy jumping tarnations!" he cried, "I'm not seeing that am I?"

"You surely are, and so am I."

"What is it, a close-up of an aurora borealis?" Delray asked.

"Umm," Douglas mumbled. "That might not be such a crazy guess at that."

"Say, you blankety fool," the other shouted indignantly, "you're not calling me crazy by any chance? If I thought you were I'd pop you out through the window and let you do some space-walking."

Before he could formulate the proper words, Douglas' retort was cut short by a frenzied pounding at the control cabin door. A muffled voice reached them: "Let me in, for God's sake, let me in!"

"Dacy?" Delray asked.

Douglas nodded.

"All right," S. D. commanded, "you open the door. I want to go to work on that dash blank dashety blank."

"He might be armed," Douglas objected. "Wait, I'll see."

He strode across the room and pulling the gas pistol from his pocket threw open the door. The huddled form of Dacy stumbled across the steel sill plate. And the gloom of the cabin was alleviated by a phosphorescent streamer that lashed and churned around in there.

"That thing!" Dacy said in a fear impelled whisper. "It's alive."

President Delray had now risen to his feet, and after a single glance into the cabin, he dragged an emergency axe from the wall and made a dash for the door. Douglas leaped in front of him.

"Now you would be crazy to do that," he said severely as if he was chastising a child instead of speaking to the man who was his superior.

Bracing his hand across the doorway, Douglas managed to restrain Delray from carrying out his wild impulse. At the same time he pulled his gas pistol from his pocket and aimed it carefully at the rapidly moving tentacle. Realizing that his chance of making a direct hit on such an uncertain target was very slim, he nevertheless pulled the trigger. Instantly some ten feet of the waving menace flashed out as rigid as a steel bar, shriveled into a mere vestige of its former self and dropped to the floor. Boldened by the success of their defense, the three stepped into the main cabin, then shrank back against the wall.

The part of the tentacle that they had severed was but an infinitesimal portion of the monster that filled the room; a huge, scintillating mass of gelatine that had oozed through the crushed glass of a port hole. It pulsated with the movements of a disembodied lung that was still breathing. The men looked out through the other ports. While at first glance the mass of the creature that filled the space without appeared to be so vast that they failed to define its shape, upon observation the lines of a huge snake, coiled around the ship, became apparent. Its head was at the position of the ship while its tail extended for at least a half mile beyond in space. A fringe of tentacles covered its body.

"Sweet spirit of tarnation!" Delray exclaimed, "it's carrying us along to the end of all creation."

"An air monster!" said Douglas. "How can such things exist up here where there is practically no atmosphere?"

"Don't know," Delray replied shortly. "I'm more concerned with how in blankety blank we can continue to exist. Just now I wouldn't bet on it even at sweepstakes odds—what was that. . . ?"

His question was prompted by a violent jar that hurled the three to the floor then precipitated them hard against the side wall as the ship came to an abrupt stop.

RISING CAUTIOUSLY to their feet, the men stepped back into the control room and looked out through the observation window. Directly in front was a barrier, a mountain of rainbow colors, translucent as clear ice, yet emitting a warmth that dispelled any illusions about having landed at the base of an iceberg.

"The ship has been released," cried Douglas. "It's free."

The air serpent having deposited them in this strange world slowly withdrew its gelatinous mass from the cabin, uncoiled itself from the fuselage and with a mighty convolution of its enormously long body, disappeared high up in space.

Now that the imminent danger from the creature was past, Dacy withdrew to one side of the control compartment and watched with narrow eyes the actions of Douglas and President Delray. These two were talking in low tones. He saw Delray nod to his pilot. The latter turned to Dacy and surveyed him as if he was seeing him for the first time and that view was decidedly unpleasant.

"Listen to me, Dacy," Douglas began, his voice like chilled steel, "there is something that you and I had better settle now without further delay. You've been confoundedly nasty. More than that you've tried your utmost to get Mr. Delray and myself. Why you should act this way I don't exactly know and I haven't time to enter a guessing contest to decide. All we want to know is how you propose to behave in the future. We've landed somewhere. We don't know what there is out there and we don't know if we will ever return to earth. But while we are together we must pull together. There must be no disharmony in our group, do you understand that?"

Dacy avoided the man's steady gaze as he weaseled with: "I wasn't myself then. I don't know what came over me."

President Delray snorted his impatience. "I see there's no use of trying to make a man out of you, you sniveling coward. Now listen, Dacy—from now on, no matter what happens we're keeping a close watch on you. Any funny business and out you go like a dash-light. That's all." And he glared at the airport superintendent until the man shifted uneasily from one foot to another.

With Dacy subdued at least for the time being, Douglas and Delray now began to devote full attention to their position. It was apparent that the air within the ship had had ample opportunity to seep out through the broken port. Yet they found no difficulty in breathing. As a precaution against atmospheric conditions outside, they took oxygen masks from the rack in the cabin and moved toward the exit door. With his mask held in readiness to don instantly Douglas swung the door open. A mellow warmth pervaded the interior of the cabin, as if they had stepped from the damp chill of a butcher's refrigerator out into the spring sunshine.

They looked down. There appeared to be nothing solid, nothing tangible below, only a brilliant shimmer of luminous colors, ever changing. Douglas was immediately reminded of Delray's comparison of this phenomenon to the flashing of an aurora borealis. He even imagined that he could hear the crackling of the electrical discharges with which the northern lights are associated.

"Well, what are you waiting for?" Delray asked. "Jump down."

"Down where? I don't want to fall on top of the north pole."

"You won't. The plane is resting on that stuff isn't it? Watch this."

Delray took a jack-knife from his pocket and allowed it to drop. The knife struck the surface with a sharp crack and then bounced into the air almost a yard.

"I'll say it's solid," Douglas admitted, "and plenty resilient. More springy than rubber. Here goes."

He lowered himself from the cabin until his feet touched the ground. But as soon as he released his hand-hold his feet shot out from under and he came down with a thud.

DELRAY'S BOOMING LAUGHTER echoed over the vast stillness. But Dacy, who had been nursing a sour expression ever since the ignominious treatment he had received, did not even smile. He stood back and permitted the president to climb out of the cabin, then with a clang that could have been heard a mile he slammed the trap door shut.

"Say, you blankety blank blank," Delray roared in the direction of the closed door. "Open that and come out or I'll come up and take you apart."

Dacy's taunting voice, muffled by the fuselage of the ship, came faintly to their ears: "If you know what's good for you you'll get going. Try anything and I'll blast both of you to smitherines. I'm taking this ship and going back to the earth. You two can pal with your air friends for the rest of your lives, which, according to my present view, is going to be mighty short."

Instinctively the two men looked up into the air. A cloud of flying creatures was coming rapidly toward them. Douglas pulled out his pistol, then realizing the futility of the gesture, he tucked it back into his pocket.

"I'll save that for later; use it as a last resort," he said grimly.

"Well, son," Delray declared, his chin squared and head held defiantly erect, "we'll at least take it like men, not like a jackal." He nodded in the direction of the man inside the ship.

By now the flying creatures were almost directly overhead, but at a still too great a distance for the men to make out their forms.

"I wonder if they have seen us?" Douglas remarked. "Or were they attracted by the ship? Let's make a dash for that crag over there where we can hide, there's no use in taking foolish chances. Dacy can stay to act as a reception committee."

While the creatures were circling downward, Douglas and President Delray shuffled across the smooth slippery surface as fast as they could. They fell at frequent intervals and made such slow progress that they despaired of ever gaining their refuge in time. Down out of the sky came the cloud. It lost its massed appearance and resolved itself into individual wriggling spirals, each one a living creature, appearing for all the world like *spirilla* bacteria viewed in the field of a gigantic microscope.

"Ugh, horrible," Delray spat in disgust. "A mass of stinking, slimy worms."

The men had now reached the hummock behind which they crouched for shelter. Horrified, yet fascinated by the sight, they followed the serpents' movements. There were literally hundreds of them, varying in size from ten feet in length to some that easily measured two hundred feet. All were composed of the same gelatinous substance as the huge air monster who had brought them there. And many of them were endowed with a fringe of tentacles.

"I've got it!" exclaimed Douglas. "Those are the young of the large reptiles. They are hatched here and are nourished by substances brought in by their parents, for there is probably nothing edible here. The ones with the fringes are apparently the males. What horrible creatures . . . . Look! They are climbing over the ship!"

"Like a nest of worms," Delray said. "Do you suppose that these air monsters could have existed all these years without any trace of them having been found on earth?"

"Quite likely. They appear to be of a very primitive class of reptile. Perhaps it was during our Proterozoic Age, a thousand million years ago when plant life on earth existed only in the form of a green scum and algae, and our fauna was a teeming multitude of unicellular creatures, that a germ of life was carried to this place either from the earth or by the agency of meteors from some outer world. And as the process of evolution raised our single-cell beings until they became huge dinosaurs and flying reptiles, so here they developed into those forms. If you remember, the earliest sea life were the jellyfish, the composition of whose bodies is much the same as that of these air monsters."

"Pure dashed speculation," S. D. snorted. "Tell me then, what is this ground or world or whatever the dang we're on, composed of and how did it get here?"

"Not having a laboratory in my pocket, I can only resort to your despised, guessing methods. Chief. This stuff was probably compounded when the earth was a swirling mass of hot gases or through some tremendous volcanic activity and was hurled out into space but not far enough to fly free of the earth's gravitational influence. So it is apparently a satellite of the earth, an unknown satellite."

"Do you mean to say that this transparent moon has been revolving around the earth without having been seen by our telescopes?" Delray asked.

"If it is where I believe it to be there is a very good chance of its remaining invisible," Douglas remarked. Then noting the puzzled expression on the other's face, he continued: "If we are somewhere above the north pole, for instance, unless at a tremendous altitude the curvature of the earth would cut off the line of vision from even our northernmost observatories; then in the second place, judging by the rapidly shifting, translucent colors, this world is a heavily charged Wimshurst machine, a huge static generator. And is it not reasonable to suppose that it causes a phenomenon not unlike the aurora borealis? Remember your first impression?" he asked. "Perhaps we are even now at the source of the northern lights!"

Delray nodded, his hesitating manner indicating that his barrier of incredulity was being slowly demolished.

All this while the two men had been watching the host of swarming air snakes. Their wriggling bodies had by now entirely covered the stratoplane until not a single square inch of its metal surface was visible. Suddenly the layer of bodies appeared to converge into a funnel near the top of the fuselage. They had found the broken port hole and were crawling into the interior

A shrill scream rent the stillness, a cry of untold agony.

"My God!" Douglas exclaimed. "Dacy. Can't we do anything for him?

Delray shook his head. "It's too late now, Doug. He should have come with us. What a horrible death."

"We can't go back to the ship and we can't stay here," Douglas reasoned after a moment's silence during which time he could not help dwelling upon Dacy's fate. "Let's follow that gorge down there. It seems to lead toward the mountain peak. At least it affords us a shelter from those monsters."

Slowly they made their way along the bottom of the ravine, keeping a vigilant glance skyward. But no living creature appeared. The ground under them maintained its scintillating color changes. In many places they trod over regions of pure transparency, regions where they could look deeply down through the substance to what might have been endless stretches of ice and snow. If they were above the north pole it was hard to explain the temperature. Even in the tropics, at an altitude of fifteen miles it was bitterly cold. And here in the upper reaches of the stratosphere it should have been near absolute zero. And the presence of air. . . . Whatever the explanation was, the two men were grateful that the mathematics of scientists were not always accurate in predicting unknown conditions.

After what must have been three hours of steady trudging on the frictionless surface where their feet constantly slipped out from under them, they reached the base of the mountain. Rising sheer above them for thousands of feet was a wall of glass that formed an effective barrier in front beyond which they could not pass.

It was at the time when the two despaired of finding some means of continuing their exploration that they discovered the valley. Following the wall of the mountain they climbed over a rise in the terrain that had shut off their view and saw below them a vast, level stretch. They slid down the rim of the crater which led into a natural bowl. Here the light was more glaring, owing to the reflection from a porcelain-white ground. And it was here, while they were stumbling along half blinded that they found it.

The bleached skeleton of a human being!

The bones had been picked clean. There was no trace of clothing, nothing but a signet ring with the initials "R. A."

"This is evidence that we're not the first human beings here," S. D. remarked in hushed tones. "I wonder if the others—Maureen—" He left the thought unfinished. Douglas shuddered. It was too horrible to contemplate. He looked ahead. Why hadn't they seen it before? Some five hundred feet away there was what appeared at that distance to be a heap of debris. They hurried toward it.

"My God," Delray cried. "The remains of a seaplane. One of those old atmospheric models they used to take such awful chances with, about the time Lindbergh flew the Atlantic. It's been crushed to bits. Even the motor is in pieces. Here's something, Doug, look."

He held out a notebook which might have served as a log. They opened it. The entries were in Norwegian. On the first page they deciphered the date, June 18, 1928, and a signature, "Roald Amundsen."

"Amundsen!" Douglas said in an awed voice. "He and Rene Guilbaud set out from Tromso in search of Umberto Nobile who had flown over the north pole in the balloon airship 'Italia'. The air monsters got him."

Although they searched the wreck there was no sign of the remains of Guilbaud. Silent and thoughtful since they had found this specter from the past, the men continued along the floor of the crater.

There was plenty to think about—the fate of crew and passengers of No. 1 and No. 7—No. 7 with Maureen Delray aboard. If they should find them in the same condition as that poor man back there. . . . And even if they were alive how could they all get back to earth? No. 7 was evidently smashed beyond repair, otherwise it might have returned.

Suddenly Delray shouted: "There's something else," and he pointed to a white shape ahead. Hurrying toward it they made out another plane, this one apparently intact. The name in French stood out in bold letters. Douglas translated it.

"The 'White Bird', Nungesser and Coli's plane! One of the first to attempt the Atlantic crossing. Lost back in 1927 wasn't it?" Douglas asked.

"About that time," the other said. And after they had searched the machine in vain for remains of the aviators he asked hopefully, "do you think we can repair the plane?"

"I'm sure that we can, but it would do us but little good. You can't fly the stratosphere in a propeller airplane, you know."

"Dash blank it, no," Delray snorted. "My brain's getting as soft as a squash."

"Uh huh," Douglas agreed absently, then aware of the significance of the glare the other gave him, he continued hurriedly: "I meant that we can still use the plane for exploring this place. That's the only way we can see what is beyond that wall," he explained, pointing to the mountain. "And maybe we'll find—someone alive."

Douglas and S. D. quickly checked over the machine. Then turning on the ignition, Delray grasped the propeller blade and pulled down on it. There was an explosion as a cylinder fired. Elated by his success, he kept turning the motor over until it finally caught. Douglas in the cockpit adjusted the throttle, then when the other had climbed in alongside, they gave it the gun and they were off, taxying over the smooth ground. Douglas' unfamiliarity with one of a model as old as this one was a serious obstacle. Time after time he tried to take off with negative results. When the last attempt resulted in a near disaster, Delray shouted above the roar of the motor: "Let me take her. I've flown some almost as old as this baby in my young days."

EITHER BECAUSE OF HIS SKILL or because of good fortune, Delray managed to get the plane into the air. Then circling around he began to climb.

From their elevation they could get a good view of the strange world they were in. It stretched for an indefinite distance until the structure of the land merged with the sky beyond. As far as they could see there was no living creature in sight. The fledgling air monsters had apparently gone back to their nest to await another consignment of provisions. The thought made Douglas shudder.

Now they had reached the top of the mountain wall. Beyond it was a terrain much the same in character as that on their side. Coming down on the far side of the mountain, they became aware of a mass of clouds lying low on the horizon.

"That's queer," Delray remarked, "the first clouds we've seen up here. I wonder if it ever rains in this place?"

"Clouds?" Douglas who was free to look around was able to focus his eyes fully on them. "They're moving mighty fast—Wait! They're air monsters! And they've seen us. Go down!" he shouted.

Reacting to the command, Delray nosed the plane down at a dangerous angle, peering anxiously over the side for a landing place. The ground below was particularly unfavorable. Sharp crags and pinnacles thrust their needle-points upward to spear anything that would attempt to descend from the sky, and deep abysses yawned dismally to entrap them. Delray levelled the plane off and soared about. Swiftly the advance column of monsters darted toward them. If the men thought the group that had surrounded their stratoplane was large, then surely this flock surpassed all imagination. The sky became black with their wriggling, serpentine bodies.

"If we don't find a spot soon it will be too late to look further," Douglas urged—then: "How about over there between those two ridges? There's just about room enough to make it."

The place to where he pointed offered a precarious landing, a thousand to one shot. But it was their only hope and Delray cut off the motor and planed down. The right wing grazed the ridge, then fortunately before the plane was thrown off balance the other wing caught on the far side, and the "White Bird," after scouring the sides of the trough, remained wedged firmly. The men hurriedly climbed out and dropped to the ground, then ran toward an overhanging rock that seemed to offer some refuge from an overhead attack. When they reached it they discovered that it was an archway leading into an abyss. Behind them they could now hear the slithering sound caused by many bodies rubbing together as the avid horde bore down upon them. It would be only a matter of moments before the end, before the horrible monsters crushed them under the weight of their slimy bodies.

Douglas wheeled around, pulling his gas pistol. Not fifty feet away one of the creatures had swooped toward him. He fired. The long serpentine body became as rigid as steel, then fell lifeless to the ground.

Plunging through the archway they looked down into the crevasse. There a hundred feet below them, was Inter-Continental's stratoplane No. 7, the ship that had been lost!

"My God!" muttered Delray, "my God!"

In one glance Douglas took in the situation. The side of the crevasse sloped down precipitously. They could never evade the air snakes and reach the refuge of the ship if they attempted to climb down.

There was but one way.

"The sides are smooth. Take it on the run and slide down," Douglas shouted. "I'll follow. Hurry," he urged.

Through the archway crowded the slimy monsters. So massed were they in their eagerness to get at these morsels of food that they had become wedged in the opening. But the leaders were already wriggling through.

Delray hit the slide feet first, and down he went. Pausing to fire several shots into the writhing bodies, Douglas followed. He landed in a heap at the bottom. The plane was a good hundred feet away. He began to rise to his feet, then sank back with a groan. His leg seemed to be broken.

"Go ahead, Chief," he urged. "You make it. I've got enough charges left in this gun to keep them at bay for a while."

"What the blankety blank do you take me for, you young squirt. Here, hold on." And bending down he lifted Douglas to his massive shoulders and started in the direction of the ship. Douglas looked toward the stratoplane. No sign of life there. It was hardly reasonable to suppose that, anyone would be left—not with the air monsters around. He looked down to the ground, then turned his eyes away. Bits of clothing and human bones, remains of the crew and passengers, were strewn about.

BURDENED WITH THE WEIGHT of Douglas' body, Delray found it hard going. The frictionless surface offered a precarious footing and he was forced to tread carefully to maintain his balance. If they reached the ship, would they be able to open the door? Every entrance seemed to be tightly closed. And even if they did gain the relative security of the interior, how long would it be before the great horde of air creatures would crush the plane under the weight of their massed bodies? Fifteen feet from the plane Delray slipped and fell heavily to his knees, precipitating Douglas' body to the ground. With a hiss the air monsters swooped down on them. Douglas rolled over and fired his pistol into them. A number fell to the ground, but there was no perceptible gap in their ranks. He fired again and again, but still they came on. Now one of them was within ten feet. It would not be long—

Even as Douglas raised his arms to shield his face from what he knew was to come, the creature overhead stiffened and tumbled to the ground almost on top of him. Then another, and another. Douglas looked toward Delray, then seeing that the man possessed no weapon, he turned toward the stratoplane. The door had been opened, and firing from it with a magazine gas rifle, was Maureen!

"Hurry, hurry, please!" she implored, never relaxing her firing.

Delray was on his feet, and once again lifting Douglas to his shoulder, covered the distance in a few moments. They pushed through the door and clanged it shut.

"Where are the others?" were Delray's first words after he had embraced his daughter.

"Out—out there," she made a vague motion with her arm. "It was horrible."

"Don't think about it, please," Douglas implored. "Thank God that you are here."

"Listen!" Maureen said.

Outside, the rain of bodies beat like hailstones against the shell of the plane. The plates began to creak with the weight heaped upon them. The ship could not long resist this tremendous pressure.

"How is it they had not attacked you before?" Douglas asked.

"But they did," the girl said. "The day we were brought here. They crushed through the after door and dragged everyone out—the crew and passengers. The chief pilot unbolted the cover of the combustion chamber and had me crawl in—just before they got him. I guess they could not smell me out. I stayed there, for days it seems, while the horrible things swarmed all over the place. I must have been unconscious, too, for a long time. Overcome by that gas they exude. When I came to, I found that they were gone. But I almost died of fright, the fear of being alone, the fear of another attack. Oh—" and she sobbed in Douglas' arms.

"How about the after-door now, Maureen?" her father asked.

"I sealed it. The only way they can get in is by breaking it down again."

From the crunching of the plates it was evident that this contingency would not be long coming. Douglas looked questioningly at Delray.

"Can't we blast our way out? The tubes seem to be intact," he said.

"We'll try it," Delray replied, "especially since the ship's wedged in so we can't use the atmosphere motors and the propellers."

With that S. D. hurried back into the engine compartment and began opening valves and preparing the propulsion tubes for the unusual service of taking off. These tubes were normally employed in the stratosphere only, where the reaction of the gas discharged at high velocities served to propel the stratoplane. On his way aft he discovered that the door his daughter had bolted back into place was far from being airtight. But fortunately the compartment in which it was located could be shut off from the rest of the ship by bulkhead doors which he now closed tightly.

ALONE IN THE CONTROL ROOM with the girl, Douglas took her in his arms for a long embrace, then sat down in the pilot's seat and grasped the starting switch.

"Strap yourself into the seat next to me, Maureen. It's going to be a rough start," and under his breath he added, "if we make it." Then into the speaker leading to the engine room he asked: "Ready, S. D.?"

Delray's booming voice came back: "All set. Give her the gun, but try her on two tubes first, son," he cautioned.

Douglas threw the main switch, then grasping the directional lever, quickly operated two buttons. There was a roar that reverberated through the vast silence, a thundering that seemed to shake the very mountain. But the stratoplane, after some convulsive trembling, became wedged only more deeply in the crevasse.

"Cut!" came Delray's voice from the speaker, "or you'll bury her in the wall of this cursed canyon. Try—" he stopped, his tone changing from one of exasperation to that tinged with alarm.

Douglas knew instinctively that the other must be exercising the greatest amount of self-control. Then Delray called:

"Douglas, come here, quick! Have Maureen remain."

The girl looked at him, her face growing white. Then, as if angry at herself for permitting this sign of weakness, she said: "Go, Doug. I'll stay. If I can help, call me."

Douglas did not trust himself to speak, but gave the girl a glance that transcended mere words. He had heard the pounding of the monsters' bodies as if they were very close indeed. No. 7 was sturdily constructed as compared with his "Stratosphere Scout," but even this ship could not withstand their impact. And something must have happened so to alarm Maureen's father.

He closed the door of the control chamber and began running aft through the main cabin. At the other end he met Delray.

"Douglas, my boy, they're in. Broke down that damaged afterdoor. They're still in the small compartment, but the bulkhead is giving. I'll show you."

One glance at the straining plates was enough. Through Douglas' mind ran a thousand and one flashes, all of which failed to materialize into anything helpful. Their gas rifles and pistols would be like toys against the vast hordes that were attacking them, seeking the flesh and the blood with which to nourish themselves while growing into those terrifying half-mile long creatures that had been preying on aviators for God knows how long. Before him marched the names of the vanished, while he was trying hard to think of a solution; Nungesser and Coli; the "Old Glory" with Hill, Bertand, and Payne; the "Sir John Carling" with Capt. Tully and Lieut. Medcalf; the "St. Raphael" with Capt. Hamilton, Col. Minchin, and Princess Lowenstein-Wirtheim and—

"I've got it!" Douglas burst out suddenly. "Remember when No. 1 came in with those living shreds from one of these monster's bodies on its landing gear? The only thing that was effective was a blow torch. We've got two tanks of that new chemical fire in the control room for emergency welding. I'll get them."

He rushed back with the tanks under his arms, quickly adjusted the nozzles and handing one to Delray, said: "I'll open the door, and when I do, you let them have it. Then I'll grab the other tank. If this doesn't clean them out—" Then he stopped and looked at the other man and in a voice that had suddenly lost its ring of confidence he said, "I—I don't know. Chief. It's a terrible risk. . . ."

"No, Douglas," Maureen's words came from the gloom of the cabin, "it's the only sensible thing to do. Hurry, I'll take the other tank while you open the door. Better to go under trying than doing nothing."

Making sure that the nozzles were ready to be ignited, Douglas unbolted the door and standing to one side, threw it open.

Immediately a long, slimy head thrust itself through the opening.

"Let them have it!" Douglas shouted and the liquid fire roared into flame. The stream of incandescent gas seared into the ugly head of the monster and at once its substance ran like putrid oil back into the outer compartment. Immediately other heads and bodies appeared, but as the fire of death struck them, they too dissolved into a fluid that sputtered with venomous intensity. The odor of burning bodies was mixed with the anesthetic gases exuded by the living serpents. Douglas snatched the tank from Maureen's hands and shouted: "Get masks, quickly!"

The girl returned not a moment too soon. By now the outer compartment, which had been teeming with the air monsters was clear except for the oily liquid that flowed in a stream out to the ground.

"We'll have to eliminate all of them, Douglas, while we can," Delray cried. "Come on." And he pushed out through the outer compartment and directed the fiery vapor toward the reptiles that were writhing on the ground. Luckily for Delray he had not stepped out of the ship, for as soon as the tongue of flame seared through the bodies and touched the ground a flash of hot gas shot up into the air. And in a twinkling the entire ground was blanketed by a wild blue flame and incandescent vapor.

Delray, blinded by the intensive flame, leaped backwards and landed in a heap on the floor, the tank falling from his grasp and rolling out through the door of the ship.

Douglas dragged the inert form of the man inside and clanged the compartment door shut. Both Maureen and he were gasping for breath, for the astringent gas had penetrated through their masks.

"Look!" Maureen cried, "their whole world is on fire!"

Out through the port hole they could see the flames creeping over the ground faster than the eye could follow.

The air monsters were in a seething mass, their body substance flashing into fluid that in another instant became nothing more than a heavy, oily vapor.

The heat inside became almost intolerable. Suddenly the ship gave a lurch and sank lower as the supporting ground under it was consumed by flames.

"Maureen," Douglas called. "I believe that we are free. Will you take care of your dad, and hold on tightly? I'm going to try the projector motors."

Back in the control room he quickly switched on the power and then threw five tubes into service. With a jar that almost tore him from his safety straps the ship leaped from the surface that was now soft and gaseous. Straight up into the air it pointed, almost causing it to go into a tail spin, until Douglas, working his controls frantically, levelled it off.

Maureen and her father came into the cabin. The man was unhurt. They looked below and saw a world as it must have appeared when it was a swirling mass of hot gases, before it had begun to congeal into a solid substance. The flames had reached even the highest peak of the mountain that the travelers had flown over only a short while ago.

SEVERAL DAYS LATER President Delray was working in his office and the door opened to admit his daughter and Douglas Carlisle.

"Ah, you young scamps, it's about time you showed up," he boomed. "Where have you been?"

"Getting acquainted with each other all over again," Maureen said, "and buying a wedding gown and charging it to your account," she added.

Delray smiled at his daughter affectionately, then turned to Douglas.

"There's no question any longer of the stratosphere and the air-lanes being free of danger from air monsters. That's cleared up, even if the papers still continue to make a seven-day wonder of it. But there is one thing that is just as much of a mystery to everyone, me included: how in tarnation did No. 1 get in here by herself and what happened to her crew and passengers?"

Douglas sat down on the edge of the president's desk.

"You wondered why it was like pulling a dinosaur's tooth to get Dacy to accompany us on our little expedition," he began. "Well, here's the reason." He removed a torn and crumpled fragment of paper from his pocket and handed it to Delray. "I picked that up in the control room of our 'Stratosphere Scout,' where Dacy had dropped it. I didn't want to show it to you before because—" he stopped and looked significantly toward Maureen, then continued, "Now I can tell all. Read it."

Delray read the words aloud:

> "Air creatures have broken in and torn everyone to pieces . . . I hid in empty tank until they were gone . . . horrible days and nights . . . to get back to earth . . . set automatic pilot . . . I must sleep, rest.
> "Atwell."

"Where in the devil did Dacy get this?" Delray asked.

"He apparently found it in No. 1 and didn't show it to anyone. Don't ask me what he had in mind in concealing it, because I can't tell you," Douglas said. "Now I might as well piece out the rest of the mystery as I see it. When the serpents left the ship, Atwell crawled out of his hiding place and assuming he was alone, took off and set the automatic controls for Long Island—"

"What do you mean 'assuming he was alone'?" the president asked.

Douglas took a deep breath before answering. "One of the air snakes must have remained on the ship. And it got Atwell. That's the reason for the skeleton. Then the monster nosed around until it found the door that had been damaged and crawled out. But it must have got the blast of one of the tubes, for all that was left of it were shreds that were found clinging to the landing gear of the ship."

THE MONSTER FROM NOWHERE
Nelson S. Bond

Chapter I
Burch Patterson Returns

ONE NICE THING about the Press Club is that you can get into almost any kind of wrangle you want. This night we were talking about things unusual. Jamieson of the *Dispatch* mentioned some crackpot he had heard of who thought he could walk through glass. "Snipe" Andrews of the *Morning Call* had a wild yarn about the black soul of Rhoderick Dhu, whom Nova Scotians claim still walks the moors near Antigonish. Then, a guy named Joe brought up the subject of Ambrose Bierce's invisible beast.

You remember the story? About the diarist who was haunted, and pursued, by a gigantic thing which couldn't be seen? And who was finally devoured by it?

Well, we chewed the fat about that one for a while and Jamieson said the whole thing was fantastic; that total invisibility was impossible. The guy named Joe said Bierce was right; that several things could cause invisibility. A complete absence of light, for one thing, he said. Or curvature of light waves. Or coloration in a wavelength which was beyond that of the human eye's visual scope.

Snipe Andrews said, "Nuts!" Winky Peters, who was getting a little tight, hiccoughed something to the effect that "There are more things under Heav'n and Earth than are dreamed of in your Philosophy—" and then got in a hell of a fuss with the bartender who said his name wasn't Horatio.

I said nothing, because I didn't know. Maybe that is the reason why this stranger, a few minutes later, moved over beside me and opened a conversation.

"You're Harvey, aren't you?" he asked.

"That's me," I agreed. "Len Harvey—chief errand boy and first scratcher-upper for the *Star-Telegram*. You've got me, though, pal. Who are you?"

He smiled and said, "Let's go over in that corner, shall we, Harvey? It's quieter over there."

That made it sound like a touch, but I liked something about this guy. Maybe it was his face. I like tough faces; the real Mc-Coy, tanned by Old Sol instead of sunlamp rays. Maybe it was the straightness of his back; maybe the set of his shoulders. Or it could have been just the way he spoke. I don't know.

Anyway, I said, "Sure!" and we moved to the corner table. He ordered, and I ordered, and we just sat there for a moment, staring at each other. Finally he said,

"Harvey, your memory isn't so good. We've met before."

"I meet 'em all," I told him. "Sometimes they are driving Black Marias, and sometimes they're in 'em. Mostly, they're lying in the Morgue, with a pretty white card tied to their big toe. Or, maybe—Hey!" I said, "You're not Ki Patterson, who used to write for the Cincinnati *News?*"

He grinned then.

"No, but you're close. I'm Ki Patterson's brother, Burch."

"Burch Patterson!" I gasped. "But, hell—you're not going to get away with this!" I climbed to my feet and started to shout at the fellows. "Hey, gang—"

"Don't, Len!" Patterson's voice was unexpectedly sharp. There was a note of anxiety in it, too. He grabbed my arm and pulled me back into my seat. "I have very good reasons for not wanting anyone to know I'm back—yet."

I said, "But, hell, Burch, you can't treat a bunch of newspaper men like this. These guys are your friends."

Now that he had told me who he was, I could recognize him. But the last time I had seen him—the only time I had ever met him, in fact—he had been dressed in khaki shirt and corduroy breeches; had worn an aviator's helmet. No wonder I hadn't known him in civies.

I remembered that night, two years ago, when he and his expedition had taken off from Roosevelt Field for their exploration trip to the Maratan Plateau in upper Peru. The primary purpose of the trip had been scientific research. The Maratan Plateau, as you undoubtedly know, is one of the many South American spots as yet unexplored. It was Burch Patterson's plan to study the region, incidentally paying expenses a la Frank Buck, by "bringing back alive" whatever rare beasts city zoos would shell out for.

FOR A FEW WEEKS, the expedition had maintained its contact with the civilized world. Then, suddenly—that was all! A month . . . two months . . . passed. No word or sign from the explorers. The United States government sent notes to the Peruvian solons. Peru replied in smooth, diplomatic terms that hinted Uncle Sam would a damn sight better keep his nutsack adventurers in his own backyard. A publicity-seeking aviatrix ballyhooed funds for a "relief flight"— but was forbidden the attempt when it was discovered she had already promised three different companies to endorse their gasoline.

The plight of the lost expedition was a nine-days' wonder. Then undeclared wars grabbed page one. And the National Air Registry scratched a thin blue line through the number of pilot Burchard Patterson, and wrote after his name, "Lost."

But now, here before me in the flesh, not lost at all, but very much alive, was Burch Patterson.

I had so many questions to ask him that I began babbling like a greenhorn leg-man on his first job.

"When did you get back?" I fired at him. "Where's your crew? What happened? Did you reach the Plateau? And does anyone know you're—"

He said, "Easy, Len. All in good time. I haven't told anyone I'm back yet for a very good reason. Very good! As for my men—" He stared at me somberly. "They're dead, Len. All of them. Toland . . . Fletcher . . . Gainelle . . ."

I was quiet for a moment. The way he repeated the names was like the tolling of a church-bell. Then I began thinking what a wow of a story this was. I could almost see my name bylining the yarn. I wanted to know the rest so bad I could taste it. I said,

"I'm sorry, Burch. Terribly sorry. But, tell me, what made you come here tonight? And why all the secrecy?"

"I came here tonight," he said, "searching for someone I could trust. I hoped no one would remember my face—for it is changed, you know. I have something, Len. Something so great, so stupendous, that I hardly know how to present it to the world. Or even—if I should.

"I liked the way you kept out of that crazy argument a few minutes ago—" He motioned to the bar, where a new wrangle was now in progress. "—because you obviously had an open mind on the subject. I think you are the man whose help and advice I need."

I said, "Well, that's sure nice of you, Patterson. But I think you're overrating me. I kept my yap shut just because I'm kind of dumb about scientific things. Ask me how many words to a column inch, or how many gangsters got knocked off in the last racket war, but—"

"You're the man I'm looking for. I don't want a man with a scientific mind. I need a man with good, sound common-sense." He looked at his wrist watch. "Len—will you come out to my home with me?"

"When?"

"Now."

I said, "Jeepers, Burch—I've got to get up at seven tomorrow. I really shouldn't—"

He leaned over the table; stared at me intently.

"Don't stall, Len. This is important. Will you?"

I told you I was snoopy. I stood up.

"My hat's in the cloak-room," I said. "Let's go!"

CHAPTER II
The Thing in the Shed

PATTERSON'S ESTATE was in North Jersey. A rambling sort of place, some miles off the highway. It was easy to see how he could return to it, open it up, and still not let anyone know he had returned. As we drove, he cleared up a few foggy points for me.

"I didn't return to the States on a regular liner. I had reasons for not doing so—which you will understand in a short time.

"I chartered a freighter, a junky little job, from an obscure Peruvian port. Pledged the captain to secrecy. He landed me and my—my cargo—" He stumbled on the word for a moment. "—at a spot which I'm not at liberty to reveal. Then I came out here and opened up the house.

"That was just two days ago. I wired my brother, Ki, to come immediately. But he—"

"He's working in L.A.," I said.

"Yes. The soonest he could get here would be tonight. He may be at the house when we arrive. I hope so. I'd like to have two witnesses of that which I am going to show you."

He frowned. "Maybe I'm making a mistake, Len. It is the damnedest thing you ever heard of. Maybe I ought to call in some professor, too. But—I don't know. It's so utterly beyond credibility, I'd like you and Ki to advise me, first."

I said, "Well, what the hell is it, Burch?" Then I suddenly remembered a motion picture I'd seen some years ago; a thing based on a story by H. G. Wells. "It's not a—a monster, is it?" I asked. "Some beast left over from prehistoric ages?"

"No; not exactly. At least, I can assure you of this—it is not a fossil, either living or dead. It's a thing entirely beyond man's wildest imaginings."

I leaned back and groaned. "I feel like a darned kid," I told him, "on Christmas eve. Step on it, guy!"

THERE WERE LIGHTS in the house when we got there. As Burch Patterson had hoped, Ki had arrived from California. He heard us pull up the gravel lane, and came to the door. There was a reunion scene; one of those back-clapping, how-are-you-old-fellow things. Then we went in.

"I found your note," Ki said, "and knew you'd be right back. I needn't tell you I'm tickled to death you're safe, Burch. But—why all the secrecy?"

"That's what *I* asked him," I said. "But he's not giving out."

"It's something," Ki accused, "about the old work shop behind the house. I know that. I was snooping around back there, and—"

Burch Patterson's face whitened. He clutched his brother's arm swiftly.

"You didn't go inside?"

"No. I couldn't. The place was locked. Say—" Ki stared at his brother curiously. "Are you feeling okay, guy? Are you sure you're not—"

"You must be careful," said Burch Patterson. "You must be very, very careful when you approach that shed. I am going to take you out there now. But you must stand exactly where I tell you to, and not make any sudden moves."

He strode to a library table; took out three automatics. One he tucked into his own pocket. The others he handed to us. "I'm not sure," he said, "that these would be any good if—if anything happened. But it is the only protection we have. You *might* be lucky enough to hit a vulnerable spot."

"A vulnerable spot!" I said. "Then it *is* a beast?"

"Come," he said. "I shall show you."

He led the way to the work shop. It lay some yards behind and beyond the house; a big, lonesome sort of place, not quite as large as a barn, but plenty big. My first idea was that at some time it must have been used as a barn, for as we approached it, I could catch that animal odor you associate with barns, stables, zoos.

Only more so. It was a nasty, fetid, particularly offensive odor. You know how animals smell worse when they get excited? Or when they've been exercising a lot? Well, the place smelled like that.

I was nervous, and when I get nervous I invariably try to act funny. I said, "If they're horses, you ought to curry them more often."

I saw a faint blur in the black before me. It was Ki's face, turning to peer back. He said, "Not horses, Len. We've never kept horses on this estate."

Then we were at the door of the shed, and Burch was fumbling with a lock. I heard metal click; then the door creaking open. Patterson fumbled for a switch. The sudden blaze of light made me blink.

"In here," said Burch. And, warningly, "Stay close behind me!"

We crowded in. First Burch, then Ki, then me.

And as Ki got through the door, I felt his body stiffen; heard him gasp hoarsely. I peered over his shoulder—

Then I, too, gasped!

THE THING I SAW was incredible. There were two uprights of steel, each about four inches in diameter, deeply imbedded in a solid steel plate which was secured to a massive concrete block. Each of these uprights was "eyed"—and through the eyes ran a third steel rod which had been hammered down so that the horizontal bar was held firmly in place by the two uprights.

And on this horizontal rod was—*a thing!*

That is all I can call it. It had substance, but it had no form. Or, to be more accurate, it had every form of which you can conceive. For, like a huge, black amoeba, or like a writhing chunk of amorphous matter, it *changed!*

Where the steel rod pierced this blob of *thing* was a clotted, brownish excrescence. This, I think, accounted for some of the animal odor. But not all of it. The whole shop was permeated with the musty scent.

The *thing* changed! As I watched, there seemed to be, at one time, a globular piece of matter twisting on the rod. An instant later, the globe had turned into a triangle—then into something remotely resembling a cube. It was constantly in motion; constantly in flux. But here is the curious part. It did not change shape slowly, as an amoeba, so that you could watch the sphere turn into an oblong; the oblong writhe into a formless blob of flesh. It made these changes instantaneously!

Ki Patterson cried, "Good God, Burch! What unholy thing is this?" and took a step forward, past his brother's shoulder.

Burch shouted, "Back!" and yanked at Ki's arm. He moved just in time. For as Ki quitted the spot to which he had advanced, there appeared *in the air* right over that spot, another mass of the same black stuff that was captured on the bar. A blob of shapeless, stinking matter that gaped like some huge mouth; then closed convulsively just where Ki had stood a moment before!

And now the fragment on the rod was really moving! It changed shape so rapidly; twisted and wriggled with such determination, that there was no doubt whatsoever about the sentiency governing it. And other similar blobs suddenly sprang into sight! A black pyramid struck the far wall of the shed, and trembling woodwork told that here was solid matter. An ebon sphere rose from nowhere to roll across the floor, stopping just short of us. Most weirdly of all, a shaft of black jolted down *through* the floor—and failed to break the flooring!

That's about all I remember of that visit. For Ki suddenly loosed a terrified yelp; turned and scrambled past me to the door. I take no medals for courage. He was four steps ahead of me at the portal, but I beat him to the house by a cool ten yards. Burch was the only calm one. He took time to lock the work-shed door; then followed us.

But don't let anyone tell you he was exactly calm, either. His face wasn't white, like Ki's. Nor did his hand shake on the whisky-and-splash glass, like mine. But there was real fear in his eyes. I mean, real fear!

The whisky was a big help. It brought my voice back. "Well, Burch," I said. "We've seen it. Now, what in hell did we see?"

"You have seen," said Burch Patterson soberly, "the thing that killed Toland, and Fletcher, and Gainelle."

Chapter III
Patterson's Story

"We found it," said Burch, "on the Maratan Plateau. For we did get there, you know. Yes. Even though our radio went bad on us, just after we left Quiché, and we lost contact with the world. For a while, we considered going into Lima for repairs, but Fletcher thought he could fix it up once we were on solid ground, so we let it ride.

"We found a good, natural landing field on the Plateau, and began our investigations." He brooded silently for a minute. Then, reluctantly, "The Maratan is even richer in paleontological data than men have dared hope. But Man must never try to go there again. Not until his knowledge is greater than it is today."

Ki said, "Why? That *thing* outside?"

"Yes. It is the Gateway for that—and others like it.

"Some day I will tell you all about the marvels we saw on the Plateau. But now my story concerns only one; the one you have seen.

"Fletcher saw it first. We had left Gainelle tending camp, and were making a field survey, when we saw a bare patch in the jungle which surrounded our landing field. Fletcher trained his glasses on the spot, and before he even had time to adjust them properly he was crying, 'There's something funny over there! Take a look!'

"We all looked then. And we saw—what you saw a few minutes ago. Huge, amorphous blobs of jet black, which seemed to be of the earth, yet not quite of it. Sometimes these ever-changing fragments were suspended in air, with no visible support. At other times they seemed to rest naturally enough on solid ground. But ever and ever again—they changed!

"Afire with curiosity, we went to the open spot. It was a mistake."

"A mistake?" I said.

"Yes. Fletcher lost his life—killed by his own curiosity. I need not tell you how he died. It was, you must believe me, horrible. Out of nowhere, one of the jet blobs appeared before him . . . then around him . . . then—he was gone!"

"Gone!" exclaimed Ki. "You mean—dead?"

"I mean gone! One second he was there. The next, both he and the *thing* which had snatched him had disappeared into thin air.

"Toland and I fled, panic stricken, back to camp. We told Gainelle what we had seen. Gainelle, a crack shot and a gallant sportsman, was incredulous; perhaps even dubious. At his insistence, we armed and returned to the tiny glade.

"This time, it was as if the *thing* expected us—for it did not await our attack. It attacked us. We had barely entered its domain when suddenly, all about us, were clots of this ever-changing black. I remembered hearing Toland scream; high and thin, like a woman. I dimly recall hearing the booming cough of Gainelle's express rifle, and of firing myself.

"I remember thinking, subconsciously, that Gainelle was a crack shot. That he never missed anything he aimed at. But it didn't seem to matter. If you hit one of those fleshy blobs, it bled a trifle—maybe. More likely than not, it changed shape. Or disappeared entirely.

"It was a rout. We left Toland behind us, dead, on the plain. A black, triangular *thing* had slashed Gainelle from breast to groin. I managed to drag him half way out of the glade before he died in my arms. Then I was alone.

"I am not a good pilot, under best conditions. Now I was frantic; crazed with fear. Somehow I managed to reach the plane. But in attempting to take off, I cracked up. I must bear a charmed life. I was not injured, myself, but the plane was ruined. My expedition, hardly started, was already at an end."

I was beginning to understand, now, why Burch Patterson had not wanted the world to know of his return. A tale as wild, and fantastic as this would lead him to but one spot—the psychopathic ward. Had I not seen the *thing* there in the shed, I would never have believed him myself. But as it was—

"And then?" I asked.

"I think there is a form of insanity," said Burch, "which is braver than bravery. I think that insanity came upon me then. All I could comprehend was that some *thing*; a *thing* that changed its shape; had killed my companions.

"I determined to capture that *thing*—or die in the attempt. But first I had to sit down and figure out what it *was!*"

Ki licked his lips. "And—and did you figure it out, Burch?"

"I think so. But the result of my reasoning is as fantastic as the *thing* itself. That is why I want the help and advice of you two. I will tell you what I think. Then you must say what it is best to do."

I poured another drink all around. It wasn't my house, or my liquor, but nobody seemed to mind. Ki and I waited for Burch to begin. Burch had picked up, and was now handling with a curiously abstract air, a clean, white sheet of notepaper. As he began, he waved this before us.

"Can you conceive," he said, "of a world of only two dimensions? A world which scientists might call 'Flatland'? A world constructed like this piece of paper—on which might live creatures who could not even visualize a third dimension of depth?"

"Sure," said Ki. I wasn't so sure, myself, but I said nothing.

"Very well. Look—" Burch busied himself with a pencil for an instant. "I draw on this sheet of paper, a tiny man. He is a Flatlander. He can move forward or backward. Up or down. But he can never move out of his world, into the third dimension, because he has no knowledge of a dimension angular to that in which he lives. He does not even dream of its existence."

I said, "I see what you mean now. But what has that to do with—"

"Wait, Len." Patterson suddenly struck the paper a blow with one finger; piercing it. He held the sheet up for our inspection. "Look at this. What do you see?"

"A sheet of paper," I said, "with a hole in it."

"Yes. But what does the *Flatlander* see?"

Ki looked excited. "I get it, Burch! He sees an unexpected, solid object appear before him—out of nowhere! If he walks around this object, he discovers it to be crudely round!"

"Exactly. Now if I push the finger farther through the hole—"

"The object expands!"

"And if I bend it?"

"It changes its shape!"

"And if I thrust another finger through Flatland—"

"Another strangely shaped piece of solid matter materializes before the Flatlander!" Ki's eyes were widening by the moment. I didn't understand why.

I said, "I told you I didn't have a scientific mind, Burch. What does all this mean?"

Burch said patiently, "I have merely been establishing a thought-pattern, Len, so you can grasp the next step of my reasoning. Forget the Flatlander now—or, rather, try to think of *us* as being in his place!

"Would we not, to a creature whose natural habitat is a higher plane than ours, appear much the same sort of projection as the Flatlander is to us?"

"Suppose a creature of this higher plane projected a portion of himself into *our* dimension—as I projected my finger into Flatland. We would not be able to see all of him, just as the Flatlander could not see all of us. We would see only a tri-dimensional cross-section of him; as the Flatlander saw a bi-dimensional cross-section of us!"

This time I got it. I gasped,

"Then you think that *thing* in the work-shed is a cross-section of a creature from the—"

"Yes, Len. From the Fourth Dimension!"

Patterson smiled wanly.

"That is the decision I reached on the Maratan Plateau. There confronted me the problem of capturing the *thing*. The answer eluded me for weeks. Finally, I found it."

"It was—" Ki was leaning forward breathlessly.

"The Flatlander," said Burch, "could not capture my finger, *ever*, by lassooing it. No matter how tight he drew his noose, I could always withdraw my finger.

"But he *could* secure a portion of me, by fastening me to his dimension. Thus—" He showed us how a pin, laid flat in Flatland, could pierce a small piece of skin. "Now if this pin were bolted securely, the finger thus prisoned could not be withdrawn.

"That was the principle on which I worked, but my task had just begun. It took months to effect the capture. I had to study, from afar, the amorphous black *thing* which was my quarry. Try to form some concept of what incredible Fourth Dimensional beast would cast projections of that nature into the Third.

"Finally I decided that one certain piece of black matter, occurring in a certain relationship to the changing whole, was a foot. How, it is not important to tell. It was, after all, theory, coupled with guesswork.

"I constructed the shackle you have seen. Two uprights, with a third that must pierce the *thing*; then lock upon it. I waited, then, many weeks. Finally there came a chance to spring my trap. And—it worked!"

Ki said, "And then?"

"The rest is a long and tiresome story. Somehow I found my way to a native village; there employed natives to drag my captive from the Plateau. We were handicapped by the fact that we could never get too near the trap. You see, it is a *limb* we have imprisoned. The head, or eating apparatus, or what ever it is, is still free. That is what tried to reach you, Ki, there in the shed.

"Anyway, we made an arduous trek to the coast. As I have told you, I chartered a vessel. The sailors hated my cargo, and feared it. The trip was not an easy one. But I was determined, and my determination bore fruit. And—here we are."

I said, "Yeah—here we are. Just like the man who grabbed a tiger by the tail; then couldn't let go. Now that you've got this *thing*, what are you going to do with it?"

"That's what I want you to tell me."

Ki's eyes were glowing. He said, "Good Lord, man, is there any question in your mind? Call in the scientists—the whole damned brigade of them! Show them this *thing*! You've got the marvel of the age on your hands!"

"And you, Len?"

"You want it straight?" I said. "Or would you like to have me pull my punches?"

"Straight. That's why I asked you out here."

"Then get rid of it." I said. "Kill it. Set it on fire. Destroy it. I don't know just how you're going to do it, but I do know that's the thing to do.

"Oh, I know what you're thinking, Ki—so shut up! I'm a dope. Sure. I'm ignorant. Sure. I don't have the mind or the heart of a true scientist. Okay—you win! But Burch said I had common sense—and I'm exercising it now. I say—get rid of that damned *thing* before something happens. Something horrible that you will regret for the rest of your life!"

Ki looked a little peeved. He said, "You're nuts, Len! The *thing's* tied down, isn't it? Dammit, man—you're the kind of guy who holds back the progress of the world. I bet you'd have voted to kill Galileo if you'd been alive in his day."

"If he'd trapped a monster like this," I retorted, "A monster who'd already killed at least three men, I'd have voted just that way. I'm not superstitious, Burch. But I'm afraid. I'm afraid that when Man starts monkeying with the Unknown, he gets beyond his depth. I say—kill it, now!"

Burch looked at me anxiously.

"That's your last word, Len?"

"Absolutely my last," I said. I rose. "And just to prove it, I'm going home now. And I'm not even going to write a damned word about what I've seen tonight. I don't care if this is the best story since the Deluge—I'm not going to write it!"

Ki said, "You give me a pain, Len. In the neck."

"Same to you," I told him, "only lower down. Well, so long, guys." And I went home.

CHAPTER IV
Terror

I KEPT MY WORD. Though I had the mimsies all night, tossing and thinking about that crazy, changing black *thing*, I didn't put a word concerning it on paper. I half expected to hear from Burch Patterson some time during the next day. But I didn't. Then, the following morning, I saw why. The *Call* carried a front-page blast, screaming to the astonished world the news that, "the missing explorer, Burch Patterson, has returned home," and that "tonight there will be a convocation of eminent scientists" at his home to view some marvel brought back from the wilds of upper Peru.

All of which meant that brother Ki's arguments had proven more persuasive than mine. And that tonight there was to be a preview of that damned *thing*.

I was pretty sore about it. I thought the least they could have done was give me the news beat on the yarn. But there wasn't any use crying over spilt milk. Anyway, I remembered that Ki's paper had a tie-up with the *Call*. It was natural he should route the story that way.

And then I went down to the office, and Joe Slade, the human buzz saw who calls himself our City Editor, waved me up to his desk.

"You, Harvey," he said, "I'm going to give you a chance to earn some of that forty per we're overpaying you. I want you to represent us tonight out at Patterson's home in Jersey. He's going to unveil something mysterious."

I said, "Who—me? Listen, chief, give it to Bill Reynolds, won't you? I've got some rewrites to do—"

"You, I said. What's the matter? Does New Jersey give you asthma?"

"Chief," I pleaded, "I can't cover this. I don't know anything about science or—"

"What do you mean—science?" He pushed back his eyeshade and glared at me. "Do you know what this is all about?"

That stopped me. I didn't want to go, but if I ever admitted that I'd known about Patterson's changeable what-is-it, and not beaten the *Call* to the streets with the story, I would be scanning the want ads in fifteen seconds flat. So I gulped and said, "Okay, boss. I'll go."

EVERYBODY AND HIS BROTHER was there that night. I recognized a professor of Physics from Columbia U., and the Dean of Paleontology from N.Y.U. Two old graybeards from the Academy of Natural History were over in a corner discussing something that ended in—zoic, and the curator of the Museum was present, smelling as musty as one of his ancient mummies.

The Press was out in force. All the bureaus, and most of the New York papers. Ki was doing the receiving. Burch had not yet put in an appearance. I found a minute to get Ki aside, and told him what a skunky trick I thought he'd pulled on me, but he merely shrugged.

"I'm sorry, Len. But you had your chance. After all, I had to think of my own paper first." Then he smiled. "And beside, you were in favor of destroying the *thing*."

"I still am," I told him dourly.

"Then what are you here for?"

It was my turn to shrug. "It was either come or lose my job," I said. "What do you think?"

Then Burch put in an appearance, and the whole outfit went genteelly crazy. Flash bulbs started blazing, and all my learned *confréres* of the Third Estate started shooting questions at him. About his trip, the loss of his comrades, his experiences. I knew all that stuff, so I just waited for the big blow-off to follow.

It came, at last. The moment when Burch said:

"Before I tell my entire story. I prefer that you see that which I brought back with me," and he led the way out to the work-shed.

Ki and Burch had fixed up the place a little; put chalk lines on the floor to show the visitors where they might stand.

"And I warn you," Burch said, just before he opened the shed door, "Not to move beyond those lines. Afterward you will understand why."

Then the crowd began to file in. From my vantage point in the rear, I could tell when the first pair of eyes sighted that *thing*—and when every subsequent visitor saw it, as well. Gasps, exclamations, and little cries of astonishment rippled through the crowd as one by one they moved into the room.

The *thing* was still suspended on its imprisoning rod. As before, it was wriggling and moving; changing its shape with such rapidity that the human eye could scarcely view one shape before that turned into another. In view of what Burch had told me, I could comprehend the *thing* better now. I could understand how, if that black blob of flesh captured by the bar were *really*—as Burch presumed—a leg of some ultra-dimensional monster, the movements of that limb, as it sought to break free, would throw continually changing projections into our world.

I could understand, too, why from time to time we would see *other* bits of solid matter appear in various sections of the room. Though these seemed disassociated with that chunk hanging on the trap, I knew it was really separate portions of the same beast. Because if a *man* were to thrust four fingers, simultaneously, into Flatland, to the Flatlander these would appear to be four separate objects; while in reality they were part of a single unit in a dimension beyond his powers of conception.

The astonishment of the professors was something to behold. I began to feel a little bit ashamed of myself, there in the background. Perhaps I had been wrong to give Burch the advice I had. Perhaps, as Ki had said, this was one of the greatest discoveries of all time. It belonged to the world of science?

One of the photographers was dropping to his knee; leveling his Graflex at the shifting, changing *thing* on the rod. I caught myself thinking, swiftly, "He shouldn't do that!" Evidently Burch had the same idea. He took a swift step forward; cried, "Please! If you don't mind—"

He spoke too late. The man's finger pressed. For an instant the room was flooded with light.

And then it happened. I heard a sound like a thin, high bleating that seemed to come from far, far away. Or it may not have been a sound at all, in the true sense of that word. It may have been some tonic wave of supernal heights; for it tortured the eardrums to hear it.

The *thing* on the rod churned into motion. Violent motion. It grew and dwindled; shifted from cube to hemisphere; back to cube again. Then a truncated pyramidal form was throbbing, jerking, churning on the steel. Where I had once noticed an old, ugly, healed wound; ichor-clotted, now I saw ragged edges of black break open. Saw a few, fresh gouts of brownish fluid well from what seemed to be raw edges in that changing black.

Burch's horrified voice raised above the tumult.

"Get out! Get out—all of you! Before it—"

That was all he found time to say. For there came a horrible, sucking sound, like the sound of gangrenous flesh tearing away; and where there had been a changing black shape swirling on an imprisoning steel rod—now there was nothing!

But with equal suddenness, several of the shapeless blobs of matter from various parts of the room seemed to rush together with frightful speed. Someone, screaming with terror, bumped against me then. I fell to my hands and knees in the doorway; feeling the flood of human fear scramble over me.

But not until I had seen a scimitar-shaped blob of black flesh reach out to strike at Ki Patterson. Ki had not even time to cry out. He went down, dead, as though stricken by the sickle of Chronos.

I cried, "Burch!"

Burch had turned to face the coalescing monster. A revolver in his hand was filling the little room with thunder. Orange gouts of flame belched from its muzzle; and I knew he was not missing. Still the *thing* was closing in on him. I saw what appeared to be four jet circles appear in a ring over the head of Burch Patterson. Saw the circles expand; and a wider expanse of black—flat and sinister—appear directly over his head. They came together with a clutching, enveloping movement. Then—he was gone!

SOMEHOW I MANAGED to struggle out of that work shed. Not that it made any difference. For with the disappearance of Burch Patterson, the *thing* itself disappeared.

I won't try to describe the frightened group of news men and scientists who gathered at the Patterson house. Who trembled and quaked, and offered fanatic reasons for that which had transpired. Who finally summoned up courage enough to return to the shed cautiously; seeking the mortal remains of Burch Patterson.

They never found anything, of course. Ki was there, but Ki was dead. Burch was gone. The air was still putrid with that unearthly animal stench. Beneath the steel "trap" Patterson had built for his *thing*, there was a pool of drying brownish fluid.

One of the scientists wanted to take a sample of this for analysis. He returned to the house for a test-tube in which to put it . . .

Maybe it was the wrong thing for me to do. But I thought, then, that it was best. And I still think so. If he had taken that sample; made that analysis; sooner or later another expedition would have set out for the Maratan Plateau in search of that *thing* whose blood did not correspond to that of any known animal. I didn't believe this should happen. So, while he was gone, I set fire to the work shed. It was an old place; old and dry as tinder. By the time he had returned, it was a seething cauldron of flame. It made a fitting pyre for the body of Ki Patterson

But—I don't know. I have wondered, since. Somehow, I have a feeling that Burch Patterson may not be dead, after all. That is—if a human can live in a dimension of which he cannot conceive.

The more I think of it; the more I try to reconcile that which I saw with that which Burch told me; the more I believe that the thing which descended upon Burch, there in the shed, was not a "mouth"—but a gigantic paw! You know, I saw four circles appear . . . with a flat black spot above. It could have been four huge fingers . . . with the palm descending to grasp the daring tri-dimensional "Flatlander" who had the audacity to match wits with a creature from a superior world. If that be so . . . and if the *thing* were intelligent . . . Patterson might still be alive . . .

I don't know. But sometimes I am tempted to organize another expedition to the Maratan Plateau, myself. Try to learn the truth concerning the *thing* from beyond the Gateway. The truth concerning Burch Patterson's fate.

What would *you* do?

THE THING FROM THE BARRENS

Jim Kjelgaard

I, George Malory, graduate geologist, could only guess about The Thing that came from the barrens. I saw the horrible outrages it committed; but never The Thing itself. Pug Davenport saw it. Now, his head literally torn from his body, Pug lies in the cemetery at North City. His should be a world-honored

grave; Pug might have saved all humanity, and certainly saved the five hundred people who made their homes in North City. He— But hear the story.

I told myself that I did not know why I was staying in North City. "Farthest north metropolis" we called ourselves, after the Blanding Corporation built our city, peopled it, and then abandoned everything when the radium ore petered out. I could have gone when Blanding quit, collected my salary, and taken a job in Russia. But I didn't go, and our so-called metropolis of five hundred people did not fold either. Some left. But others drifted in to take their places and the population remained static.

I lived because I had an independent income, others did whatever there was to do. Pete Gallagher set up his store, Joe Urschel came along with his saloon, a few men did odd jobs, and most of the remaining 300 adult males went into the barrens to trap. That was a hard life, the trappers would be gone for weeks and sometimes months with no intercourse whatever with other human beings. But they brought in plenty of white foxes, ermine, caribou hides, wolf pelts, fisher, and wolverines.

Though I often went into the barrens to hunt caribou and wolves, I did no trapping. Frankly I lacked the hardihood to start out with a few dogs and a three months' supply of grub to spend a three-month-long night facing the lashing gales and everything else that could roar across the winter-bound arctic. Then I did not need the money. It was a dull life, but I had never intended to make it a permanent one. I read my books, and imported new ones, to keep abreast of developments in my own field.

But when I told myself that I did not know why I was staying in North City it was a lie because I did know. I stayed because of Marcia Davenport. That's right, a girl. Ask me why and I cannot answer you. I had dined and danced with what supposedly are the most beautiful and charming women in the world, those found in the salons of New York, Paris, Santiago, Moscow. And I was madly in love with the little daughter of a fox trapper, a girl so devoted to her drunken and worthless father that the most she had ever given me was a friendly smile and a kind word. But I could neither help myself nor leave North City without her, and if Pug Davenport had taken his daughter and gone to the North Pole I would have followed and built my igloo as close to theirs as possible. It was that way.

Marcia and Pug had blown into North City with the first settlers Blanding had sent in. Pug was a wizened little man with a cross batch of red veins hopelessly netting his features. He was supposed to be an explosives expert. But I suspect that, back in what must have been a very checkered career, he had been an expert on anything you'd want to name, including safe-blowing and larceny. When Blanding pulled out, Pug stayed in the house they gave him and went in for fox-trapping. Marcia—

How can I tell you about her? Does it mean anything to say that she was a girl, almost twenty years old, beautiful, tall and lithe, with raven hair through which shone coppery overtones? That doesn't express it. All I can say is that what happens to maybe one man in a million had happened to me. I knew that I could never go anywhere unless she went with me. To have her as my wife would be the consummation of everything. If I could not have her, to be near her was second choice.

But all during the twenty months since they had come to North City, Marcia's time had been given to Pug. She took him home when he was drunk, which was whenever he had any money. She nursed him through his hangovers, and when he was home spent all her time making for him the things he liked. When he was out on the barrens she worried about him. That little, drunken, worthless father of hers had woven such a spell about her that she seemed unable to think of another man.

But yet she *must* think of other men! She was young, alive, human! Someday, I hoped, she would break the shell she had built around herself and let me in. That was the day I lived for. Meanwhile I had danced with her a few times, and when Pug was out on the barrens I could go see her once in a while. That was what kept me hoping.

The fox trappers had been out on their lines for six weeks now, and the half-light of winter had blanketed North City for two, when I stepped out of my house into the street. There was not much snow, farther south they get more of that than we do and most of what falls here is blown away by the wind. That had been from the east for the past twenty days, and there were deep drifts along the eastern walls of all the houses.

I had intended to go down and see Marcia when I dimly made out a dog team lying in front of Joe Urschel's saloon. As soon as I was close enough, I saw that it was Pug Davenport's team. That was a surprise. In spite of his habits Pug is tough and hard, and usually stays out on the barrens as long as anybody. This time, I figured, his thirst must have become unbearable. Evidently he had just blown in, and Marcia didn't know he was here. But she would appreciate somebody's giving him a hand, and I went into Urschel's.

URSCHEL HAD HIS OWN POWER PLANT. Every spring the *Nanook*, North City's supply ship, brought him twenty fifty-gallon drums of gasoline to run it. I blinked in the unaccustomed glare of electric lights, and looked at the bar. Two of North City's winter residents, Moose-Hide Allen and Al Pettigrew, were hanging over it. Urschel would have starved if he depended on winter trade; his big killing was made when the fox-trappers came back. Furs were currency, and he was getting rich. Now there was a great pile of white fox furs, bigger and silkier than I had even seen before, on one end of the bar. I stepped up.

"What'll you have, George?" Urschel asked.

"Make it scotch."

I fingered the drink he poured, and looked at the pile of foxes. A white fox is a little thing, some of them aren't much bigger than cats. But those pelts were nearly wolf-size, and yet definitely they were foxes. Pug Davenport, somewhere out on those lonely barrens, had found a breed of foxes the like of which man had never seen before.

Don't smile at that. Spread a map of the North American continent before you. From Key West, Florida, to Point Barrow, Alaska, you cannot find an unnamed place. You can then understand why cartographers, and even some explorers, have declared the world an open book with no new frontiers. Actually nothing could be farther from the truth. Even though it takes you only a tenth of a second to move your pointing finger, from one named place to the other, it might take you one hundred days to walk between those same places. That's what we had around North City. Men had gone into the barrens, but not into all of them. Even in thickly populated states, there are still places where no man has set foot. A lot of things that we never dreamed existed are yet going to be found right in our own back yards.

I looked at the pelts again, noted their size and texture. Ordinarily it pays to give strict attention to your own business in North City, but I asked Urschel:

"Where'd you get 'em?"

"Pug Davenport brought 'em in. Said I should send half the money for 'em down to Marcia and he'd drink up the rest."

"Wow! He should be able to drink until July!"

Urschel looked at me, his eyes hard, "He will be."

"No offense meant," I told him. "Give me another drink."

I took the drink he poured and backed against the bar to look around the unlighted back end of the room. Pug Davenport sat at a corner table, the darkest and most inaccessible one he could find, with a bottle of whiskey before him. As I looked he tilted the bottle to his mouth and drained out a teacup full, I waited a minute—Pug can be ugly when he's drunk—then took my drink and walked over to him.

"Hello, Pug," I said,

He looked at me, and shrank as far as he could down into his chair. His trembling hand strayed out to grasp my sleeve.

"Zhorzhe," he said unsteadily. "Sit close to me, Zhorzhe."

He pulled a chair around and me down on it. Again he raised the bottle, took a drink that would have floored an ordinary man, and his right hand, took a firm grip on my left arm. I frowned. There was something here that should not be. I had known Pug Davenport to be almost anything except afraid. He went farther out on the barrens than anyone else and laughed at those who dared not go with him. Always he had been ready to face anything. But now, both from the way he gripped my arm and in the way his eyes met mine, I knew that he was terrified. I told myself that he was probably in the first stages of the D.T.'s. But when I moved he whispered again:

"Zhorzhe, don' leave me alone!"

For a second, I don't know why, I was very disturbed. But I fought for a grip on myself and tried to talk him out of it.

"You certainly brought in a wonderful catch of foxes," I tried to be casual. "Where'd you get 'em?"

He looked at me, staring as though he hadn't the least idea of what I was talking about, and let his glance rove to the pile of furs on the bar. For a full minute he didn't say anything. Then he shuddered violently.

"It's the duckfoot," he whimpered. "The duckfoot an' the stick. You should shee what it done to Matt Brazeal."

"What duckfoot and what stick, and what did it do to Matt Brazeal?"

Pug stared into space. "I tried to shake it off," he whispered. "I tried to. The trees was all green there, big tall trees. Thass where the foxshes lived. I tried to shake it off but it followed me. It caught Matt Brazeal, and you should shee what it done to him. It will come here."

That was nonsense. In the first place there aren't any trees in the arctic. In the second place this talk of a duckfoot and a stick doing something terrible to Matt Brazeal, another North City fox trapper, was just the inane ramblings of a trapper who had too much to drink. As for the duckfoot and the stick following Pug to North City— Marcia was needed here. I stood up, put my hand on Pug's shoulder, and shook him. He blinked into drunken attention.

"Pug," I said dearly, "sit right where you are. No duckfoot and stick can get you in here. The door's shut."

A PATHETIC EXPRESSION of hope and relief crossed his eyes. He mumbled something that I did not hear.

"I'm going to get Marcia," I said. "We'll keep you safe from the duckfoot and the stick. Don't move until I come back."

I pulled my parka about me and went back into the wind-blasted street. Pug's four huskies were stretched in their traces, sleeping, and they raised indifferent heads when I came out. I had seen them before, but only now did I notice how thin and worn they were, and the blood that stained the snow beneath their paws. For a moment I looked uneasily at them. Wherever he had come from, Pug had certainly given the dogs a lot of punishment. I— That was silly. There couldn't be any truth in the wild, disconnected story he had told. Tall green trees, foxes big as wolves, and a duckfoot and a stick that had done something terrible to Matt Brazeal. Only the foxes were real and—

Exactly where had Pug Davenport taken those pelts? Certainly no other man had ever seen foxes like them. Somewhere back in those God-forsaken barrens Pug might even have found trees. But the duckfoot and the stick—

I broke into a run. The darkness seemed unreal, full of moving things. Deliberately I slowed to a walk. A man had to keep his head and there was nothing with which he could not cope as long as he let nothing excite him. Whatever Pug Davenport had seen on the barrens—

"Cut it out," I told myself. "He didn't see anything."

I swerved to Marcia Davenport's lamp-lighted house and knocked on the door. Marcia opened it, and a gust of wind blew sugar-like snow across the kitchen floor. I slipped inside, shut the door behind me, and let my hungry eyes feast on her. Somehow the loveliest pictures my mind ever drew were never quite so lovely as she herself. And always, when I was near her, I wondered why she should even think of marrying me or any other man. A god would be a more fitting mate for Marcia Davenport. She smiled.

"Hello, George. Take off your parka."

I stood against the door, the parka swinging about my knees. For a second I groped for words, wondering how to break gently to Marcia the news that Pug was back and having a real bender up at Urschel's. Common sense came to my resale. In a good many ways Marcia was exactly like Pug, not afraid of much and seldom hesitating to tackle anything.

"Pug's back," I told her.

She nodded, grasping at once everything I meant. "Is he bad?" she asked quietly.

"Quite bad. You'd better come."

"All right. Just a minute."

She went into another room, and when she came out she was wearing the exquisite fawn-skin parka that Pug himself had made for her. Marcia smiled at me, and grasped my elbow reassuringly. I groped happily beside her, thoroughly ashamed now of my own near-panic. Somehow it seemed that nothing could ever go wrong as long as Marcia was near. There was something deep inside her that seemed incapable of being moved or even ruffled by anything from the outside, a quiet strength. Whatever came, Marcia could face and cope with it. And right at that moment I thought more strongly than ever that this girl beside me represented not only the highest type of womanhood but the highest of humanity.

TOGETHER WE WALKED up the street, Marcia, bending her head against the wind and holding tight to my elbow to steady herself. We were nearly opposite Urschel's when I had on almost irresistible impulse to cross to the other side of the street.

There seemed to be something over there overwhelmingly magnetic, something that I could not see but only feel. Marcia was one step ahead of me, pulling me by the arm and looking questioningly up into my face.

"Come on," she made herself heard above the steady roar of the wind. "I must go over there!"

I took another step forward and stopped in my tracks. Deliberately, forcefully fighting some mighty summons that pulled me forward, I took two steps backward and the pressure lessened slightly. A cold hand seemed to be stroking my spine, a clammy breath pouring down my neck, I recognized those symptoms as the awakening of fear, terror such as that which was reflected so plainly in Pug Davenport's face. I tried to summon reason to my aid. But all I could be sure of was that, though I did not know what lay on the other side of the street, I did know that it was something to be very much afraid of.

"Come on!" I shouted. "Pug's in the saloon!"

"But I must go across the street!"

"Come on!" I screamed.

Fighting for every inch, doing my utmost to resist the powerful impulse that said I must cross the street, I half dragged her toward the saloon. When we had gone ten feet farther, we seemed to pass out of the orbit of whatever had tried to influence us. So strong had been my pressure on Marcia's arm that immediately we both stumbled into the snow.

We arose and brushed ourselves off. Marcia, puzzled, turned around.

"I don't know why," she said. "But I had the strangest feeling back there that I must cross the street."

"Nonsense!" I told her. "Come on."

We reached the saloon. Joe Urschel had no sign in front of his establishment. But he did keep an electric fan turned on the window before the bar in winter so that frost would not cloud it and passers-by could readily see a place of refreshment. I glanced up at that window to see the faces of Al Pettigrew and Moose-Hide

Allen plastered against it. Their eyes were staring, their mouths agape. Plainly they had had some terrific surprise of shock. Careful to swing Marcia the other way when we entered, I pointed to the back end of the room.

"Pug's there," I said.

She hurried back, and I approached the two men who were staring out the window.

"What's wrong?" I asked.

"Ur—Urschel!" Al Pettigrew ejaculated.

"What's the matter with Urschel?"

"He—he floated away!"

"What!"

"That's right," Moose-Hide said. "He was goin' over to Pete Gallagher's for a set of hinges. But as soon as he got across the street he turned an' went down it, right to that little black stick layin' that. He stood thar a minute or more, rockin' back an' forth an' like to fall. Then he floated away! His laigs was two feet off the ground."

"You're crazy!"

"George, I ain't crazy an' I ain't drunk!" Moose-Hide said angrily. "Urschel's parka was wrinkled, like a rabbit's fur when a wolf's haulin' it. But nothin' carried him. He floated!"

SOMETHING SEEMED to pervade the room, a cold and fear-inspiring presence that had no shape or form, but yet had definite being. I turned around to see Marcia bent over her father, stroking his temple with her hand and swinging the bottle of whiskey behind her. Pug groped for it like a pleading child, and Marcia permitted him a short drink. Pug fell across the table, hopelessly drunk, and Marcia sat down opposite him. I walked back.

"How is he?"

"He'll be all right, George." Marcia smiled at me and I felt weak all over.

"Did he tell you anything?"

"He had some story about a duckfoot and a stick, and said that I must keep away from the stick or I'd never get away. I think he's more bushed-out than drunk."

"Yes, that's it," I agreed. "He's bushed-out."

That's a term we apply to anybody who's been out in the barrens too long, and has gone a little crazy as a consequence. Association with others generally fixes them up. But I knew that Pug Davenport was not bushed-out and now I knew also that, wherever he had caught those foxes, he had also met some unreal, inhuman thing about which the whiskey that fogged his brain prevented his telling us. Doubtless the surprise had been mutual. But whatever the monster was, it had followed Pug back to North City and was preying on human beings! I walked to the front of the saloon and looked thoughtfully at Urschel's 30-06, hanging on a rack of caribou horns over the bar. Al Pettigrew sidled down to me.

"Wha—what do you s'spose it is, Doc?" he asked.

"Nothing at all, Al. By the way, what became of Pug's dog team?"

"They took off down the street, sled an' all, howlin' like banshees. Doc, there's somethin' out there!"

"Nonsense!" I snapped—anything to avoid a panic. "What could be out there?"

"You ain't foolin' me," Al said suddenly. "I seen it."

"What did you see?"

"N— Nothin'."

"There you are. Don't go starting crazy rumors. I'm going out there."

"I'm stayin' here," Al mumbled.

"Keep the door locked if you're afraid."

"I aim to."

"I'll go with ye," Moose-Hide offered.

"No thanks. You needn't."

I took Urschel's big 30-06 from the rack and stepped out on the porch. My intention was to stand there, and blast the stick with a soft-nosed bullet from the gun. But when I looked the stick was not there. Nor was there any indication of the powerful force that had tried to drag Marcia and myself across the street. Carefully, the gun leveled, I walked to where the stick had been. A strange, musty odor, vaguely like that of an aroused ermine, pervaded the air. Slowly, a step at a time, I went forward. The snow was blowing down the street, a fine mist of hard flakes. But it had blown over the place where the stick had lain, and I stopped short. Just ahead of me were half a dozen long, triangular tracks almost exactly like those that might be left by a duck walking in the mud. But these tracks were longer than my own, and proportionately wide.

I gasped, and raised the rifle for something to shoot at. But there was nothing, only the musty odor and the half-dozen tracks, that were lost in snow-blown nothingness. Slowly I turned around, saw Swede Thomas' half-breed daughter step out of her house at the end of the street. A slim girl, with her father's coloring and her mother's patient acceptance of whatever came, Lorna turned suddenly and walked to the other side of the street. She stopped short, swaying back and forth, coming dangerously near falling but always rising again. It was then that I saw the black stick, directly between her feet.

I yelled, and ran as fast as I could. But before I was able to cover half the distance I saw Lorna Thomas rise in the air. Her parka was wrinkled, as though something had hold of her there. The little black stick was on the other side, floating through the air about three feet from the ground. I flung myself to one knee and levied the rifle. But at once the futility of my own position became apparent.

There was nothing to shoot at, nothing except the dangling girl and the little black stick. I sighted squarely between them and pressed the trigger. A hollow, chuckling sound rose high above the seething wind and floated back to me. Whatever carried Lorna Thomas broke into a run so swift that I was unable to keep them in sight. I shot again and again, and ran as fast as I could.

But all I found was the line of huge duck tracks that again faded into wind-blown snow.

I WAS TERRIBLY SHAKEN when I got back to the saloon. For a few seconds wild hysteria threatened. I grabbed a bottle, took a long pull, and slammed the bottle down on the bar. Al Pettigrew sidled up to me.

"I told you," he leered. "There is somethin' out there, ain't there?"

That, more than anything else, sobered me. Al Pettigrew was the sort of nameless spawn, product of a father who had never seen him and a mother who had never wanted him, that you'll find in the north or anywhere else. He had a weak and flabby face in which abject terror lived. I, product of a high-class home and the finest scientific training man can provide, was supposed to be just a little better than that.

"Yes!" I snapped. "There is something! Now shut up!"

Again I tried to bring reason to my aid, calling up and rejecting every scientific rule and theorem I had ever heard of and inventing a few on the spot. But nothing applied. There was no precedent for this. All I knew was that a monster had come among us, a monster with a trap that held people helpless. The trap was easier to figure out. Doubtless it was some sort of metal with a very strong magnetic attraction for living flesh. Neoglaunce had properties similar to that, and probably this was some variety of such a metal. The creature that bore it must have form and substance, but was of a pigmentation that could not be discerned by the human eye. Certainly every resident of North City was doomed unless we could find a way to stop it. But how can you take action against that which you cannot see? Now that The Thing had discovered human haunts, when it was finished with North City it had only to go south. Then—?

I walked back to where Marcia was still sitting beside the drunken Pug. Now the arctic day had changed to the deeper gloom of night, and the lights glowed brightly. Marcia had folded her parka into a pillow, placed it under Pug's reclining head. Pug began to snore.

"Is he all right?" I asked.

Marcia smiled, and again I felt that curious weakness. I would have licked her boots for her any time, and when she smiled I would have cut off my own arm if she'd asked me to.

"He's all right," she said. "Let him rest, I don't think he's slept in the past two weeks."

"Okay," I tried to sound casual. "Let him spend the night in his chair. But hadn't you better lie down? There's a cot in the backroom."

"'No, thank you," she smiled again. "I'll sit with him. I'm really used to it, George."

"Good enough."

I returned to the front of the saloon, for the first time thankful that this girl had been so engrossed with her sick father that she'd scarcely noticed anything else. Al and Moose-Hide looked uneasily at me as I laid the 30-06 across my knees and pulled a chair in front of the door. If anything came in that door, I determined, it was going to cross my dead body before it got to the girl in back.

"Ain't—ain't you takin' this a mite serious?" Moose-Hide demanded.

"Lie down," I said. "Try to get some sleep. We've a job to do in the morning."

"Well—I s'pose it's all right if you say so."

All night I kept vigil before the door, the cocked rifle across my lap. It seemed unreal, almost ridiculous. I, George Mallory, waiting with a rifle across my lap for something that I could not see when it came. As the slow hours dragged by it seemed sillier than ever, and all my thoughts of last night even more silly. No, there had to be some more reasonable explanation of everything. The thin gray daylight crept upon us, and I think that is the time when I dozed off.

I was awakened by a rush of cold air in the face, and jumped up. Moose-Hide sat on the bar, nonchalantly swinging his legs. I looked toward the back end of the saloon, saw Pug still sprawled across his table.

"Where's Marcia?" I demanded.

"Why, she said she was goin' to take an' get Pug some hot vittles," Moose-hide drawled.

"When did she go?"

"Mebbe two minutes past."

I sprang to the door and looked out, just in time to see Marcia Davenport, across the street, standing directly over the little black stick. She bent forward, until her head almost brushed the snow, and straightened. I gasped, took one step toward her. But, even as I did, I saw her lifted into the air and begin to float away. The little black stick floated beside her.

I WAS ICE COLD. If Marcia Davenport was not alive in it, I knew that the world would offer no more inducement for me to stay alive. But yet I did not run after her. I was thinking more completely and swiftly than I had ever thought before.

I raced to the back of the room and slapped Pug Davenport across the cheek. He mumbled, and shifted his head to the other arm. I slapped him again and again, and when slapping did no good poured a bucket of cold water over his head. Pug awoke slowly, and blinked at me.

"Pug!" I screamed. "Listen! The duckfoot and the stick, they have taken Marcia!"

Never before have I seen so swift a change in any man. Pug leaped erect, there was no trace of fear in him now, no hesitation. And at that moment I was very proud to be a human being. This little derelict had come in from the barrens, terrified by something that had taken place out there. But when the same thing threatened his daughter, Pug could forget his own fear to go to her aid. He snatched the 30-06 from my hands and raced out the door.

Though my legs are longer than his, it was very hard just to keep up. Again, as soon as we got outside, there was an aura of ermine musk. A hollow exclamation, a parody of that which might come from a human hunter who has just bagged an especially fine head of game, seemed to linger in the air. And there were the duck tracks, huge triangular marks in the snow. If I breathed any sort of prayer it was one of thanksgiving that there was no blowing snow this morning to cover them.

We raced out of town into the barrens, stopping where The Thing had stepped, running as hard as we could. And it was a half-mile away, almost in North City's back yard, that we came upon the snowbank. Something huge and powerful had piled that snow, and I looked with glazed eyes upon the things that were hanging from it. The skins of Matt Brazeal, Joe Urschel, Lorna Thomas, stretched on the snow as we would stretch bear skins! The frozen, nude carcasses were cast haphazardly into the snow before it. I gasped. A trapper that sought the skins of human beings just as we sought those of foxes. I saw Marcia.

She was hanging, head down, from the snowbank. The black stick, on top of the bank at her feet, seemed to be holding her up. There was absolutely no evidence of anything else, yet I knew something was there. From Pug Davenport's throat there rolled a hoarse, terrible, snarling, animal cry.

"Aaaa-gh!"

HE THREW HIMSELF DOWN on one knee and leveled the rifle. I could still see nothing, but he took a steady aim. He pressed the trigger, the rifle blasted. At the same time a fine spray erupted from the snowbank. I saw Marcia slide from it, crawl a little way through the snow, and get up to run toward me. More snow flew, there was a great threshing, as though up there near the bank some mighty animal was in its death throes. Pug shot again, and again. A wild scream split the air. I saw a line of duck tracks coming toward us, and Pug shot again. He clubbed the rifle and raced forward to give battle to whatever opposed him. A huge bloodstain spread on the snow.

I heard Pug gasp, saw him borne backwards on the snow. His throat seemed of its own volition to be constricting, his eyes bulged, and horrible, gasping breaths sputtered from his open mouth. I sprang forward, receiving a mighty blow that sent me reeling back. When I had recovered, Pug Davenport lay quietly on the snow.

The line of duck tracks, marked frequently by huge splashes of blood, was wobbling across the barrens. I saw them reach the Sheep River, and another terrible scream floated back as the ice parted and the river's freezing waters opened to receive The Thing. When I looked for the little black stick it was nowhere to be seen.

Marcia was coming toward me, like one awakening from a dream. She looked down at Pug, and I saw the agony that crossed her eyes. Just as swiftly I saw her conquer it. She shook her head.

"Wh—what happened!" she asked. "I left Urschel's, and that's the last I remember."

I stared past her, fascinated by the black, gaping hole in the river where The Thing had gone down. With an effort I tore my eyes away from it, looked back at Marcia. Strength returned, and with it came sense. I looked straight into her eyes, anything to keep her from turning her head to see what was left of the three human beings trapped by The Thing.

"He—" I began, and stopped, "Marcia, when grief is gone let pride replace it. North City lives because Pug Davenport died. I—"

I dared not continue, to blurt out the truth and have this girl who to me meant more than anything else on earth question my own sanity. At the moment I questioned it myself.

But not after Marcia walked up to me, buried her face in my chest, and parted to cry. Then I knew that at last Marcia Davenport had given herself to me, that happiness and delight would spring out of the seeds planted by death and terror. I looked once more at the tracks and the great blood splashes in the snow. The wind would cover them, the Sheep River did not give up its dead. As I gathered Marcia a little closer to me I looked down at the face of her father. For the first time it seemed a peaceful and a happy face.

And I blessed the thought that had bade me wake Pug Davenport up, and set him out to rescue his daughter. The Thing was of no color that normal eyes could see. But Pug's eyes were the only ones in North City that did not react normally. Of all the men who had ever been there, he was the only one who was totally color blind.

THE ISLE OF DOOM
Robert Moore Williams

Chapter I

THE TOWN OF TOM'S LANDING, at the edge of the Big Cypress swamp in the Florida Everglades, looked like the thing it needed most on earth was a good hurricane to blow it to hell and gone off the planet. Mark Redding stood on the dilapidated board-walk that ran down one side of the dirt road that served as a street and looked at the nine wooden shacks that made up the residences in this community. The only living creatures in sight were a scattering of scrawny chickens visible under the house across the street, a lean hound dog that looked like he wished an alligator would catch him and save him the trouble of starving to death, and a razorback hog. Redding turned to look at the store. It was a single wooden building and it was ready to fall apart. Its back end rested on piles driven into the water. The launch that had brought him here across the swamps was tied up at the back end of the store and its garrulous owner was inside the building.

The faded sign on the joint said:

JENKIN'S STORE
*Groceries, fishing tackle, dry goods,
and snuff*

A second smaller sign hung under the first one. The small sign said:

U. S. POST OFFICE

Well, this is it, he thought. *This is the post office. This is the place I'm looking for.* He pushed open the door of the store.

As he entered the front door, the owner of the launch that had brought him here came in through the back door.

"Hi, Zack. Hi, Ned. How're you, boys?" the launch operator sang out to two men in the back of the store. "Seen any more swamp ghosts lately?"

The owner of the launch was kidding. He got a short answer for his efforts.

"Shut yer mouth, you danged fool!" one of the two men told him. "There's some things in these swamps that people who got any sense don't talk about."

Redding stepped into the room. At the sound of his footsteps, the two men looked up quickly. Their unshaven faces turned instantly blank when they saw a stranger. The behavior pattern of the swamps is the same as the hills: keep quiet when a stranger comes around.

The launchman recognized Redding. "Hi," he called out. "Here's my passenger. I want you to meet a couple of the boys. This is Zack and this is Ned. They're alligator hunters. That is—" He winked broadly at Redding. "they hunt gators exceptin' when the ghosts run 'em out of the swamp."

"Hello," Redding said. The two men nodded, said nothing. One of them, Zack, glanced sideways at the launchman. If looks could have killed, the launch tied up at the back of the store would have been in need of a new owner.

The launchman was determined to have his joke. "They're a little sensitive about ghosts," he said, winking again at Redding. "But they're good fellers and if the man you're looking for is anywhere around these parts, they'll be able to help you out. Know every hole and gator hideout in these swamps, the boys do. Well, I gotta get that stuff unloaded. Can't stay here and talk all day."

Grinning, the launch owner hustled into the back room of the store.

The two men eyed Redding. Their gaze went over his lean, bronzed face, took in the sport jacket he was wearing, noted his slacks, his sport shoes. They looked a long time at the beaten brown canvas bag he was carrying. Then Zack's eyes came back to the slack coat, searched for the bulge under the arm that would mean this stranger was carrying a gun.

There was no bulge under the arm. The gun was in the canvas bag.

"You lookin' for somebody?" Zack said at last.

"Yes," Redding answered.

"Who?"

"The postmaster."

"Oh."

"Either of you in charge of the post office?"

"Nope," Zack said. "Ab Jenkins is the man you want. He's in back checkin' groceries."

"I'll wait for him," Redding said. While he waited, he looked around the store. The post office occupied a small corner of the room. The rest of the store was devoted to an amazing conglomeration of goods. There were cheap shoes, a barrel of salt pork, fish nets, gig heads, snuff, twists of chewing tobacco, bolts of calico, galvanized iron buckets, pencils, pens, tablets of writing paper, blue denim overalls, blue work shirts, and other items essential to the trappers and fishermen who lived in the swamp.

One showcase fascinated Redding. It contained a collection of fish hooks of various sizes, yellow candy made to resemble peanuts, boxes of snuff, sacks of smoking tobacco, a box of cheap cigars, shoe laces, pocket knives—and an expensive miniature camera with a price of $5.00 scrawled on the tag attached to it.

The camera had an imported F 3 lens. A light meter and range finder were mounted on the sides.

A camera like this would cost $200.00 in New York. Second-hand, it could easily cost $100.00. It was for sale in this store for $5.00.

Looking at the camera, something inside Redding began to turn cold. He knew what it meant to be cold. He had been cold on the Anzio beachhead, he had been cold in southern France, he had been cold in front of the Siegfried Line when an 88 was zeroed in on his platoon. All during the war—and he had seen it all—he had been cold. It was the same kind of coldness he felt now.

A step sounded behind the counter. "Something I can do for you?" a heavy voice said. Redding looked up.

Ab Jenkins, the postmaster and store owner, was a big man. A two days' growth of tobacco-stained whiskers covered his face. He spat on the floor behind the counter.

"I'd like to look at this camera, if it's for sale."

For a second, Jenkins hesitated. His heavy eyes studied this customer. Then he shrugged, took the camera out of the show-case. "Everything in here's for sale."

Redding took the camera, turned it over and over, studied the lens and the exposure meter. He didn't give two hoots in Georgia about the lens and the meter. He wanted to see if there were two initials scratched inside the case but he didn't want to be in a hurry about looking.

"I'll buy it," he said at last. He took a five-dollar bill out of his wallet. While Jenkins was putting the bill into the money drawer, Redding opened the camera, looked inside it.

Scratched on the black enamel on the inside of the box were the initials J. R.

They stood for Jim Redding, Mark Redding's brother.

"Where did you get this camera?" Redding asked.

"A gator hunter found it on an island out in the swamp," Jenkins answered. "He owed me a bill and I took the camera as part payment."

"I see," Redding answered. He studied Jenkins. The store owner's face was impassive and revealed nothing. He might be lying. He might be telling the truth. Or his story of how he had obtained the camera might be part lie and part truth. Redding had no way of knowing.

"Anything else I can do for you?" Jenkins asked.

"Yes. You're postmaster, aren't you?"

A look of irritation crossed the storekeeper's face. "You ain't another danged inspector, are you?" he demanded.

Redding grinned. "No. I'm looking for some information on a man who mailed a letter from this post office on December 2, 1941."

"Huh?" The request surprised, startled Jenkins. "A man who mailed a letter here in 1941! Mister, that's five years ago!"

"I know it is. The man is my brother. I had a letter from him in December 1941 and I haven't heard from him since. I came down here to look for him. Here's the letter."

Redding took a big envelope from his inside coat pocket, opened it, removed a smaller envelope. The postmark, Tom's Landing, Florida, December 2, 1941, was faded but still visible on the small envelope. Redding laid the letter on the counter.

In the back of the room the two alligator hunters suddenly stopped talking.

Jenkins looked at the letter but made no move to touch it. "You waited five years to come lookin' for your brother," he said. The tone of his voice was an accusation.

"I was in the Army," Redding said. Bitterness crept into his voice. "They don't give you time off from the army to go looking for missing brothers. After I was discharged, I had to spend some time looking after my business. I got here as quickly as I could."

Jenkins listened in silence. He looked at the letter, found courage to pick it up. He turned it around in his fingers, studied the postmark and the address.

"I wouldn't have to see the man who mailed this letter," he said. "He might have come in here and dropped it in the box without my seeing him. Or he might have gave it to someone else to mail and never came in here at all."

"Then you don't remember my brother being in here?"

"I sure don't," Jenkins said flatly. His gaze went regretfully to the camera tucked under Redding's arm. That camera made him a liar and he knew it, but he obviously intended to stick to his story.

"He was a member of a scientific expedition," Redding continued. "There were two other men with him. One of them, Roger Nash, financed the trip. Did you ever hear of him?"

Jenkins shook his head.

"No?" Redding said. "The third man was Sidney Gulick. Did you ever hear of him?"

Sudden rage knotted Jenkins' face. "I never heard of any of them!" he shouted. "And if you want my advice, you'll go back where you came from and stop asking these damned fool questions. I ain't got any more time to talk to you."

He stalked out of sight into the back room of the store. Redding let him go. If Jenkins wouldn't talk, well, there were other people in the town of Tom's Landing. He turned to question the two alligator hunters.

The cane chairs where they had been sitting were vacant. The alligator hunters had cleared out the side door. Redding went to the door and looked out. He didn't see them. He saw something else.

Drifting in across the swamp, its motor throbbing as it headed for a landing in the vacant lot beside the store, was a helicopter. Coming up the bayou channel was a powerful cabin cruiser.

A ten-year old youngster, attracted by the sound of the 'copter's motor, dashed out of a house across the street. He looked at the plane, then at the launch.

"Gulick!" he yelled back to someone still inside the house. "Gulick is coming!"

Running as fast as his skinny legs would carry him, he dived into the horseweeds across the street and disappeared.

The helicopter slid down to a landing in the vacant lot. Almost before the vanes had stopped turning, Redding was at the cabin door. He could see the pilot inside. The door opened.

"Are you Sidney Gulick—" he began, then stopped as he realized his mistake. Wearing a leather helmet, the pilot had looked like a man. As she got out of the plane, he saw she was an uncommonly attractive girl.

"No," the girl answered. She looked curiously at Redding. "I'm Gerry Nash. Mr. Gulick is in the launch. If you will wait he will be here."

She walked across the lot and entered the side door of the store.

The launch pulled up at the little landing behind the store. A heavy-set man clad in gray flannel trousers climbed out of it.

Redding waited.

CHAPTER II

"REDDING? JIM REDDING? Hm." Gulick pressed thick lips into a line as thin as the edge of a knife. His gaze went out across the swamp, across the cane and the occasional cypress trees, focused on a buzzard wheeling on lazy wings in the bright blue sky. Something about the carrion bird seemed to fascinate him. He did not look at his questioner. "You are Mark Redding, you say? Jim Redding was your brother, you say?"

"Yes," Redding answered. The way Gulick kept repeating "You say?" angered him. It sounded like Gulick was trying to make him out a liar. "He was with you and Nash on an expedition that Nash financed to explore the swamp. At least that's what he wrote me."

"Nash? Oh, yes, Nash. Nash was interested in investigating certain forms of living creatures found in the swamp. He had the theory that life originally emerged in swamps such as this millions of years ago. He thought the process might be continuing still, that somewhere in the swamps the processes of creation might be working even now, and that careful investigation might reveal new life forms emerging. Ha. Hm. You're scarcely interested in that, however. Jim Redding, you say? Let me think. What was the name of that young fellow—"

His eyes were still on the buzzard. Redding waited patiently. A step sounded behind him. It was the girl pilot of the helicopter. Gulick greeted her effusively.

"Gerry, my dear! You're looking fine, fine indeed." He slipped an arm around her, kissed her with every sign of affection. She accepted the kiss but did not respond.

"Hello, Sid," she said. "Have a nice trip?"

"Very satisfactory trip."

"Ready to go?"

"Yes, my dear. Yes, indeed. Just as soon as you get the—ah—eggbeater started, I'm ready." Opening the door of the plane, he stood aside for her to enter.

"You haven't answered my question," Redding spoke.

"Your question?" For a moment Gulick looked blank. "Oh, yes. You must excuse me for neglecting you. I'm a little absent-minded.

You're looking for—what was the name now? Jim Redding. Ah, yes. My dear," he spoke to the girl, "do you remember anybody by the name of Jim Redding who was with us in 1941? I can't seem to place the name."

The girl had one foot on the step that led to the cabin of the helicopter. She seemed to freeze in place. The knuckles on the hand that grasped the handhold turned white. Slowly she took her foot from the step, turned to Redding.

Her face was paper white. Her eyes, as blue as the sky overhead, were alive with sudden fear.

When she spoke, her voice was calm.

"Redding? At the moment I don't seem to recall anyone by that name. Was he a friend of yours?"

"My brother."

"Oh!" Fear deepened in the eyes.

"I've got it!" Gulick spoke suddenly. He snapped his fingers. "Redding was with us before the war. He left us to enter service. I remember him now. In January, I think it was, of 1942, he left us to go into the Army. Volunteered for the air forces. Fine boy, mighty fine boy. I've often wondered what happened to him. You haven't heard a word from him, you say? Too bad. So many fine young fellows—"

"He went into the Army—" Redding exploded, then caught himself. This was neither the time nor the place to reveal that Jim Redding had volunteered for service on two separate occasions, and had been turned down both times, because of a punctured eardrum and a heart murmur. Whatever had happened to him, he hadn't entered the army. No doctor on earth would ever have passed him for service.

"Sorry I can't help you any more," Gulick said, helping the girl into the 'copter. "Sorry. Please stand back now. The vanes are rather dangerous. What's this? Something for me? Ah, thank you, Jenkins."

THE STOREKEEPER had come running up to the ship. He handed an envelope to Gulick. The latter glanced at it, thrust it into his pocket without opening it.

The ship's motor roared. Vanes spinning madly, the eggbeater dragged itself into the air, moved slowly out across the swamp, then went straight as an arrow toward its unknown destination.

"I thought you said you didn't know Gulick?" Redding said.

"Gulick? Did you ask me about Gulick? I didn't understand you." Jenkins turned and walked back into his store. He slammed the door behind him.

A wind, tangy with the odor of stagnant water and Spanish moss and decay, moved across the swamp. Somewhere in that deep fastness of water and cane and tangled jungle growth, a bull alligator bellowed softly. The buzzard that Gulick had watched was wheeling in smaller circles now and was nearer the ground. A second buzzard had joined the first one.

Redding, his face tense with baffled anger, stared in the direction in which the helicopter had vanished. Gulick had lied to him. Jenkins had lied to him. Why? The girl pilot had showed sudden fear at his questions. What was she afraid of? For that matter, what was Jenkins and the two alligator hunters afraid of?

He tried to remember what his brother had told him about Sidney Gulick. It hadn't been much. Gulick was a biochemist employed by Nash, a sort of a hired hand who did routine laboratory analyses. Nash had been the important member of the expedition Jim Redding had joined. Jim's letters had been full of Nash. Redding had gotten the picture of a benevolent, wealthy old scientist, eccentric but lovable, who poked around in swamps looking for the origin of life. If anybody could give him information about his brother, Nash would be the man. Where could he find Nash? He was so busy wondering where he could find the scientist that he didn't hear the man scream.

He did hear the sound of running feet. He turned, searching for the origin of the sound. Zack, the alligator hunter, was running down the main street of Tom's Landing. Redding had seen men run with machine gun bullets zipping around them, he had seen the Supermen run from Sherman tanks—and that was really some running—but he had never seen a man run any harder than this alligator hunter. Zack's tongue was hanging out, his face was contorted as he fought for breath, he was covering more than ten feet at a single stride, and his feet were tearing up the sandy soil.

"What the devil? Oh, oh—"

Floating through the air behind Zack, keeping pace with him but apparently not able to overtake him, was a globe of shining mist the size of a basketball. It was mist and yet it wasn't mist. It looked like a ball made up of thousands of strands taken from spider webs, each single strand covered with microscopic globules of dew that glittered in the sunlight.

Zack saw Redding. "Willo!" he screamed. "Run, you fool!"

As he screamed the warning, he tripped and fell headlong.

The misty globe dived toward him.

The hunter rolled frantically, saw it hanging in the air over him, screamed again. Redding had the dazed impression that the doors of several houses had opened and as hastily slammed again as the people in them looked out to see what the shouting was about. One look was all they needed to slam and bolt the doors. No one came out to help. The sound of slamming windows rattled the air. Redding raced toward the fallen man.

Zack seemed to be doing a dozen different things at once. He was trying to get to his feet, he was trying to kick at the ball of mist, he was trying to slap at it, at the same time. The ball was following him like a hound snapping at a cornered rabbit.

Redding vehemently wished for the gun in his bag. Lacking the pistol, he slapped at the ball.

A jolt of icy numbness seared all feeling from his arm.

HISSING LIKE A FRIGHTENED SNAKE, the ball spun upward. It had no eyes but it looked at Redding and Redding knew it was looking at him. When he slapped it, it had seemed to melt away from his hand, to bounce like an extremely spongy rubber ball. Except for the numbing shock to his hand, he was not certain he had touched it.

It hung in the air, regarding him. Redding stared at it. He didn't know what to do next.

Zack scrambled to his feet.

"Run!" he hissed. "Follow me!"

He dived headlong toward the nearest shack. Redding learned later the shack belonged to the hunter. Now it merely seemed the nearest place of refuge. He followed the hunter. The shining ball of dancing mist darted after them.

Zack kicked the door open, scrambled inside. Redding was right behind him. The hunter slammed the door. It was a one-room shack with a ragged bed in one corner, a cookstove in the other, a table and several chairs between. There were two windows. Zack slammed them shut. His tortuous breathing was loud in the room. Outside the door was a hissing sound that resembled high pressure steam escaping from a small jet.

"What was that thing?" Redding demanded.

"Willo," the hunter gasped. "We—we were dead monkeys. Or I was."

"What the hell is a willo?"

Zack shook his head. "They come out of the swamp. That's all I know. You see 'em sometimes at night. First time I ever saw one in the daytime. First time I ever saw one here in town. Come here and look." He pointed out the window.

Redding looked out through the dirty glass. The willo was hanging in the air ten feet above the ground. It seemed to be resting. The microscopic points that looked like dew glittered along the strands of spider web that formed its body.

"We're safe here. They can't come through glass or through walls. Watch!"

A lean razorback hog ambled between the two houses. The ball of mist tensed when the pig came into sight. Like a panther, it seemed to be gathering itself to spring. It darted downward.

The hog didn't see it coming and probably would have paid no attention if it had seen the incredible creature in the air above it. The ball of mist settled gently on the animal. The hog stopped dead still. Something had happened to it, it didn't know what. Nose down, ears still, four feet firmly planted on the ground, it stood without moving. Either it did not know what was happening or it was paralyzed. The bail of mist seemed to sink partly into the pig. Slowly the hog's four feet spread out. The leg muscles seemed to relax gradually. The hog toppled over, did not move.

Two, three, four minutes passed. The ball of mist seemed to feed on the pig. Then it floated free. Moving with renewed energy, it darted into the air, passed above the tree tops and was gone.

A dead hog lay in the yard.

The fifteen or twenty inhabitants of the town of Tom's Landing huddled in their houses, knowing that death had walked among them. Redding went slowly out into the yard, examined the hog. There was not a mark on its body. For all he could see, the hog had just laid down and died. If he hadn't seen the tragedy happen, he would have sworn it hadn't, couldn't, happen. But the hog was dead.

"That would have been me, if I hadn't seen it coming," Zack spoke. He looked out across the swamp. His face was gray with fear.

<h2 style="text-align:center">Chapter III</h2>

Late afternoon came slowly over the swamp. Somewhere off behind the house a catbird trilled sleepily. The bull alligator was still mumbling morosely to himself off in the fastnesses of water and weeds.

"Nope," Zack said, for the fifth or sixth time. "You saved my worthless carcass and I thank you kindly for it but I ain't takin' you out in that swamp to look for anybody, not for a million dollars. You can stay here in my shack as long as you like, I'll dig up vittles for you and I'll find some corn to go along with 'em, you can have my boat or my gun or anything else I've got, but I ain't takin' you out to Gulick's island, or anywheres near it."

The hunter wiped the mouth of the jug, tilted it across his arm, let the liquor flow down his throat. He handed the jug to Redding. There was corn whiskey in the jug. Redding drank slowly.

"Why not?" he asked.

"You helped me drag that hawg off, didn't you?" the hunter answered. "Then you know why not!"

"Is that the only reason?"

"Ain't that enough reason?"

"But there may not be any more of those things and anyhow, we could outrun them. You said yourself it was possible to outrun them, that they couldn't fly very fast."

"Not out there you can't outrun 'em. And if there is only one, that's too many."

"Okay, okay," Redding agreed. "Do you know anything else about my brother?"

"Only what I told you. He was in here two or three times with Gulick and Nash. After the war started, I never saw him again. I ain't seen Nash in a couple of years."

"How do you think Jenkins got his camera?" Redding questioned.

"Mark, I don't know. That camera was in the showcase for a long time. I haven't the foggiest notion where he got it. Jenkins and Gulick have always been pretty thick. Maybe Gulick gave it to him."

The hunter was willing to talk. The fact that Redding had saved his hide had opened his mouth. He just didn't know any more. Jenkins might be able to tell him something but Jenkins wasn't talking. Gulick might know something but he wasn't talking either. That left Nash, if the scientist could be found.

"I guess I'll have to find the way myself," Redding decided.

"You can go if you want to," Zack said, a little sullenly. "But if I was you, I'd go in the other direction. That's what I'm goin' to do as soon as I can get out of here. There's plenty of other places where I can hunt gators besides Tom's Landing. Hey. What's that?"

A far-off drone was audible inside the shack. Redding went to the window and looked out. The helicopter was dropping down for another landing beside Jenkins' store. The girl was at the controls again. She brought the ungainly ship to a perfect landing, stopped the vanes, went into the store. Redding and the hunter watched her.

"I'd like to know where she fits into this picture," Redding said.

Zack shook his head. "I wouldn't know. This swamp is thick with mysteries and she's just another one that I can't figure out."

A few minutes later Redding saw the girl come out of the store. She came down the street, into the yard, knocked on the front door. Zack opened it.

"Jenkins said I could find Mr. Redding here. Could I speak to him?"

"Certainly," Redding answered for himself. "What can I do for you?"

"Mr. Gulick sent me back for you," the girl answered. "He remembered that your brother forgot some personal belongings at the island when he left. Mr. Gulick thought you might like to have them."

Redding took a deep breath while he tried to grasp the meaning of this new turn of events. Gulick had sent his helicopter back for him. Before he could answer, Zack was speaking.

"Don't you do it, Mark," the hunter said. "Don't you go near that island. Whatever your brother left there, leave it where it is. You don't need it bad enough to go after it. Let 'em bring it in here, let 'em bring it to you. Don't you go after it."

"Nonsense," Redding answered. He turned to the girl. "I'll be glad to go. Wait until I get my bag."

Ignoring the hunter's frightened warning, he picked up his bag, followed the girl out to the ship. She paused at the cabin door.

"Your friend back there gave you some good advice," she said, "Do you want to take it?"

Redding stared at her in blank astonishment. Slowly he shook his head.

"Okay. Get in," she said. Her voice was bright and hard without the slightest trace of emotion in it. Only after the ship was in the air did he see the tears running down her cheeks.

Mark Redding did not know much about girls. He had been in the army so long he scarcely remembered that women existed. The tears made him realize that this girl had been putting up a front. She had been pretending to be brave and competent, to be strong and fearless, when underneath she was just an extremely frightened little girl.

"Can I do something to help?" he asked gently.

She shot a startled glance at him out of the corner of her eyes. He got the impression that maybe this was the first time in her life anybody had offered to help her.

"You could have stayed back there at Tom's Landing," she answered. "Better still, you could have gone back north. That would have been the sensible thing to do because you can't do anything to help down here. All you can do is get yourself—" She hesitated, changed her mind about what she was going to say.

"Killed?" Redding supplied. "All I can do is get myself killed? Is that what you were about to say?"

"Yes," she bluntly answered.

Redding chuckled. "Thanks for the warning," he said. "Thirty minutes after I arrived in Tom's Landing I realized I had come to a fine place to get myself killed. *Is that what happened to my brother?*"

Like bullets out of a gun, he shot the words at her. In his mind was the grim suspicion that this girl knew more than she was telling. He hoped to startle information out of her.

It worked.

"Yes," she said. "No, no, no!" she gasped, a split second later. "I didn't mean that. I don't know—"

"I heard you the first time," Redding answered. He leaned back in his seat, stared from unseeing eyes at the swampy jungle below the slowly moving ship. So he had it. Jim was dead. The news did not exactly surprise him. He had suspected as much all along. But the confirmation of what had been only suspicions tightened a cold knot around his heart. His brother was dead.

"How did he die?"

"I—"

"Was he murdered?"

"That—"

"Who did it?"

"But—"

"Did Gulick do it?"

"I never—"

"Did Nash kill him?"

"Nash!" Surprise showed through the misery on her face. "Mr. Redding! Don't you know my name?"

"No, I don't."

"I'm Geraldine Nash. Roger Nash is my father. He didn't kill your brother. Don't you say he did. Don't you dare say it. Don't you even think it."

"Uh!" Redding gulped. So this girl was the daughter of Roger Nash! "I'm sorry," he fumbled for words. "Please forgive me, Miss Nash. I didn't have any idea that Nash was your father. All I knew was that you were here and that you obviously knew something you wouldn't tell. I'm sorry for the third-degree technique but I had to know."

"It's all right," she dabbed at her cheeks with a tiny handkerchief. "Now that you know you—can't help any—do you want me to turn around and take you back to Tom's Landing?"

"What?"

"I'll take you back. No one will ever know the difference. I'll say you had already gone."

"Thanks."

Her face lightened. "You mean I can take you back?"

"Yes," Redding answered. "You can take me back, when I know how my brother died. Do you want to tell me?"

"I—I can't—"

"You mean you won't?" he challenged.

"No, it isn't that," she flared. "I can't. There are good reasons why I can't talk to you or to anyone else. I've already told you too much."

"Oh. Perhaps the sheriff or the state police or whoever the local authorities are in this area would be able to find out for me."

"That's why you're here now," the girl answered. "To keep you from going to the authorities. The note Jenkins gave Gulick said you had bought your brother's camera and knew too much. If you hadn't bought that camera, you wouldn't have been able to prove anything and you wouldn't have been bothered. Don't you realize, Mr. Redding, that I'm taking you back to the island to keep you from taking that camera and your story to the authorities? *Now* do you want to go on or do you want me to turn back with you?"

In a dozen ways, she had tried to warn him. Redding knew she was trying to help him, she was trying to save his neck. He shrewdly suspected she was risking her own life in trying to help him. He remembered the note Jenkins had given Gulick. The latter had thrust it into his pocket without reading it. Later, when he read it, he had sent this girl back for Redding. When Jenkins had sold him the camera he hadn't known who the purchaser was. The storekeeper must have realized too late that Redding had recognized the camera. He had promptly given this information to Gulick. And Gulick had acted.

A hundred warning impulses told Redding he ought to do what Miss Nash suggested, he ought to turn back. Out there in the swamp was danger. Up ahead of them on the mysterious island that was their destination was danger. If he went ahead, his life was probably not worth a plugged dime.

He shrugged. If he turned back, he would never know. And he had lived so long with danger all around him that his senses were dulled.

"I'm going with you," he said.

She seemed to sag a little at the words but she did not reply.

"I want you to know that I appreciate what you've tried to do," he continued. "I'll be on guard."

She shook her head.

"One other thing," he added. "I think you're in trouble, serious trouble. I would like to help you, if you will let me and if I can."

A tiny smile danced on her face. "Thank you," she said. "Will you take this?"

She reached down into a compartment on the left side of the pilot's seat, pulled out a box about the size and shape of a cigarette case. It was made of aluminum.

"Put this in your pocket and keep it there. Don't let anybody see it and don't ever move out of your room without it. Put it in your pajama pocket when you go to sleep at night."

"Thanks," he said. "What is it?"

"It's a present. That's all I can tell you. And if anybody discovers you have it and asks where you got it, tell them you found it. But don't ever tell anyone that I gave it to you."

HE ACCEPTED the strange cigarette case, dubiously slipped it into his pocket. Ahead of them, out of the growing dusk, an island was emerging. A few twinkling lights glistened among the trees.

"That long low building where you see the lights is our living quarters," Gerry Nash said. "The big dark building off to the right is the laboratory. This is the island."

"Um. Quite a big place," Redding said. He was staring at the island but out of the corner of his eye he was watching something that had appeared from nowhere and was struggling desperately to keep up with the moving helicopter.

It was one of the glowing basketballs that had attacked the alligator hunter back in the town of Tom's Landing. In the dusk it looked like a dim will-o'-the-wisp that are occasionally seen floating over swampy country. Redding had never seen a will-o'-the-wisp but he had read about them.

Redding watched it, said nothing. He reached down into the bag at his side, stealthily extracted the gun and an extra clip of cartridges from it, slipped them into his pocket.

The floating ball gave up trying to keep up with the helicopter, veered off, and then suddenly vanished into the darkness.

Under Gerry Nash's skillful handling, the eggbeater dropped to a landing without a jar.

CHAPTER IV

GULICK WAS WAITING in the shadows for the helicopter to land. The vanes had barely stopped turning before he was opening the cabin door. He glanced at Redding, nodded, then spoke to the girl.

"Gerry, my dear. Come here. I want to talk to you."

Helping her from the plane, he took her arm and led her off into the darkness. Redding unashamedly followed. For once in his life, he was grateful for his army training. It had given him the ability to move with the stealth of an Indian. Many times in the past few years his life had depended on his ability to move without sound. His hunch was that this was another one of those times. When he stopped moving, he was lying under a tree in a clump of grass beside the path Gulick had taken. He could have reached out and touched the girl with his hand.

"Where are we going, Sid?" he heard Gerry Nash ask.

"To Cuba," Gulick answered. "Sometime tonight. I want the plane ready to leave at a moment's notice. From Cuba we're going into South America. Your father is in the laboratory packing the equipment he wants to take with him."

"South America!" Surprise was in the girl's voice. "We can't do that, Sid. We'll need passports."

"I have them. I arranged everything while I was away. And I have something else, Gerry!" Exultation showed in his voice. "A letter of credit for almost two million dollars. I succeeded in disposing of all the gold the submarine brought, got it transferred into dollars. When we clear out of here, my dear, we'll be taking a fortune with us. Think of that! We'll be rich!"

Redding whistled silently. Two million dollars brought here by submarine! Two million in gold! It was a fortune worth fighting for. But where had the gold come from? Why had it been brought here? Redding's mind raced madly, seeking an answer to the mysteries hidden here in the swamp. A secret laboratory, a fortune in gold, a submarine, an unwilling but strangely cowed girl, floating balls of mysterious death. What was going on here?

"But Schultz!" the girl protested. "And Wasser. What about them? They claim this gold belongs to—"

"I don't care what they claim," Gulick snapped. "They brought the gold here to pay us, didn't they? That makes it ours, doesn't it? They have no right to the gold. It's m— ours! And I intend to keep it."

"They won't like it," Gerry Nash slowly said.

"What do I care what they like?" Gulick answered. "They're not going with us."

Silence. Redding could almost hear Gerry Nash thinking.

"Sid. Does that mean—" she whispered.

"Never mind what it means!" Gulick answered. "You go get the helicopter ready."

"But—"

"Do as I say!" the biochemist snarled, his voice harsh in the darkness. "I'll take the responsibility. You just do as you're told!"

FOR AN INSTANT, Redding thought she was going to slap the man. Silently he prayed for her to tell Gulick to go to hell. If she would only smack him, tell him off—Redding silently thumbed the safety on his gun. If she would defy Gulick, he would come out of hiding and help her.

"All right, Sid," Gerry Nash answered in a voice with tears in it. But she didn't defy Gulick. Instead, she turned and walked back toward the helicopter. Gulick went in the other direction, disappearing toward the dark building that served as a laboratory.

Redding swore silently but did not move. A dark shadow lifted itself from the ground not ten feet from him, slipped furtively away toward the living quarters.

"Holy hell!" Redding thought. "Somebody else was listening in too!"

Somebody—he couldn't guess who—had also overheard Gulick and the girl.

Redding slipped back toward the plane, then walked boldly up to it. Gerry Nash was sitting in the cabin crying.

"Oh, hello," she said. "Take your bag up to the living quarters. Sam, the Negro cook, or Frances, his wife, will show you your room. Dinner will be ready soon."

Redding lifted his bag out of the ship. "Okay," he said. He glanced back at her. "You coming too?"

"I'll be along soon," she answered.

Redding pounded on the door of the long, low building that served as living quarters for whomsoever lived on this mysterious swamp island, was admitted by a ponderous colored woman, followed her heavy footsteps through what was apparently a living room into a long narrow hall.

"This be your room," she said, stopping at a door at the end of the hail. "We's fixin' to eat right away. You come out soon as you's ready."

She waddled off, apparently in the direction of the kitchen, leaving Redding to his own devices. The room contained a cot, a washstand, a chair, and a closet. It was hot and stuffy in the place. Redding went to the single window to open it. The window was nailed shut and a complete pane of glass was missing. There was no screen.

"Mosquitoes will eat me alive in here," he thought. "That is, if I stay alive long enough for the mosquitoes to get a crack at me!"

He did not doubt that he was in deadly danger. Danger brooded over this lonely swamp island like fog over the jungle. Somewhere in this place a trap was set for him. He knew too much. Because he knew too much, he was to be swept aside as one smashes a stinging mosquito. Oddly, he did not know what it was he knew that made him dangerous. Of course, he knew enough to demand an investigation. Gulick certainly did not want the state police to do any poking around on this island. And yet—what was Gulick doing here that he did not want investigated? What was the secret of this swamp island that the biochemist was so carefully hiding? What was the source of his power over Gerry Nash? Where did the two million dollars in gold fit into the picture? Where—what—he shook his head. Questions. No answers.

Nor did he get any of the answers at dinner. But he did meet Schultz and Wasser.

Gulick greeted him when he entered the dining room. "Ah, Redding. Those things that belong to your brother, I know they're here but I haven't had a chance to find them. I'll look them up tomorrow for you. In the meantime, I should like to have you consider yourself my guest."

So I am to stay tonight, Redding thought. *And tomorrow you will be gone.*

"Thank you," he said aloud. "Be glad to stay."

DINNER WAS A SILENT AFFAIR. Gulick sat at the head of the table, Gerry Nash at the end. Schultz and Wasser sat directly across from Redding. Of the mysterious scientist, Nash, there was no sign. They were served by Frances, the ponderous colored woman who had shown Redding to his room.

It was one of the strangest meals Redding had ever eaten. No one said a word.

"I saw a strange sight this afternoon," Redding ventured at last.

"Um. What was that?" Gulick asked.

Redding described the incredible ball of floating mist that had attacked the alligator hunter in Tom's Landing. He was curious to see how Gulick and the others would react to the story.

The reaction was even deeper silence than had existed before. Even the occasional scrape of silver on china faded away as if each person in the room was suddenly trying to eat as quietly as possible. Gerry Nash looked fixedly at her plate. Schultz and Wasser seemed not to have heard what he had said. Gulick frowned.

"What do you think that thing was?" Redding persisted.

"Um," Gulick answered. "Had you been drinking?"

"No, I hadn't been drinking," Redding answered. "I saw the thing. I helped drag the dead hog away."

"I have no idea what it was," Gulick answered. The tone of his voice indicated the subject was closed. Before he had finished speaking, Gerry Nash had abruptly risen and left the room. Gulick stared at her but said nothing. Two minutes later Schultz and Wasser rose and excused themselves. Gulick hastily gulped the rest of his food.

"Excuse me, Redding. Got some work that simply has to done. Make yourself right at home. You'll find some excellent books in the library. Read if you would like until you are ready to turn in."

Redding was left alone at the table.

"Would you be wishin' anything more?" the colored maid asked, entering the dining room.

"No, thanks," Redding answered. He rose from the table, lit a cigarette, went out on the porch. Around him the swamp was still. There was no sign of Schultz, Wasser, or Gulick. They had left the building and the night had swallowed them.

"I wonder where that booby trap is," Redding thought. "I wonder where it is."

He found it in his room sometime around midnight. In spite of his intention to remain awake, he had dozed. He awakened with the sound of high pressure steam in his ears, high pressure steam escaping from a tiny jet. Grim experience had taught him how to be wide awake instantly. No amount of experience would ever teach him how to control the flow of cold sweat that poured over him when he heard that high pressure hiss.

He opened his eyes a slit. And saw it. A dimly luminous ball of pale light was floating through the window. The missing pane of glass! That had been the booby trap! The glass had been deliberately removed from the window so this thing could enter!

Redding moved so fast his body was a blur of motion. In less than split seconds he was off the cot, across the room, and had the doorknob in his hand. Zack had said these things couldn't pass through walls. With the door behind him, he would be safe.

The knob wouldn't turn as he twisted it. He shook it savagely, realized then that the door was locked.

Somebody was making damned certain he wouldn't escape!

Feeling like a rat in a trap, he dropped flat on the floor. As he fell he was reaching for the gun in his pocket. He had lain down with all his clothes on. The gun was in his pocket. He yanked it free, thumbed the safety off, knowing that even if bullets would stop the creature that had come out of the night, it was already too late to use them. Deep in his mind his sense of time was telling him he ought to be paralyzed, he ought to be dead, by now. He might have beaten the floating basketball to the door, but when he couldn't open the door, it should have struck him instantly.

It hadn't struck him. It wasn't even trying to strike him. He gasped in astonishment when he saw what it was doing.

It was trying to escape from him! It was inside the room but instead of attacking him, it was dashing madly from corner to corner seeking a way out. The hiss of its motion was shrill with—fear!

It was afraid of him. It was trying to get away. It darted back and forth, apparently so crazed with fear that it had forgotten the window where it had entered. Redding didn't move. In his mind was the thought that his life had been saved by a miracle. As he watched, the ball remembered the window, darted down to it, hissed out into the night. He caught a glimpse of it burning the wind as it lifted over the trees.

He crept silently to the window, peered out.

"Mr. Redding," a faltering voice whispered. "Are—are you all right?"

The whisper came from under his window. Out there in the darkness, Gerry Nash was speaking to him.

CHAPTER V

"WHAT MAKES YOU THINK I wouldn't be all right?" Redding said. There was savagery in his voice and he made no attempt to conceal or control it. He was still badly scared. Somebody had tried to kill him. He was not at all certain that Miss Gerry Nash did not have something to do with the creature that had been in his room. In his present shaken mental condition, he was not certain of anything. "Why wouldn't I be all right?" he repeated.

"I'm so glad!" she answered. "I got here as quickly as I could but I saw it leave just as I arrived. I didn't know until I saw it leave—"

"You didn't know what?" Redding interrupted. He was standing at the edge of the window taking care not to expose himself. The gun covered the spot where her voice was coming from.

"I didn't—didn't know what was going to happen to you."

"But when you saw that floating death ball leave, you knew all right?" "Y—es. That is—"

"Then you know what that thing is!"

"Y—es."

Redding laughed, a sound without mirth in it. "I suppose you're going to tell me next that you came here to save me from it!"

"Y—es," she faltered. The scorn in his voice was stinging her. "That is—you weren't in any danger."

"No? I saw what one of those things did to a hog. You tell me they're not dangerous."

"They're dangerous all right," she admitted. "They're a hundred times as deadly as a rattlesnake. But *you* weren't in any danger, not from it."

"No?" Her sureness shook him. He was being unfair and he knew it, but he was still so badly scared he couldn't completely control his reactions.

"It didn't attack you, did it?"

"After it got into the room, it tried to get away, didn't it?"

"How did you know?" he faltered. "Were you watching?"

"No. I saved you from the gas balls this afternoon."

"What?"

"The little aluminum box that looks like a cigarette case," the girl explained. "No gas ball will even come near you as long as you're carrying that."

"Huh?" Redding grunted. Until this moment he had completely forgotten the little aluminum box. He felt hastily in his pocket. It was still there. "You mean this box saved me from that thing? How the devil could it?"

"That box contains an ultra high-frequency miniature radio transmitter. I have one of them, Sid—all of us have them. We couldn't work with the gas balls without them. Occasionally the gas balls escape. One of them would kill all of us if we didn't carry the little radio transmitters to drive them away."*

"Holy hell!" Redding breathed. They *worked* with the luminous balls! The monstrosities belonged here on this island!

---

* *Radio Death Rays:—The radiations from the miniature radio transmitters were in effect death rays to the gas balls. The life energy of the gas balls was a radio frequency vibration high in the ultra frequency ranges. The radiations from the tiny transmitters disrupted the functioning of this vital life process of the gas balls and drove them away from the transmitters.—ED.*

The implications back of her words made his mind reel. She was speaking again.

"Listen, Mr. Redding, I haven't time to explain everything. I came to get you. We've got to get away from this island and we've got to do it right away!"

"You came to get me!" Somewhere inside of him he was aware of a warm feeling. She had come to help him. That was good. In giving him the little radio transmitter in the aluminum box, she had already saved his neck once. The good feeling grew. There were questions that went with it, lots of questions, but they could wait until later. For the moment at least, he was convinced of the honesty of Gerry Nash's intentions. Whatever part she was playing in this amazing adventure, he felt, in this moment at least, that she was on his side.

"Wait a minute," he answered.

The lower window frame had four panes of glass in it. One was missing. The door was locked. The window was nailed down. He snatched the blanket from the cot, stuffed part of it out through the opening where the pane was missing, grasped the frame in the middle, pulled vigorously. The breaking panes of glass, muffled by the blanket, made very little noise as they fell inward. He stepped through the shattered window, dropped lightly to the ground.

"Okay," he said. "Where do we go now? You know this place. You'll have to lead the way."

"We'll take the 'copter," Gerry Nash's suddenly soft voice answered. "Sid may hear it start but we'll be gone before he can stop us."

She turned, tugged at his hand for him to follow her.

"One question," Redding's voice stopped her. "This evening, no matter how much you seemed to dislike it, you obeyed Sidney Gulick's orders. Tonight you're running away from him."

"Early this evening my father was alive," she answered. "Now he's dead."

Pain and hurt and fatigue were in her voice, all the pain in the world. She was suddenly a little girl, a very frightened little girl, crying in the darkness.

"I'm sorry," Redding said gently. "I did not know."

"For over three years Gulick has held my father prisoner on this island. I obeyed him, because I knew what would happen to my father if I didn't obey. Now my father is dead and I no longer have to obey."

"Oh," Redding said. Sympathy and understanding welled up in him, found expression in the single syllable that he spoke. At last he understood why this girl had obeyed Sidney Gulick. The biochemist had been holding her father a prisoner. She either did what he told her to do, or else! Redding had been inside Germany long enough to know how easy it was to hold someone prisoner and from that fact to command the unquestioning obedience of the prisoner's relatives.

"I'm sorry," Redding whispered. "I'm very sorry. I did not know. Did Gulick—your father—"

"My father died the same way your brother died—because somebody tampered with the radio transmitter that protected him from the gas balls."

"Somebody!"

"I don't know who. I only suspect. Your brother objected to the use Gulick proposed to make of the gas balls my father discovered. After he objected, he died. Of course it could have been an accident, but—"

"He died," Redding said. "That's the important thing: he died." The old savagery had crept back into his voice.

"I'll tell you the whole story later," Gerry Nash whispered. "But we've got to get out of here, and we've got to do it right away, or we may never get out."

Desperate urgency was in her voice. She tugged at his hand. Redding followed her.

Sitting in the little clearing that served as a landing field, the helicopter was a shadow that looked like a Rube Goldberg invention. A gas ball darted over them as they approached it, veered down, then fled away as the radiations from the miniature radio transmitters repelled it.

"Some time I want you to tell me all about those things," Redding said, involuntarily ducking.

"Later," Gerry Nash answered hastily. She opened the door of the ship, slid into the pilot's seat. Redding slipped into the seat beside her.

The starter ground. And ground. And ground.

The motor refused to start. "Something's wrong," the girl whispered. "I'll look."

Jerking a flashlight from its holder beside the seat, she lifted the cover off the motor. The flashlight beam poked into the mechanism.

"The distributor arm is gone," Gerry Nash said.

"Gone?" Redding echoed.

"Somebody removed it. Somebody who didn't want this ship to take off."

Rising above the fatal words, Redding heard the sound of running feet coming up the path from the laboratory.

He swung himself out of the cabin, dropped to the ground beside the plane, rolled in the other direction.

A flashlight beam stabbed through the darkness, clearly revealed Gerry Nash as she stood up beside the motor.

Chapter VI

"What's going on here?" Sidney Gulick demanded. His flashlight covered Gerry Nash. Redding, lying flat on the ground, could see the gun glinting behind it. Gulick was interested in the girl. Redding began to crawl.

"Sid!" Gerry gasped. "Where did you come from?"

"I heard someone trying to start the helicopter—"

"I'll take the gun," Redding said.

With the muzzle of his own pistol he jabbed Gulick so hard in the back that the bones creaked. Reaching around him, he jerked the pistol from the biochemist's grasp, stepped back, a gun in each hand.

"If you move before I tell you to, I guarantee your guts will be so full of holes in thirty seconds that they will leak forever. Just stand still, Sid. That's all you have to do."

Over his shoulder Redding called. "Gerry. Come and get his light."

Gulick appeared dazed as she took the flashlight from his shaking fingers.

"Surprised to see me?" Redding said. "You thought I was dead, didn't you? Ain't it too damned bad I'm not!"

"Where—where did you come from?" Gulick stuttered.

"That's the sixty-four dollar question, Sid. Where did I come from? And here's the $128.00 question, Sid: Where is that distributor arm?"

"Wh—what?"

"Don't stall. I'd like nothing better than to save the State the expense of hanging you. Produce that distributor arm. Miss Nash and I are clearing out of here. Of course, now that you've come along, we'll take you with us—but not to Cuba, Sid, not to Cuba tonight. Something tells me that if you ever get to Cuba it will be in the spirit world. Where is that distributor arm?"

"I—I don't know what you're talking about."

"The hell you don't! You fixed the ship so nobody would leave here without you. A little insurance to protect you if anything went wrong, eh, Sid? Where is that arm? I'll give—"

Sock!

Something hit Redding from behind, descending with crushing force.

Men who live through battles often find they have developed a sense of danger, a feeling that they had better duck at the right time. Redding had lived through many battles but he didn't need his keenly developed sense of danger here. The sound of a stealthy step behind him told him the blow was coming. He rolled with it. The club knocked him head over heels, splintered his vision with thousands of shooting stars, dazed him, but did not knock him out. He rolled like a tenpin hit by a bowling ball and he did not get to his feet, but when he stopped rolling and sat up, he was shooting.

The shadow that had hit him ducked. Gerry Nash screamed and threw the flashlight at it. It ducked again. Redding took a second snap shot at it. The shadow hit the ground.

Gulick ran like a fool. The second after the first shot split the night, he was gone—toward the laboratory.

Redding shot at the ground where the shadow had fallen. He had seen too many men hug the ground when bullets were coming at them, hit the dirt when they weren't hit, to believe that his dazed aim, shaky from the blow on the head, he had scored a hit. He shot again.

Over in the dark shadow of the trees at the edge of the little landing field, a machine pistol let go. The air around Redding sounded like it was being torn as the slugs ripped through it.

REDDING THREW HIMSELF FLAT on the ground. He got a mouthful of dirt as a bullet hit the sandy soil inches in front of his face. He fired at the flash of the machine pistol.

The pistol abruptly was silent. He couldn't tell whether or not he had hit the man who held it. All he knew was that it was silent.

"Gerry!" he whispered.

"Yes," she answered from somewhere in front of him.

"Crawl back along the path," he ordered. "I'll cover for you."

He heard the rustle of her body as she slid along the ground. Redding waited. Far off in the swamps a bull alligator was bellowing. The night wind sighed through the scrub pines beside the clearing. The helicopter was still a Rube Goldberg invention in the night.

Redding slipped a fresh clip of cartridges into his pistol. Somewhere in the clearing he could hear a man crawling stealthily. The man was going farther away. Redding began to edge along the ground following the girl. He did not dare risk giving that machine pistol another chance at him. He had seen one of those pistols cut a man in two with the murderous stream of bullets it threw.

"Gerry," he whispered.

"Yes," she answered.

"You all right."

"I'm alive. But my nervous system will never recover."

"Who the devil was it that hit me with the club? And who was using that machine pistol?"

"Schultz," she answered. "I caught a glimpse of him as he hit you. That was Wasser with the pistol."

"Holy hell!" he muttered. "They were trying to help Gulick."

"I don't think so," Gerry Nash said. "I think they know that Gulick intended to leave them here, with you, and my dad. I think they're the ones who removed the distributor arm, so nobody could use the helicopter without them."

"I still don't get it," he frowned. "Who are they? Scientists who were helping your father?"

"Hardly," she answered. "I don't question their technical ability but they weren't helping dad. They're a couple of agents sent over by the Nazis to buy the gas balls from Gulick. Using someone in South America, he got in touch with the Germans, told them what he had, offered to sell. Schultz and Wasser came over by submarine to investigate. They saw the gas balls would be an extremely powerful weapon—thousands of those things sprung in a surprise attack would demoralize an opposing army—but the war ended before they could return to Germany with their information. Schultz and Wasser are still here."

"Hell on earth!" Redding whistled. "A couple of Nazis. And I thought I had heard and seen everything! That's where the gold came from that Gulick has."

"Yes. They paid off in gold but he has had a lot of trouble getting it changed into more negotiable currency. The government asks questions if you try to turn gold in at a bank these days. Gulick would have been gone long ago if he could have managed to convert the gold into money he could use. But—" she seemed mildly perplexed. "—How did you know about the gold?"

"I eavesdropped," he answered. He told her how he had listened to her conversation with Gulick when she first brought him to the island. "And there was someone else listening too," he added, suddenly remembering something that had risen from the ground.

"Probably Schultz or Wasser," Gerry Nash said. "That's how they knew Gulick was planning to leave tonight."

"Hm. Can either of them fly that helicopter?"

"No. They're tricky things to handle. I'm the only pilot here."

"Then it stacks up like this," Redding said slowly. "They've got the distributor arm, but they can't fly the ship. We've got the pilot, but we haven't got the missing distributor arm, so we can't fly. It's a stalemate. Gulick can't take a hand in the game because he has neither the pilot nor the missing part. We're all marooned here and we're all just begging for the chance to cut each other's throat. What a fine setting for murder!"

The night wind went whispering through the scrub pines.

"What about a boat?" Redding asked. "If there is a boat around, we could use it to get away."

"There's a launch," Gerry Nash answered. Hope suddenly sounded in her voice. "We might—if we don't get lost in these blasted swamps—"

"Lead me to the launch," he said. "I'll take a chance on getting lost."

"The launch is tied up at the little dock on the other side of the laboratory," Gerry said. "Come on."

THE LABORATORY was a dark shadow huddled close to the ground. They moved silently toward it. As they drew near, a luminous ball of light suddenly appeared over the building.

Redding dived for the ground, then sheepishly got to his feet.

"Sorry. My reflexes are working a little too good tonight. When I see danger I hit the dirt first and think afterwards. I keep forgetting those things can't harm us. Hello! There's another one. I won't duck this time."

A second gas ball had leaped up over the building. It gyrated, dancing like some monstrous hound exulting because it has been freed from the leash.

Behind it came a third one. Then a fourth! A fifth. The air was full of the things. Redding stared at them. He could smell danger. "What the hell—"

"Sid has turned them loose," Gerry Nash swiftly said. "They're bred there in the laboratory. There's hundreds of them in there and he's turned them all loose. I wonder why?"

Uneasiness had crept into her voice. "They can't hurt us. They can't touch us. They won't come near us—" Suddenly her voice was frantic.

"Check your radio generator. Is it working all right. Here! Let me have it."

She jerked the cover from the little aluminum box, held it to her ear. "It's dead. The batteries are worn out. Mark! Mark! We've got to get under cover. Those things—"

"How about your generator?" he demanded.

She fumbled inside her dress for It, pulled it out, jerked the cover off.

Her voice was hollow with fear.

"It's dead too. Mark, this isn't an accident. Gulick did this. He changed batteries on every miniature transmitter on the island. He planned to turn the gas balls loose and kill us all. He was going to kill all of us tonight, including me!"

"Back inside the living quarters!" Redding snarled. "Back while we have the chance."

Chapter VII

Before they reached the clearing that served as a landing field for the helicopter, a gas ball came up the path behind them. They ducked into the brush. It did not see them. Redding watched it float on up the path. At the clearing it zoomed high in the air, hung poised there like a hawk watching a rabbit on the ground below, then, again like a hawk, it dived straight down, a flaming streak splitting the darkness.

The night was suddenly hideous with the sound of a man screaming.

"It got someone," Redding whispered.

"Schultz or Wasser," Gerry answered. "Their radio transmitters aren't working either, but they didn't know it—until now!"

The screams stopped as suddenly as they had begun.

"We—we should have warned them," Gerry whispered.

"I should warn a Nazi he's going to die!" Redding grunted. "I spent too long killing them, trying to keep them from killing me, to care if the gas balls get every damned Nazi on earth. Come on. We've got to get under cover."

Over the laboratory the darkness was bright with the floating gas balls. They had gone into a sort of a dance. The darting,
spinning, whirling luminous balls would have been beautiful if
they had not been so monstrous.

"Can he get those things back in the cage after he's turned
them loose?" Redding asked, as they slipped silently toward the
house.

"Sometimes they come back. More often they don't. Once
they're turned loose, they do what they please."

"Well, all I can say is, with those things loose, times are going
to be mighty tough in this swamp. There will be dead hunters,
dead trappers, dead fishermen, from here to Miami. When those
things start running up in the resorts, there will be the damnedest stampede north this country ever saw!"

"They won't live long," Gerry Nash answered. "The first hard
thunderstorm will kill them. That's something Gulick never told
the Nazis, you can bet, when they came here to see what he had.
He took their money all right but he didn't tell Schultz and Wasser that the violent electromagnetic disturbances—static, you
call it in your radio—resulting from lightning tears the gas balls
to pieces. Lightning affects them the same way the little radio
transmitters do. Radiations from the little transmitters merely
drive them away. Lightning, being much stronger, kills them.
The first hard thunderstorm that comes along will clear them
out of the swamp."

"Then all we have to do is pray for rain," Redding said, looking up. Overhead a million stars sparkled in the black vault of
heaven. There was not a cloud in sight.

"Here's the house. We'll go in through the kitchen and wake
up Sam and Frances and warn them."

In the kitchen they discovered they would never warn the
Negro cook and his fat wife. Both were stretched cold and lifeless on
the floor. A swift examination disclosed what had happened. The
protective miniature radio transmitters each carried were dead.

"If I needed anything to prove Gulick planned to kill us all,
this does it," Gerry Nash said slowly. "The batteries in these
little sets will last thirty-six hours. There were two sets of trans-

mitters for everyone. We got a fresh transmitter every evening at 6 o'clock. Daddy changed the batteries every afternoon and brought the sets up here for us to pick up. Every morning he took the old sets back to the laboratory. All Gulick had to do was to put worn-out batteries in the sets, then turn the gas balls loose. We would never know we didn't have any protection—until we were dead."

REDDING CAREFULLY CLOSED the kitchen door. "Well, we're here. The gas balls can't get in. Gulick is down at the laboratory. I'll bet the batteries in *his* protective transmitter are all right. Somewhere outside there is one dead Nazi and one live Nazi who probably has a machine pistol. We can't go outside. Gulick can't come inside, not while I have a gun. The gas balls can't come in either. Is there food and water in here?"

"Plenty of both," Gerry said.

"Then all we have to do is stay inside until the next thunderstorm kills off the gas balls. After they're gone, I can go outside and give Sidney Gulick a lesson in stalking. Oh, no. Too bad you can't come in but the windows and doors are closed."

He was speaking to the gas ball that had come up to the window. It hung in the darkness outside the panes of glass like a cat at a rat hole.

"Sure, I'll admit I'm a rat," Redding murmured. "But even rats like to stay alive."

Spang! Off in the night a rifle barked. Before he heard the sound of the gun, Redding heard something more horrible—the tinkle of broken glass.

The bullet hit the opposite wall. Redding ignored it. In front of his eyes, a window pane had exploded. The gas ball was already moving toward the opening left by the broken glass.

Redding grabbed Gerry Nash, jerked her through the door that led into the butler's pantry. From the pantry a second door opened into the dining room. They stood in the hot stuffy darkness, scarcely daring to breathe. Through the closed kitchen door they could hear the hiss of high pressure steam escaping. The gas ball had entered the kitchen.

Off in the darkness the rifle barked again. Again the explosion was followed by the rattle of breaking glass.

"It's Gulick," Redding breathed. "He knows we're in here. He's shooting out the windows, so the gas balls can come in and get us."

Gerry Nash's frightened breathing was the only sound.

Again the rifle spoke.

"Why I didn't kill him when I had the chance, I'll never know," Redding whispered. "He stays out there and shoots the windows out, and we stay in here and wait. Sooner or later he's bound to knock the window out of this pantry—"

He didn't want to think what would happen after that.

"Will a bullet stop those gas balls?" he questioned.

He felt rather than saw the shake of her head.

"Will anything stop them?" he continued.

"Nothing on earth except radio frequency radiations."

Redding sighed. He could feel sweat running down his face, he could feel it running down his chest.

He opened the door to the kitchen a crack, peeped through, hastily slammed it shut.

"It's still out there," he said.

"I know," Gerry answered. "I can hear it."

"Gerry, what are those things? Where did they come from? Maybe, if you tell me all about them, I can think of something."

"They are, or their remote ancestors were, will-o'-the-wisps," Gerry Nash said. "My father—I guess you don't know about him—was a scientist, one of the greatest of them all. He was a biologist who spent his life investigating life forms. It was his hope, his dream, that new life forms were still evolving here on earth. Somewhere in some swamp he thought he could find a place where life was coming into existence, where inert atoms were building up into live molecules, the molecules in turn building up into complex living substance. That's all life is—a subtle electro-chemical reaction. I'm talking of the mechanics of living matter now, not the spirit. He didn't find what he was seeking but he did discover the will-o'-the-wisps."

THE RIFLE BARKED AGAIN, talking of exploding violence in the darkness. The tinkle of falling glass answered the report of the gun.

"Go on," Redding urged. As long as she talked, she wouldn't be thinking.

"Will-o'-the-wisps have been seen around swamps for centuries. Superstitious people thought they were ghosts. Another explanation was that they were balls of marsh gas. My father found a few of them here and began to study them. He discovered the things were alive."

"The devil!" Redding said.

"They're really not gas at all," Gerry Nash continued. "They're charged electric fields and they're true parasites that they draw the source of their energy from living creatures. They kill by sucking every tiny bit of electrical energy out of living bodies. My father spent years studying them. By careful breeding he managed to develop a new strain, much more agile and more deadly than the original will-o'-the-wisps. He wasn't trying to create a deadly killer; he was just trying to find out how the things worked. They can move against gravity: he wanted to know how they did that. They are intelligent in some weird way: he wanted to know how their intelligence worked. It was his dream that by studying the will-o'-the-wisps he could make a great and lasting contribution to human progress."

She sounded very sad. Something of her father's dream was in her. Outside in the night every crack of Gulick's rifle was bringing closer the time when her father's life work would destroy her. Roger Nash had never dreamed of that!

"I'm sorry," Redding said softly. "I see now why Jim thought your father was a wonderful man. I wish I could have known him."

"You would have loved him."

The rifle cracked again. Gulick had moved around to the other side of the house and was breaking the windows there. He didn't know in what room they were hiding. He only knew they were somewhere inside the building. If he broke all the windows, he couldn't miss.

"I've been thinking," Redding said. "There's a table here. Why can't I use it to board up the window? Then when he breaks it, our little friends won't come boiling through. Will that help us any, do you think?"

"Mark! Why didn't I think of that instead of sitting here like a ninny! Of course it will help. They can't go in through any solid substance."

Working frantically, he tore the top from the table, fitted it against the window. Boards from the cupboard plugged up the openings at the sides and the top.

They settled down in the darkness to wait. Even if the gas balls couldn't get into the room, Redding knew their fate was only a question of time.

Crack! The window in the pantry tinkled as a bullet hit it. Gulick had moved back to their side of the house. They could hear the soft hiss of the gas balls outside, could catch vague glimpses of them in the cracks around the window, but the hideous monstrosities could not get into the room.

Redding sighed. He began to hope they would see the sun rise again.

The rifle was silent. Now and then they could hear Gulick moving around outside. They kept as quiet as mice. Then Redding smelled smoke.

"I've been thinking," Gerry Nash said. "Sam always kept a flashlight here in the pantry."

Redding wasn't listening. He sniffed again. There was no mistaking the odor. Now he could hear the faint crackle of flames

"Gerry," he whispered. "Gulick has set the building on fire. We're not only rats in a trap but the trap is going to turn into a furnace."

Chapter VIII

The odor of smoke was strong in the room now.

"I'm going out there," Redding said. "I can outrun those gas balls, or dodge them, long enough to get Gulick—"

"Wait a minute," the girl protested.

"We don't have many minutes left," he answered.

"Let me see! Dad used tiny little cells no bigger than a lead pencil. He used two of them in each set. They furnished three volts—"

Redding rose to his feet. "We're going out," he said.

"We can't go out, not without protection from the gas balls."

"We can't stay here, not without asbestos suits," he grimly answered.

"But I tell you Sam—"

There were shelves on each side of the pantry. She was rummaging through them.

"Light a match," she whispered. "Quick!"

Redding lit the match. Gerry snatched at the flashlight the flickering flame revealed, squealed with joy. "Mark! Give me your miniature transmitter. There isn't a second to lose. Quick! Give it to me."

She snatched it from his fingers, tore her fingernails prying the cover off. "Light another match. Keep on lighting them. Find a piece of paper and light it. I've got to see."

There was a magazine lying on the shelf over the cabinets. Redding snatched a page from it, rolled it into a tube, lit the end. By the tiny light from this flickering torch, he watched what Gerry Nash was doing.

From clips inside the miniature transmitter, she gently removed two little dry cells, each about as big as a pencil and about half an inch in length. Then she screwed the end from the flashlight, slid the cells out of it, and Redding realized what she was trying to do.

Gerry was trying to substitute the good cells from the flashlight for the dead cells in the protective radio transmitter.

"Good girl!" Redding whispered. "If that will only work! But how are you going to fit those flashlight batteries into the transmitter? They're three times as big as the little cells that came out, too big to fit inside the case."

"I'm going to tape them on the outside of the case and run wires from them to the terminals on the inside. Tape? I haven't any tape!" She glanced frantically around the room. "I've got to have something— Mark! Give me your shirt. I'll tear strips from it. Here, I'll hold the light."

Redding probably bettered the world's record in getting his coat and shirt off. She snatched it from his hands, ripped inch-wide strips from it.

Smoke was flowing through the cracks in the door that led to the kitchen. Gulick had set the fire at the back end of the house. Through the cracks at the window, Redding was beginning to catch glimpses of the trees outside. The air in the pantry was getting hot and heavy with smoke. Redding coughed, rolled another page of paper into a tube, lit the end. Gerry Nash worked.

This girl was a first-class technician. She didn't have any tools except a bobby pin and a knife that Redding supplied but she knew her way around inside the miniature transmitter. Redding realized she must have had a first-class technical education. In addition, she had unquestionably helped her lather with his experiments.

She needed wire. Six inches of wire was enough but there was no wire in the pantry. She got the wire she needed from her own protective transmitter.

"Hey!" Redding protested.

She didn't answer. Taping two of the flashlight cells to the back of the little aluminum case, she tied the contacts into place, held the device to her ear. A soft, almost out of hearing hum, was dimly audible. Her eyes glinted.

"It works," she said.

Slipping the cover into place, she bound it into position with another strip of cloth, then handed the generator to Redding.

"Here," she said.

Redding stared at her. "What about your generator?" he demanded. "What about fixing it up too?"

"There are only enough batteries for one. Anyhow I had to use wire out of mine to fix this one. You take it. It will protect you. I'll try to slip out—"

"Not this century!" Redding exploded. "I go out and save my neck and you stay here and burn to death!"

"I'll be all right, Mark. I feel I let you get into this—"

"*You* let me get into this!"

"Yes. I didn't have to bring you out here. I could have come back and said I couldn't find you."

"Gerry," Redding said softly. "Remind me sometime to tell you what I think of you. Right now all I can say is you're talking nonsense. We're in this together. Together, you understand. Will this generator protect both of us?"

"Yes, but—"

"But what?"

"We'll have to stay within two or three feet of each other. We'll be tied together. I'll be like a ball and chain around you. You can't move without me—"

"I can't imagine anything I would like better. Come on."

"But Gulick is out there. You'll have to move freely."

"So Gulick is out there," Redding answered. "And he has a gun." There was a thoughtful note in his voice. He reached for his coat, took out of the pocket the gun he had taken from Gulick at the helicopter. "Here. You take this gun. You take the generator. If I get shot. . . . No, don't try to argue me out of it. The generator ties us together. If I get shot, you run. You'll have a chance this way."

He pressed the protective transmitter into one hand, the gun into the other. She took the pistol readily enough but she didn't want to take the generator. Redding pushed open the door that led to the dining room. A gas ball swirled toward him.

He faced the luminous monstrosity. There was no point in trying to evade it. If the hastily improvised transmitter wouldn't protect them, they might as well die now.

The ball darted at them. Then, as it felt the subtle radiations from the little transmitter, it shot up to the ceiling, pulled back from them.

Redding sighed. "We're over that hurdle," he whispered. "Come on."

They went out the front door of the building. Flames leaping high over the kitchen threw grotesque dancing shadows on the ground. A gas ball saw them, darted at them, drew back before the radiations from the transmitter, followed along above them. Trying to keep in the shadow from the burning building, they raced for the trees, running hand in hand. If Gulick saw them, he did not chance a shot in their direction.

They reached the trees, dived out of sight among them.

"Gerry!" Redding exulted. "We've made it! We're out of the furnace and we've got protection from the gas balls."

"'Alten!" a harsh voice said near them. "Don't move. A machine pistol covering you I have got!"

"Schultz!" Gerry Nash gasped.

The Nazi agent was invisible in the darkness but Redding did not doubt the machine pistol was trained on them.

"Hah!" the Nazi grunted. "Those guns, drop."

Redding hesitated.

"I shoot!"

REDDING LET his pistol slide from his hand. He heard Gerry's gun thud softly on the ground.

"Hah! Waiting I have been for Gulick to roast you two out of there. You, Geraldine, you I want. You can fly the plane."

"Schultz!" Gerry Nash gasped. "I thought—"

"You thought I was dead? No. Wasser is dead. When I saw him die, I realized something was wrong. Only a minute was needed to detect what it was. Then, naturally, I substituted flashlight batteries the dead cells for."

The German was no fool. He, too, had discovered that his protection was gone and had taken steps to remedy that defect.

"Now, we must go," Schultz continued. "But first, Geraldine, stand aside for one moment."

"What?"

"Stand aside."

"What for?"

"He wants you to stand aside so he can shoot me," Redding said. "He doesn't want the helicopter overburdened. Well—"

Crack!

Off in the darkness Gulick's rifle spoke again.

The bullet pinged within feet of them.

Schultz let go with the machine pistol, firing at the flash of Gulick's rifle. The rifle bullet had startled him. Automatically, without stopping to think, he answered the shot.

Like a leaping cat, Redding dived at him. The flash of the pistol revealed where Schultz was hiding. Aiming at the hand that held the gun, he struck downward with all the strength in his arms.

He hit the Nazi's wrist, knocked the gun from his hand.

"Donner—"

Redding was behind him, one arm around his throat, yanking him backward. They fell heavily.

The miracle was that the fall did not break Schultz' neck. It didn't. It didn't break Redding's hold either. It enabled him to jerk his elbow up under the German's chin, lock his hands together in the terrible strangle hold that is either broken quickly or has only one ending.

Schultz arched his back, tried to leap upward. He tried to kick backward, he clawed fiercely at Redding, pulled his hair, tried to find an eye to gouge. His breath was coming in great gasping sobs. Redding held grimly on. His biceps muscle was directly across the other's windpipe. He tightened his grip. Schultz stopped breathing, then a little by little he stopped struggling, and lay still. Redding held on. Only when the other's body was dead weight in his arms did he release his grip.

"Gerry?"

"Yes."

"Stay here with this monkey. If he revives, crack him on the head with your gun."

Redding was already searching through the Nazi's clothes for the protective transmitter. He found it. Flashlight batteries were wired across the back. He searched for the gun he had dropped, found it.

"Remember, if he moves, bop him. Let him have it, hard," he said.

"I'll keep him quiet," she promised. Redding disappeared into the darkness.

"Good luck," her whisper followed him.

There, Redding thought, is a woman! She didn't ask him any questions, she didn't try to hold him back. She said, "Good luck," and let him go, and she knew where he was going.

THE WHOLE BACK END of the living quarters was on fire now, the crackling flames curling upward in long tongues of yellow blaze. The gas balls seemed to be attracted to the fire. They were circulating over the entire area, globes of light revealed them drifting above the trees, slipping along a loot above the ground, but always they came back to the burning house as though fascinated by the heat or the light. They never entered the flames but occasionally one would dart upward with a tongue of blaze. They seemed to think the flames were alive, and possibly prey.

Redding watched the weird dance around the house. He shivered, then turned resolutely away. Somewhere within a circle not over two hundred yards in diameter, was Gulick. If he was looking for Gulick, Gulick was also looking for him.

In a hard school, Redding had learned to crawl silently. Keeping flat on the ground, he slipped away from the burning house. He wanted to get out into the darkness and look in toward the blaze. Then, when the biochemist moved, his body would be silhouetted against the flame, an easy target. Once he had located the biochemist, the stalk could begin.

Fallen logs, wiry grass, brush, barred his way. He crawled over or around the logs, the grass he crawled through, the brush he went around. Always he used his fingers to feel the way ahead of him. They were sensitive antennae, revealing obstructions, enabling him to move in absolute silence.

Under an old pine tree his probing fingers revealed a six-inch-in-diameter fallen limb ahead of him. A split second before the limb moved, he knew this limb hadn't fallen from any tree. It wasn't a limb. It was a man's leg.

Gulick had been sitting with his back against the pine tree, quietly waiting for his enemy to reveal himself outlined against the light of the burning house. Redding had crawled directly into him before either realized the other's presence.

Redding's pistol flashed upward.

Gulick kicked him in the face.

Redding dropped the pistol. He dived at Gulick's legs. The rifle thundered over his shoulder as he hit. His arms went around the biochemist's middle.

Gulick grunted. He tried to strike downward with the rifle barrel but Redding's head was buried in his chest, too close to use the barrel. He used the butt. Stars exploded inside Redding's head. He held on, shoved forward.

Gulick tripped, fell. Redding landed on top of him. The gun flew out of Gulick's hands. His fingers reached for Redding's eyes. Redding's fingers closed around his throat.

For a man with fat on him, Gulick had amazing strength. He grabbed Redding's wrists, broke the grip on his throat. Threshing on the ground, they struggled in the darkness. Each knew that no quarter would be asked and none given. Redding could hear Gulick breathing heavily. The biochemist rolled. Redding ended up on the bottom. Gulick tried to jerk loose. He managed to get to his feet. Redding realized the biochemist was trying to get away. He grabbed him around the legs, threw him heavily.

Gulick grunted. Redding grabbed him around the middle. In the side pocket of Gulick's coat, he could feel a hard, flat object like a cigarette case.

Gulick never did know what happened. To him, it seemed that he was able to wrench free from the arms that were holding him. Freedom was what he was seeking. He had lost his rifle but there was another rifle in the laboratory. He knew he didn't have a chance in a rough and tumble fight against the iron-hard man who fought so silently and with such ferocious strength. If he could get away and get the rifle—

When he managed to wrench himself free, he ran, stumbling through the darkness. Suddenly shots sounded behind him. Heavy slugs drilled the air around him, thudded into trees, screamed as they bounced off. He knew Redding had found a gun and was shooting at him. He ran faster.

The gas ball came down from over the trees and dropped on him. He screamed. And screamed again. Amazed, incredulous terror was in those screams. The gas ball fastened on to him, seeped into his body—

Redding lowered the smoking pistol. He listened to the screams. He saw a second gas ball follow the first, a third follow the second. Then they came in droves, diving downward like hawks screaming after their prey.

The screams sobbed into sudden silence.

Redding stood without moving. He looked down at the little flat cigarette case in his hand. It was a protective radio transmitter. He had stolen it from Gulick's pocket while they were struggling.

"He never knew I had it," he whispered. "He never knew I had his protection. . . . I wonder if he ever knew he got exactly what was coming to him—"

Flames from the burning house leaped higher into the sky. Most of the gas balls had left the flames now. They were all clustered around a certain spot off at the edge of the darkness. Redding watched in silence, then turned and walked back to where Gerry Nash waited. He walked erect, making no effort to move quietly. She was still waiting.

* * *

LATER, WHEN THE HELICOPTER LIFTED from the swamp island, the flames from the burned house had died down. Off toward the east another brighter fire was burning—the rising sun.

COACHWHIP PUBLICATIONS
CoachwhipBooks.com

FLORA CURIOSA
Cryptobotany, Mysterious Fungi,
Sentient Trees, and Deadly Plants in
Classic Science Fiction and Fantasy

COACHWHIP PUBLICATIONS
CoachwhipBooks.com

BOTANICA DELIRA

More Stories of Strange,
Undiscovered, and Murderous
Vegetation

COACHWHIP PUBLICATIONS
COACHWHIPBOOKS.COM

ARBORIS MYSTERIUS
Stories of the Uncanny and Undescribed
from the Botanical Kingdom

COACHWHIP PUBLICATIONS
CoachwhipBooks.com

ZOOLOGICA FANTASTICA
An Anthology of Strange Creatures
in Classic Cryptofiction

COACHWHIP PUBLICATIONS
CoachwhipBooks.com

Bestiarium Cryptozoologicum

*Mystery Animals and Unknown Species
in Classic Science Fiction and Fantasy*

BESTIARIUM CRYPTOZOOLOGICUM
Mystery Animals and Unknown Species
in Classic Science Fiction and Fantasy

COACHWHIP PUBLICATIONS
CoachwhipBooks.com

CETUS INSOLITUS
Sea Serpents, Giant Cephalopods,
and Other Marine Monsters in
Classic Science Fiction and Fantasy

COACHWHIP PUBLICATIONS
CoachwhipBooks.com

SAURIA MONSTRA
Dinosaurs, Pterosaurs, and Other
Fossil Saurians in Classic
Science Fiction and Fantasy

COACHWHIP PUBLICATIONS
CoachwhipBooks.com

INVERTEBRATA ENIGMATICA
Giant Spiders, Dangerous Insects, and Other Strange Invertebrates in Classic Science Fiction and Fantasy

INVERTEBRATA ENIGMATICA
Giant Spiders, Dangerous Insects, and
Other Strange Invertebrates in
Classic Science Fiction and Fantasy

COACHWHIP PUBLICATIONS

COACHWHIPBOOKS.COM

THE LAST MAMMOTH

CPSIA information can be obtained
at www.ICGtesting.com
Printed in the USA
LVHW011519280621
691349LV00012B/688